Fairford Affairs

Book 3

SAVORING

Addison

BAY SINCLAIR

To Hugh, for showing me the best way to look at the world.

And to Jason, for his kind and beautiful soul.

CHAPTER 1

Addison

Addison did her level best to not think the words *at least it can't get any worse*. The last thing she needed was to jinx the ever-loving shit out of herself.

It could always get fucking worse.

But damnit, her life was shaping up to majorly suck right now. The café where she worked her ass off for the last nine years would close its doors for good on Christmas Eve. And because the universe had a dick sense of humor, her roommate Kate asked her last night to move out by January sixteenth. Thirty days to find a new place to live when she was a week away from unemployment. Yippee.

"I know it's shit timing," Kate had said, genuine guilt in her eyes and filling her voice. "Noah's lease is up on January twentieth, and we're ready to move in together. We don't want to wait another year. I'm so sorry."

Addison couldn't even be mad at her best friend. Kate and Noah were the most adorable couple on the face of the planet. Deliriously in love with each other, respectfully talking out disagreements instead of fighting, and splitting things like cooking and housework 50/50.

Hell, the guy regularly wore a T-shirt that said *On Wednesdays We*

Smash the Patriarchy. Her bestie had found one of the good ones, and she wasn't about to stand in their way.

Addison had no doubt they'd let her stay longer if her only other option was a bench in Central Park, but it would be better for everyone if she got her shit together ASAP. Their Upper East Side apartment wasn't much bigger than a walk-in closet, and it had taken months to get into a routine with Kate where they weren't constantly in each other's way. The three of them wouldn't be able to manage for long—especially since Noah worked from home ninety-nine percent of the time.

Sighing, Addison finished wiping down the café's kitchen counters, tossed her apron into the half-full washing machine for Lola to run later, and clocked out. It was only a few minutes shy of noon. At least that gave her the rest of the day to search for a new job.

She was the head (and only) baker at Lola's Café on Second Avenue, and arrived by five every morning to make the day's assortment of breads and pastries. Seven days a week for the last nine years, without ever even taking a vacation day, because she thought she and Lola were in this shit together. That if she paid her dues, Lola would let her take over the mortgage payments and run the café when she retired.

The little coffee and pastry shop had done good business for the last nine years, even staying afloat during lockdowns thanks to delivery services, but it never quite reached the level they expected. They remained consistently in the black, but barely. The only way for Lola to get the cash she needed to spend her golden years soaking up the rays on a beach was to sell the property, and Addison had no chance of getting approved for a loan that big.

Fucking hell, she couldn't even be mad at Lola. The woman just celebrated her seventieth birthday. She deserved to retire down in Florida, and it wasn't her fault things worked out the way they did. They'd both put everything they had into making the café a success, but life doesn't always go as planned.

It was just so goddamn unfair. Addison was getting fucked over from every side, and she didn't even have anyone to blame.

Burying the urge to scream and throw shit, she headed out into the dining room. Fuck, she'd miss this place. The metal tables and chairs that looked like they belonged in an old movie set on the streets of Paris. The faded cream wallpaper with little blue flowers she and Lola picked out together. The gleaming display case she stocked with freshly baked goodies every morning.

The ambiance.

The smell.

I will not cry.

She recognized two of the three people sipping coffee at the little round tables. They were among her most loyal customers, a stunningly beautiful couple who came in almost every day—often with their two-year-old daughter, who inherited her father's sandy blond hair and her mother's brown eyes. They apparently lived in one of the massive brownstones close to the park and were two of the nicest people despite being crazy rich.

Another few days and she might never see them again.

Addison wanted to grow old in this tiny café—wanted it so damn badly, her chest ached with the loss. She rubbed her sternum with the heel of her hand, not that it helped. She'd never been in love, but she had a feeling this was what heartbreak felt like.

Gritting her teeth, she tried to hold it together as she made her way up the café's long, narrow dining room. Their two part-time employees, Joey and Alyssa, both started new jobs within a week of the big announcement, so Lola was the only one behind the counter. "See you in the morning," Addison said, managing to sound almost normal.

Lola wasn't looking at her, though. Her gaze was locked with the third person in the dining room—the one she'd never seen before. Addison glanced between them, frowning when Lola mouthed the words, *That's her.*

The man stood, easily blocking her narrow path. Holding out a hand, he said, "I'm Gabriel. I'd like to talk to you about a potential employment opportunity if you have a minute."

Addison glanced over her shoulder at Lola. The older woman grinned, nodding encouragingly at her startled expression.

"Ms. Walker?"

Turning, Addison threw on her best approximation of a smile. "It's nice to meet you," she said, shaking his hand. "Sorry about that. I'd love to talk about this opportunity." A little warning would've been nice, but she wasn't exactly in a position to turn away potential job offers at this point.

"Why don't you two head out back for a little privacy?" Lola suggested, her lips pursed into a half smile, one of her snowy white brows arched. "I'll bring you back some refreshments."

Addison frowned. This was starting to get weird. "Uh, sure. Right this way."

As they settled into a pair of chairs at the back of the kitchen, Lola brought over two steaming mugs of tea and a couple of cocktail napkins. Addison's brows shot up when she also put a plate on the break table, nearly overflowing with bite-sized samples of everything she baked that morning.

A tasting tray? Maybe this man wanted her to cater an event. She had no idea how she'd manage that without a proper kitchen, but Lola seemed to think this wasn't a waste of time.

"How can I help you, Gabriel?" she asked, studying him as she sipped her tea. If she had to guess, she'd say the man was in his early to mid-fifties. Faint wrinkles lined his round face, and most of his black hair had gone gray. But with his trim waist and broad shoulders, he didn't look old. Too old for her, but the term silver fox bounced around in her brain.

"Ms. Walker—may I call you Addison?"

She nodded.

"Addison," he started again, plucking a flakey bite of chocolate croissant from the tray, "you have a true gift." He popped the bite into his mouth, closing his eyes as he chewed. "Absolutely divine."

Her cheeks flushed with pleasure. "Thank you."

"I'm the head chef at a high-end resort called Fairford Manor, and I've felt for a while that our breakfast pastry and bread selections are lacking." He chose a long, thin sliver from a raspberry babka, moaning softly as he chewed. Meeting her gaze as he swallowed, he said, "You may be exactly what we're missing."

"Wow," she said, trying her best not to sound too excited. Playing hard to get might result in a better offer. "Thank you. It really means a lot to me that you like my food."

4

Addison's head spun. Could this be real? This might be the answer to all her problems.

Then it hit her—he'd called this place a resort, not a hotel. Which meant it definitely wasn't in New York City. The excitement left her like air leaking out of a balloon. "Where is Fairford Manor exactly?"

He ate a small bite of a cream puff before answering. "It's in northern Vermont, about six hours from here."

Throwing on her best customer service smile, Addison held out her hand. "Thank you very much for your interest, but I don't intend to leave the city."

Gabriel looked down at her outstretched hand for a solid five seconds, and then chose part of an orange cranberry muffin from the tray. "I'd appreciate you at least listening to my offer."

Flattening her lips into a tight line, she let her hand fall to her lap. "I don't think—"

"I was speaking to Lola just now," he interrupted, pulling a pen from an inside pocket of his jacket and taking the topmost cocktail napkin. "She told me the café is closing in a week, and you haven't yet found a new job."

"I'm not moving to Vermont," Addison insisted, crossing her arms over her stomach. She didn't have time for entitled men who didn't know the meaning of the word no. She had shit to do.

Gabriel scribbled on the cocktail napkin as he spoke—an obvious attempt to bait her. She refused to look down at it out of principle. "She also mentioned you have thirty days to find a new place to live," he said.

Heat flashed across the surface of her skin, and she knew she was blushing from head to toe. "Lola had no business telling anyone about that." She hated the catch in her voice. "Least of all a perfect stranger."

"I'm not a perfect stranger." He said it with such a plain, matter-of-fact tone, she sifted through her memories, trying to figure out when they might have met. "Though I'll admit I've never met you or Lola before today."

She pressed her lips back into that tight, unamused line. "If there's another definition for stranger, I've never heard it."

Gabriel chuckled, which only made the anger flare up in her even more. "I'm starting to think they were wrong." His bright blue eyes

5

danced with mirth. "You don't seem to have a submissive bone in your body."

"Excuse me?" Addison stood so abruptly her chair toppled back onto the tile floor. Her hands curled into tight fists at her sides. "I don't know what the fuck this is, but I want you out of my kitchen. Now."

Her anger didn't seem to bother him in the least. Putting the pen back in his pocket, he picked up his tea, watching her over the rim of the ceramic mug as he took a long, slow sip. After returning it to its spot on the table, he leaned back in his chair and sighed. "I'm here as a favor to Sophie and Leo. As I said, perhaps they were mistaken."

Confusion took over until there wasn't any room left for her fury. "Sophie and Leo?" Her gaze darted toward the dining room. Those were the names of the gorgeous, rich couple sitting right on the other side of that door. "What do they have to do with this?"

"They're partial owners of the resort where I work." He folded the napkin he wrote on in half, and then in half again. "When Lola told them she was closing the café, they asked me to come down and try your food. See if you'd be a good fit."

Good God, this conversation was like being on a carnival ride, spinning so fast you can't see or think straight anymore. "What does that have to do with whether or not I'm—" Heat flooded her face, but she refused to let this man render her too embarrassed to speak in her own damn kitchen. Squaring her shoulders, she forced out, "Submissive."

"Leo and Sophie saw you at Luciana's Lair a few months ago, though they don't believe you saw them. That led them to think you'd fit right in at the Manor, and since you're now in need of both a job and a new place to live . . ." He let the sentence trail off, watching her with a placid expression.

Addison's mouth hung open. Luciana's Lair was a famous BDSM club in midtown. They had a whole team of Doms and Dommes who could give you almost any kind of bondage or punishment scene you were willing to pay for. She'd been going there every month or two for almost seven years now—the one extravagance she allowed for in her budget. Ever since her last Dom told her she worked too much and found someone with more free time, she needed to take the edge off somehow. At least dropping a couple hundred bucks for an hour of pain was cheaper than retail therapy.

Never in a million years would she have suspected Sophie and Leo were also customers.

"Do you, perhaps, wish to deny any association with Luciana's Lair?" Gabriel asked, his pursed lips not quite hiding his amused smile.

She felt her face turn bright red again—the curse of fair skin. This man didn't seem to be judging her, though, and if Sophie and Leo were also kinky . . .

"I'm not denying anything," she said at last.

Gabriel tilted his head to one side, regarding her. A decision flashed through his bright blue eyes, and he said, "Yes, I think you'll do." Gabriel gestured toward the fallen chair. "Why don't you take a seat and let me finish explaining."

Part of her wanted to march out of the kitchen without a backward glance. This was, beyond a shadow of a doubt, the weirdest conversation of her life, and she hated that he knew things about her that weren't any of his damn business.

But he'd said just enough to intrigue her. Setting the chair back on its legs, she sat, folding her hands in her lap. "I'm listening."

"Fairford Manor is an exclusive BDSM resort up in the Green Mountains, in the middle of nowhere." One corner of his mouth lifted into a wry smile. "So I'm sure you can understand why we can't hire just anyone. No one outside the lifestyle would last very long."

Was he serious? He wanted her to work at a kinky sex resort? "I don't know if there's been some kind of misunderstanding, but I was a customer at Luciana's, not an employee. I have no intention of—"

He waved his hands, cutting her off. "I'm not asking you to be involved in any scenes, Addison. For the most part, I suspect you won't even see the guests. As I'm sure you can imagine, the Doms and their guests tend to burn the midnight oil. You won't have to make nearly as much food as you do here to keep the Manor staff and guests fed, so if you start early enough, you can be done and gone before most people are even awake."

"And where would I go?" she asked, arching her eyebrows. "You said this place is in the middle of nowhere."

Gabriel had the good grace to look mildly chagrined. "Admittedly, accommodations are fairly limited in the immediate area, but we have several suites up on the top floor, away from the guests. You'd be welcome to stay in one of those until you find something more suitable."

"Let me get this straight," she said, doing her best to keep all inflection out of her voice. "You want me to leave my entire life behind, move into a sex resort, bake for a bunch of fancy Doms and their subs every morning, and then hide up in the attic for the rest of the day."

"No one will ever ask you to hide, Ms. Walker." There was a hint of censure in his voice. "The whole point of Fairford Manor is *not* having to hide."

The blush returned with a vengeance, but she refused to look away. He could use whatever pretty words he wanted. That didn't change the fact that, in her opinion, she'd done a damn good job summing up his job offer.

"But otherwise, yes, that's more or less correct. Why don't you come up for a trial period. Let's say . . . three months? I'll make it very much worth your while."

It took a great deal of self-control to keep from rolling her eyes. "I don't care what you're willing to pay me. I'm not moving out to the country to work at a kink hotel."

"I think you'll find life at the Manor is nothing like what you're imagining." His eyes seemed to pierce her, as if he could look right into her brain and see all the rude, judgmental thoughts there.

She clenched her hands over her thighs to resist the urge to fidget.

"Three months, room and board included, and if you hate it, I'll even pay your moving expenses to come back. As I understand it, you don't have a lot of other options right now, so what do you have to lose?"

Addison took a deep breath, willing herself to stay calm. "It's a really interesting offer, and I do appreciate you taking the time," she said, the customer service smile back on her face. "But I'm afraid I have to say no. My whole life is here. I'm sorry you came all the way down for nothing."

Gabriel's answering smile looked completely unbothered, like he hadn't a care in the world. "Not at all. I always love visiting New York. Some of the best food in the world is made right here."

Standing, he shook her hand again, pressing something soft into her palm. As he strolled out of the kitchen, she stared down at the folded napkin in her hand.

Addison very nearly tossed it into the trash. She'd made her decision and had no interest in this obvious last-ditch attempt to convince her otherwise.

In the end, her curiosity was too great to ignore.

Unfolding the napkin, she flattened it as best she could against the tabletop and stared at it with wide, uncomprehending eyes.

Gabriel had written a dollar amount.

A fucking absurd dollar amount.

He would pay her this much just to live in the middle of nowhere and bake for three months? No fucking way.

With this amount of money, it would be a piece of cake to get her own apartment in the city once the contract was up. Hell, it might even be enough to open her own café if she played her cards right.

Lola came into the kitchen, leaning against the wall by the door. "Nice man, Gabriel," she said, her eyes sparkling with excitement. "As I understand it, he was planning to make you an offer. How did you feel about it?"

Looking back down at the rumpled cocktail napkin, her gaze tripped across the phone number scrawled beneath his offer. Addison found her lips spreading into a wide grin. "I feel like I'd better go home and start packing." She met Lola's gaze, her heart beating too hard, too fast. "It seems I'm moving to Vermont."

CHAPTER 2
Mason

Saturday meetings were Mason's least favorite part of his job, something every other Dom at Fairford Manor knew. Even if he didn't bitch every time one rolled around—which he absolutely did, at length—he gave each of them a mug printed with *This Meeting Could've Been an Email* for Christmas last year.

Subtlety wasn't exactly his strong suit.

Yet Jonathan insisted they all meet in the dining room at least one Saturday a month, after all the guests checked out at eleven. He always gave some bullshit line about the partners needing to meet face-to-face to ensure their business relationship stayed strong and the Manor ran smoothly. Even though Leo, the only silent partner, attended a few times a year at most, and Jonathan didn't seem to give a flying fuck.

Mason ignored the Manor's senior partner and head Dom as he prattled on about the New Year's Eve party he'd given Zach, Nell, and Olivia permission to throw. As if Mason cared. New Year's Eve was in three days. Even if he did have objections, it was too late to do anything about it.

"How long has this party been planned?" Mason interrupted, doing his best to sound bored. Acting never came easily to him, though, so he mostly just sounded pissed off.

A muscle in Jonathan's jaw ticked. "The three of them asked for permission shortly after the Halloween party," he said, his arched brow clearly adding, *Are you seriously challenging me about this? Of all fucking things?* "Given how successful that was, I saw no reason to deny them."

"Oh yes, very successful," Mason drawled. "I especially enjoyed the attempted kidnapping of one of our guests."

Rafe, the oldest of the Manor Doms, who Mason and the other founding partners brought in a couple years after they opened, practically growled in response. "Leave Nell out of this."

It had been nearly two months since Nell, Rafe's guest-turned-girl-friend, almost got kidnapped by her stalker ex during the party. Not that it was her fault. That guy was an abusive motherfucker to the highest degree, and Mason had been more than happy to restrain him while they waited for the police to arrive.

In all honesty, even he enjoyed the party before that all went down.

Which meant he was bitching for the sake of it, and he damn well knew it. He just couldn't stand things that wasted his time.

Skipping breakfast this morning definitely didn't help matters.

Looking Rafe in the eyes, he said, "Sorry. I shouldn't have said that. You know how much I like Nell." It was just weird as fuck that his friends/business partners started pairing off in the last year and a half. First Aiden fell head over heels for Olivia, and the two were sure to announce their wedding date any day now.

Then Rafe got involved with Nell. Zach, the Manor's receptionist and overall boy Friday, confided that he suspected the pair planned to leave Vermont sometime next year. How they could even consider it when they'd only known each other for two months was beyond him, and it would majorly fuck over the Manor.

Rafe took a deep breath, letting it out slowly. "It's fine. But maybe keep in mind that these meetings you complain about so much last longer because of all your whining." What sounded like months of pent-up frustration spilled into the man's voice. "If you just shut your damn mouth and let Jonathan say his piece, we'll be out of here in ten minutes."

"I don't—" Mason let the objection trail off, knowing anything he said would be a lie. Lying never came easily to him either.

He didn't even know why the meetings pissed him off so much. They didn't used to—not for the first several years. It was only within the last year or so that any mention of the mandatory monthly meetings made his teeth grind.

"Sorry," he said again, not quite able to meet any of their eyes. "Maybe I need to stop skipping breakfast on Saturday mornings."

"Did I hear that someone's hangry?" Gabriel said in an annoyingly cheerful voice.

Mason whipped around in his chair in time to see the head chef bustle through the kitchen door with an enormous wooden tray.

Laughing, Camden asked, "Were you listening at the door, waiting for the perfect time to make an entrance?"

Gabriel grinned in response, the smile lines around his eyes long and deep. "A tasty treat for you," he said, depositing his tray in the middle of the table. Five salad plates held cinnamon rolls the size of softballs and slathered in icing. Gabriel handed them out around the table, followed by silverware, and finally mugs of coffee prepared to each Dom's personal preference.

The fact that they were all in *This Meeting Could've Been an Email* mugs didn't improve Mason's mood in the least.

"To what do we owe this lovely surprise?" Aiden said, cutting away a bite and popping it into his mouth.

Rather than answer, Gabriel watched intently as Aiden started to chew, then froze, his eyes going round. The chef's smile grew even wider, delight filling his bright eyes.

"Holy shit," Aiden said, already cutting off another huge bite. The others followed his lead, hurrying to test out Gabriel's newest creation, each making a similar declaration upon tasting their cinnamon rolls.

All except Mason. His gaze remained locked on Gabriel, watching the look of triumph on his face grow stronger and stronger as the men ate. What the fuck was he up to?

"Dude, this is incredible," Camden said, cutting off another huge chunk and loading up his fork. "This might be my new favorite breakfast."

"I'm very happy to hear that," Gabriel said, clasping his hands behind his back and looking like the cat who just caught the canary. "Since I already hired the woman who made it."

Aaaand there it is.

All of them stared at Gabriel now, each with varying levels of surprise written all over their faces. Except for Mason, who only narrowed his eyes.

Jonathan recovered first, giving the chef a look somewhere between irritation and amusement. "I beg your pardon?"

"Her name is Addison," Gabriel said, not even pretending to feel guilty about hiring a whole-ass new staff member without permission. "She's here on a trial period of three months. Since we can't exactly expect her to find housing around here for such a short time, I helped her move into one of the bedrooms on the third floor last night."

Even Mason's eyes widened at that one. The audacity of it all was almost impressive. *Almost.*

"Hell, she can have my suite so long as she keeps making shit like this," Camden said, shoving the entire last quarter of his cinnamon roll into his mouth.

Jonathan rolled his eyes. "Yes, I'm sure your guests for the next three months would love that."

Amusement danced in Camden's blue eyes, and he gave that fuckboy grin the guests all loved so much. According to Zach, there was a whole thread on the Manor's subreddit, r/SordidFairfordAffairs, devoted to Camden's dimple.

Glancing around the table, Mason realized none of the others were nearly as annoyed as they should be. Hell, even Rafe devoured his cinnamon roll with an amused tilt to his lips. That man had hardly bothered to smile in the last five years—at least not before Nell came along.

Mason reached deep inside for the cool, calm demeaner he preferred to present to the rest of the world. His mother had been overly dramatic to a painful degree, flying into fits of histrionics over every little thing. She was the kind of person to burst into tears and yell for a manager over minor mistakes or perceived slights. To constantly have one or more feuds going with various family members or neighbors—sometimes without the other person even knowing about it.

She'd lock herself in her room for hours if she thought Mason or his dad had even considered criticizing something she did, while lamenting that no one but Mason's little brother cared about her at all.

Chaos would never seep into his life again. He'd made damn sure of that.

Gabriel prattled on about the Manhattan café where his new baker used to work, as if Leo and Sophie liking her scones would make them all agree. Was it supposed to impress him that she worked in a coffee shop? For what Gabriel agreed to pay the girl, they could probably hire the entire staff of the nearest Starbucks. Both things seemed equal wastes of money to him.

"You don't have the authority to create new positions at the Manor without authorization from a majority of the partners," Mason said the next time Gabriel came up for air. "You need more than just Leo's vote."

"Mason." Jonathan's voice held a clear warning.

Ignoring his best friend entirely, Mason kept his gaze locked with Gabriel's. "You overstepped."

"I have total authority over my kitchen," Gabriel said, raising himself up to his full height. "That was the agreement when I came here."

"And you do." Not liking the hint of frustration in his voice, Mason strove for cool indifference when he added, "Within the agreed upon budget."

"The budget is inadequate."

"Something you should've brought to our attention, rather than hiring someone behind our backs."

Aiden snorted. "Yeah, because you run it by us every time you spend a shit ton of money on the Manor card."

Pressing his lips into a flat line, Mason waited until he forced his anger under control before responding. "That's irrelevant. They're two completely different things."

"Really?" Gabriel said, all traces of his deep smile lines long gone. "Because when you spend money it's automatically a good idea, but when I do it's automatically a bad one?"

This was getting fucking ridiculous. "I didn't say anything remotely—"

"Enough!" Jonathan pinched the bridge of his nose and attempted to massage away a headache. "Jesus fucking Christ, Mason. Why do you even care?"

The truth was, he didn't know. Just like with the Saturday meetings, there was nothing necessarily wrong. If Gabriel pulled this stunt a year or two ago, he suspected he wouldn't have given two shits.

But right now, he just . . . did.

Since that made him sound every bit as overly dramatic as his mother, he chose to go on the offensive instead. "I just don't see a need here. Our breakfast is already excellent." He pushed his untouched plate toward the center of the table. "If our guests really want cinnamon rolls, they can get Cinnabon at the airport on their way home. It'll probably taste better anyway."

Only after he finished speaking did he realize no one was looking his way anymore. All eyes were directed over his shoulder toward the kitchen door.

Well, fuck.

With a slow, steadying breath, he twisted in his chair a second time. A woman stood just inside the dining room, her honey blonde hair pulled back into a messy bun and cheerful yellow letters on her apron spelling out *Lola's Café*.

Her beauty took his breath away for a moment, even with the scowl narrowing her eyes and forming harsh lines around her pursed lips.

"Gentlemen, I'd like to introduce Addison Walker," Gabriel said in a clipped tone.

Addison and Mason stared at each other, the ticking of the antique grandfather clock in the corner the only sound in the room. Everyone else seemed to be holding their breath as they waited to see what would happen next. Christ almighty, could this get any more uncomfortable?

After the longest, most awkward silence of his life, Addison forced her features into a calm, serene mask. Her hands remained fisted at her sides. Turning to Gabriel, she said, "I hope I didn't upend my entire life and move up here for nothing." Then she stalked from the room with quick strides, disappearing in the direction of the lobby.

Mason stared after her long after she left, afraid to look at the others still in the room. This was *not* going to go well.

With a sigh, he forced himself to face the music. Straightening in his chair, he folded his hands on the table in front of him and said, "I apologize. I definitely could've handled that better."

"Ya think?" Aiden said, rolling his eyes. At least he seemed to be lingering somewhere closer to exasperation than actual anger.

Gabriel was a different story entirely. With his gaze focused solely on Mason, he looked about ready to spit fire. "Let me make one thing perfectly clear," he said in a low, dangerous tone. "I've put everything I have into this kitchen. It's been my entire life since the Manor opened. I've been here nearly every goddamn day for seven fucking years. I've worked my ass off to give you the gourmet food you wanted, and not once in all that time did we get a single bad review. And you know what? I'm fucking tired. I deserve a break every now and then. So you either give me this or you can find a new head chef." He stalked out of the room without a backward glance.

"Wow," Camden said, reaching for the abandoned cinnamon roll in the center of the table. "Gabriel De Leon pissed off and giving ultimatums. Never thought I'd live to see that day."

Well, at least one of them was too distracted by food to rip him a new one. He'd take what he could get.

Steeling up his courage, he forced himself to look at Jonathan. The cold fury filling his friend's eyes sent guilt spiraling through him. "I'm sorry," he said softly.

"Fix this," was Jonathan's only reply. Then he swept his gaze around the table. "Meeting fucking adjourned." Snatching his car keys off the table, Jonathan left the room with long, swift strides, clearly too angry to deal with Mason's bullshit.

Mason felt pretty much the same way. But how did one stop their own stupid bullshit when they never intended to do it in the first place?

Heaving a deep sigh, Rafe stood as well. "I'm heading home to Nell. I'll see you guys later." He didn't meet Mason's eyes before he walked away.

"I'm sorry," Mason said again, looking at the other two.

"I know," Aiden said, his voice kinder than all the others. "Maybe you need a break. Do you have one of your trips coming up?"

Mason took time off to travel every two to three months, each time choosing a random place on the map. The only thing these places had in common? They were all somewhere he'd never been before. His vacations were the only thing he loved more than his job.

"Not until the last week of February." The trip to Chile had been booked for months now. He couldn't fucking wait to explore that new corner of the world.

The look in his friend's eyes made it clear he thought that wasn't nearly soon enough. "Well, I'm not sure what's been going on with you recently, but I'm here if you ever want to talk, okay?"

Mason opened his mouth to speak, but he couldn't figure out what to say. Deny anything was wrong? Apologize again? Thank him for the offer and then politely decline out of some idiotic sense of masculinity?

In the end, he only nodded.

"All right," Aiden said, getting to his feet. "My next guest doesn't get here until Tuesday. See you then."

"Here," Camden said once it was just the two of them, sliding the plate back across the table. "I saved you a couple bites. Eat this, admit you were wrong, and everyone will calm the fuck down."

With a resigned sigh, Mason picked up his fork and stabbed one of the remaining gooey bites. Camden was right. Whether he thought the angry blonde was worth what Gabriel wanted to pay her or not, he could only fix this one way.

When the bite hit his tongue, he tasted exactly what he expected to —cinnamon, brown sugar, and a cream cheese glaze. It was tasty enough, sure, but he didn't see why the others went gaga over it. He felt almost vindicated about the Cinnabon comment, even if he did know it was a dick thing to say.

As soon as he started to chew, everything changed.

Instead of the pure sweetness he expected, it had a warm, almost spicy undertone. Ginger maybe? And what he thought were raisins burst on his tongue with the tartness of dried cranberries.

Eyes wide with surprise, he pulled apart the layers of the final bite. Tiny pieces of candied ginger hid in the filling. And the dough . . . so ridiculously light and fluffy it almost felt like eating air.

"See?" Camden said, sitting back in his chair. His smile was encouraging though, not smug. Camden might be a pain in the ass sometimes, but he never gloated. "I've never tasted anything like it."

An image of Mason licking tiny, sparkling pieces of candied ginger from Addison's skin flashed through his mind. Where in the actual fuck did that come from? Shoving it into a box at the back of his mind and slamming a lid down over it, he focused on the task at hand—undoing his fuck up.

"It's incredible," he agreed, gathering everything left on the plate into a final bite and closing his eyes as he chewed. Certainly a step or three above the Manor's current breakfast pastry offerings.

Fuck.

Still smiling, Camden got up and headed toward the doorway. "Well, see you tomorrow night. Good luck with Gabriel and—" He paused, frowning. "What was her name? Allison?"

"Addison," Mason corrected. Addison Walker, a truly gifted baker to whom he owed a genuine apology.

Mason trailed behind Camden until they reached the lobby. While his friend headed straight out the double front doors and off toward the parking lot, Mason made his way upstairs instead. He hoped he'd find her up on the third floor. If she already said fuck it and left, Gabriel would probably poison his next dinner. Or, even worse, follow through on his threat and quit.

At the far end of the second-floor hallway, Mason pushed open the last door, heading up what had once been the servant's stairs. The enclosed staircase did a one-eighty halfway up, before finally letting him out at one end of the long, narrow third-floor hallway. No guests ever came up here, which allowed for a more relaxed atmosphere than the rest of the house—a sharp counterpoint to the old-world elegance and rich decadence of the lower floors.

The soft gray of the birch hardwood floors went perfectly with the light blue walls. Photos of the Manor in different seasons hung within simple black frames. The overall effect was incredibly soothing, something they all needed from time to time when dealing with difficult guests.

Though someone had plugged cheap, ugly nightlights into almost every outlet down the length of the hall. He'd have to talk to house-keeping about removing those. They threw off the whole ambiance.

For now, though, he had much more important matters to deal with. Mason frowned at the eight closed doors lining the hallway, four on each side. Where would Gabriel have put her?

Three of the rooms were obviously out. One was the office where Zach sorted all the applications of potential guests into different categories for the Doms to look through. When one of them chose a new guest, he put his name at the top of the first page and left the application in the Accepted box so Zach could send out one of his fancy, hand-written acceptance letters. If, on the other hand, a Dom knew the applicant wasn't for him, he put his name on the bottom of the final page. Once all five Doms passed, Zach sent out a polite rejection instead.

Another door led to a large break room, complete with a leather sofa and matching overstuffed chairs, a full-size fridge stocked with drinks and snacks, and a seventy-five-inch flatscreen—the only TV in the house.

The last door on the left led to what was a bedroom once upon a time. In the seven years since the Manor opened, it turned into a giant storage closet, with several rolling racks and boxes of costumes for various types of roleplay; spare sheets, pillows, and duvets; assorted seasonal decorations not currently in use; and even bankers boxes full of financial documents from previous years.

Which left five possible bedrooms for Addison. Wanting to get this over with, Mason strode down the corridor, knocking on the doors as he passed. He'd taken two steps beyond a door in the middle of the hall when it swung open behind him. Turning in a slow, dignified manner, Mason faced the blond baker.

At least she didn't scowl at him like she had downstairs, though she certainly didn't look happy to find him knocking on her door. She leaned against the doorframe with her arms crossed over her stomach, eyes cool and assessing, chin lifted in a clear challenge. "Can I help you?" she said, her voice as cold as her eyes.

Fuck, she really was beautiful, her hazel eyes an incredible mix of green, blue, and gold that seemed to change color in different light. Soft tendrils of hair escaped her bun and framed her face, curling slightly at the ends. And her lips . . . so full and soft and perfect, he found himself wishing she was a guest, not an employee. As a guest, he'd likely be able to join in one of her scenes. But as an employee, his chances of kissing those perfect lips stood distressingly close to zero.

Especially since she hated his guts.

Realizing the silence had already dragged on far too long, he said, "I want to apologize for my behavior downstairs. I assure you it had nothing to do with you or your food."

She arched her honey blond brows at him and waited, not saying a word.

Seriously? For fuck's sake. Why not just take the win and move on?

Dragging a hand through his hair, he forced himself to add, "I was in a bad mood and felt like complaining. I did try your cinnamon roll after you left, and it was delicious. Clearly the, uh"—*Jesus Christ, this was awkward*—"the Cinnabon comment was uncalled for. Again, I apologize."

"Hmm." She pursed her lips again, but some of the tension eased out of her shoulders. "Which one are you exactly?"

"Mason St. John," he said, holding out a hand.

Addison looked down her perfect nose at his hand for several agonizing seconds before finally shaking it. "Pleasure." She said it like it was anything but. "Now if you'll excuse me. Since it seems I'm staying after all, I'd better finish unpacking. See you around." With that, she slammed the door in his face.

Staring at the white-painted wood, he clenched and unfurled his hands several times. Every dominant bone in his body longed to crash through that door and turn Addison Walker over his knee.

Yes, he'd been rude. But he fucking apologized for it. Maybe he could've done a little bit better with some time to plan out the wording, but really, what more did she want from him?

And not for nothing, he was partial owner of the Manor, which made him her fucking boss. Social norms weren't always his strong suit, but he was almost sure an appropriate response would've been to politely accept his apology and agree they could start over from scratch.

Yet here he was, glaring at a door only inches from the tip of his nose, his palm itching to dole out a punishment he couldn't deliver.

Especially since he knew virtually nothing about her. What if she wasn't a sub, or even kinky?

With one more long, slow exhale, he stepped away and headed back toward the stairs. With any luck, she just wanted revenge for the way he ruined her big entrance downstairs. He supposed that was only fair.

His palm still itched, though.

No amount of logic or calming breaths stopped him from wanting to spank the brattiness right out of her.

CHAPTER 3

Addison

I f Addison didn't stop taking her frustration out on the dough, her artisan bread would be tough and dense—not at all the light, fluffy consistency she required of her best work.

It wasn't a big deal when she kneaded the dough an hour ago, giving it several satisfying punches. But she already set it aside to rise by this point. Nothing ruined artisan bread faster than knocking all the air out of it while shaping the loaf.

Willing herself to focus on the smell of yeast and the feel of soft dough between her fingers, she grabbed a piece from the outside of the misshapen ball, pulling it up toward the center. At the last second, she couldn't help picturing Mason's stupid, superior face right in the middle. She pushed her hand down on top of the dough far too hard, knocking the air out for at least the fifth time.

"Calm the fuck down," she muttered, forcing herself to continue the process with slow, careful movements. Artisan bread was delicate, and she wasn't about to give Mason the satisfaction of seeing her fuck up. Especially not on her first day serving guests.

When the dough no longer stuck to the marble countertop, she flipped the ball over and transferred it to the waiting proofing basket. After washing the flour off her hands, she covered the basket with plastic wrap and placed it to the side. Setting a timer for thirty minutes, she began cleaning up her mess and getting her station ready for the next order of business—dark chocolate orange scones. She had just set aside the orange zest and started dicing some candied orange peel when the kitchen door swung open.

Addison looked up, expecting another member of the kitchen staff. She looked forward to finally meeting Luca and Kendra, who worked breakfast and lunch during the week.

Mason St. John strolled through the door in his perfect, stupid suit, with his perfect, stupid face and that thick, perfectly wavy brown hair that practically begged her to run her fingers through it.

Absolutely not. Mason was a giant dick, and she refused to waste her time lusting after him. She'd learned her lesson about fooling around with sexy assholes with her last Dom. Ryan never gave a fuck about anything but his needs and desires, and she had a gut feeling Mason was cast from the same mold.

"Good morning," she said, going for politely bland, but ending up somewhere closer to frosty disdain.

Mason's brows arched slowly upward, and he looked at her in that way all truly spectacular Doms could. The way that made her want to drop to her knees and beg forgiveness.

Yeah, no thanks.

"Breakfast isn't served until eight," she said, happy when she sounded significantly less hostile.

"I own one-sixth of this resort. I know what time breakfast is served." One corner of his mouth twitched. "I'm only here to get some coffee while I wait for my guest to wake up."

Heat climbed up her neck and flooded her cheeks, making her want to disappear. "Right," she said, returning her attention to the candied orange peel she made yesterday. Gabriel and his dinner staff didn't arrive until two on Sundays, so she spent the previous morning familiarizing herself with the kitchen and prepping things she needed in the coming days.

"Addison, look at me." When she ignored him, he added a softer, "Please." Only the barest hint of a command lurked in his voice.

With a sigh, she put down her knife and raised her gaze to his perfect, stupid eyes. Goddamn, they were gorgeous. A deep, riveting blue, the color of lapis lazuli. "How can I help you?" she asked, trying and failing to look anywhere but his eyes.

"I know we got off on the wrong foot." Mason's gaze skittered away from hers before he added, "And I know it was my fault."

He didn't sound like he thought it was his fault. In fact, he sounded like he just swallowed a bug. He still had that infuriating superior look on his face, too, the bastard. Unable to help herself, Addison narrowed her eyes.

Clearly noticing the change, Mason's brows shot up again. "Are you always this terrible at accepting apologies?" he said, his voice cold enough to freeze water.

Planting her hands on her hips, she fired back, "Are you always this terrible at making apologies?"

Mason's nostrils flared—the only outward sign he'd even heard her. He took several deep breaths, his eyes boring into hers the entire time. At last, he said, "I was rude, and I apologize. You can either accept my apology and we can start over, or you can continue being a hypocritical brat. It's your call."

"Excuse me?" Addison said, her spine stiffening. "I am *not* a hypocrite."

"You're mad at me for being rude to you when I didn't even know you were there. In retaliation, you're being rude to me on purpose. How is that not hypocritical?"

Never in her life had she wanted to slap someone across the face before. And yet the desire coursed through her like a raging fire. "You were rude before you even knew anything about me, and you did it behind my back." She did her best to look down her nose at him, even though he loomed over her by a foot or more. "At least I have a reason, and I'm honest enough to do it to your face."

He reeled back as if she actually hit him. It took him several seconds to recover, which gave her a surge of pleasure. She had a feeling it was about time someone put him in his place.

That pleasure melted away when he gave her a cool, icy stare and said, "Be that as it may, I'm still one of the Manor's partners, which makes me your boss. You don't have to like me, but you *will* show me the proper respect."

"The proper respect?" She forced out a harsh laugh. "Respect is earned, asshole." And despite the voice of reason in the back of her head —the one screaming at her to stop while she was already behind, before she got fired—she gave him the finger.

Mason sped across the kitchen in four long strides. For a fleeting moment, she thought maybe she should turn tail and run out the kitchen's back door. It was about twelve degrees outside, but hiding in the snowy garden seemed like a much better idea than waiting around to see what that steely glint in his eye meant.

Something kept her rooted to the spot, though. It wasn't fear. Even though the reasonable part of her brain informed her she should be afraid.

She held her breath as Mason whirled her around, bending her over the counter. Holding her in place with a hand splayed between her shoulder blades, Mason brought his other hand down across the center of her ass.

Addison's eyes drifted closed.

"Do. Not. Disrespect. Me. Like. That. Again." He punctuated each word with another hard spank, spreading them around her bottom and the tops of her thighs. Then he kept right on going, kicking it up another notch in intensity.

Holy fucking hell, he was a hard spanker. The Doms at Luciana's Lair would never punish her quite as hard as she wanted, no matter how much she begged. They hardly even left bruises.

But this . . . she'd have to find a full-length mirror somewhere in the Manor so she could check her ass later. He had to be leaving marks even through her pants.

It took all her self-control to hold in a disappointed groan when he finally stopped. Hell, the spanking could've lasted several more minutes and she still would've been disappointed. She couldn't remember the last time she felt this good. It was almost like that perfect state between buzzed and drunk, when she felt like her feet were about to float right off the ground.

Spinning her back around, Mason gripped her upper arms, leaning down until their noses nearly touched. "This is my fucking house. If you want to remain here, I suggest you at least figure out how to hold your tongue in my presence. Do you understand me?"

"Yes, Sir." It slipped out before she could stop it. She drew in a sharp breath, as if doing so would somehow suck the word back in. But it was too late for that, and she damn well knew it.

Mason blinked in stunned silence for the space of three ragged breaths.

Then his mouth crashed down over hers with enough force to bend her backward over the counter. Her lips parted for him without putting up even a token fight.

Stop! He's your fucking boss!

That part of her brain had zero control over her body right now. Burying her hands in his ridiculously thick hair, she held on for dear life as he claimed her mouth with commanding strokes of his tongue. No one had ever kissed her like this. Like he'd been searching for something his entire life, and she was his answer.

Like she was his only source of air.

"Fuck," Mason ground out, wrenching his mouth away from hers. "This is a mistake." But his hands still dug into her hips, like he feared what would happen if he let go. Not that it made a bit of difference. His gaze pinned her in place all on its own.

God, his eyes were so intense. She couldn't even fucking breathe while he looked at her like that—like he could see right into her soul and read all her deepest, darkest secrets as easily as reading a book.

Why did she feel the urge to shrink away from him, as if something about her past was shameful? Fuck that. She may have lived through hell, but despite everything that happened, she grew into a strong-ass woman, thank you very much, and she was proud as fuck. No self-important gazillionaire Dom who probably never struggled for anything in his fucking life would make her feel otherwise.

Arching her brows ever so slightly, she stared back at him, doing her best to not even blink. "Stop overthinking this and fuck me, goddamnit."

An icy fury blazed in his blue eyes a second before he spun her back around. Lifting her up, he flattened her whole torso against the countertop, leaving her short legs dangling. Reflex had her kicking out, but he easily trapped her legs with his own, pressing them against a cabinet door.

Mason pressed his hips forward, letting her feel the hard bulge of his cock as he leaned over her. "We're going to have to do something about that filthy mouth of yours," he whispered in her ear.

"I can say whatever the fuck I want," she shot back, bucking her hips. Not that it did any good. All she managed to do was grind his cock harder against her ass.

With a rough growl, Mason straightened, holding her in place with a strong hand at the small of her back. With his other hand, he wrenched her pants and panties down to her knees. "I'll teach you some fucking respect if it's the last thing I do." Grabbing a large wooden spoon from a nearby crock, he brought it down hard against her exposed ass.

"Fuck!" Addison yelled, kicking and squirming.

He held her in place as easily as if she were a small child. "Still not learning, I see," he said cooly, bringing down the spoon again, peppering her ass with sharp stings.

"Fuuuuuu—" She let it trail off that time, squeezing her eyes shut and grinding her teeth together. Goddamn, this hurt. And yet it felt . . .

So.

Fucking.

Good.

Shit, shit, shit, she shouldn't be doing this. Not with *him*. A total dickface *and* her fucking boss. Why had she goaded him to keep going when he tried to stop? Why couldn't she ever just keep her big mouth—

"*Oh my God!*" she screamed when he brought the spoon up between her legs, landing soundly on her clit.

She couldn't stop moaning and her heart fucking raced and sweet fucking Jesus, if he didn't fuck her soon, she would die.

"Finally," Mason said with a frustrated sigh. Then with the swish of a zipper and rustle of cloth, he pushed into her, and holy mother of God, she hadn't been fucked in so long.

"Holy shiiii—" She caught herself at the last second.

Apparently not quickly enough. Mason grabbed a fistful of her hair and yanked, arching her head backward. "What have I told you about your language?"

"I'm sorry, Sir." Fuck, why did it feel so good to call him that? "I'll try harder, I promise." She'd promise him anything to ensure he didn't stop fucking her.

With a rumble of approval, he released her hair and took firm hold of her ass, prying her cheeks apart. Good God, he'd be able to see everything from back there. Shouldn't she be mortified? This was a near stranger. Her fucking *boss*.

Yet her pussy clenched tighter around him, and a mangled, "*Please*," tumbled from her lips.

Mason drew back his hips slowly before slamming back in. Again and again and again, the force of it crushing her upper thighs against the edge of the countertop, eventually drawing a pained cry out of her.

For one horrifying moment, he stopped. "Are you—"

"Mason, I swear to God, if you stop now, I'll literally die."

That was all the permission he needed. He fucked her into the countertop like his life depended on it, each harsh stroke sending her higher and higher. When he wrapped an arm around her hips, reaching in to pinch her clit, she completely fucking exploded. If her scream didn't wake the whole house, she didn't know what would.

Mason pulled out of her at the last second, snatching a hand towel off the counter. With his weight lifted, she finally managed to slide off the island and back to her feet. When she turned, Mason stood tall and proud in the middle of the kitchen, his head thrown back as his body jerked with his orgasm.

God, he was glorious. She'd never seen anything sexier in her whole life.

It took a long time for their breathing to return to normal. Only then did Mason slowly open his eyes, as if coming out of a trance. His gaze lowered to where his hand still held the towel around his cock, and he stared for several seconds before finally letting go.

Mason opened his mouth to speak, but closed it again without making a sound. After only a few more awkward seconds, he set his clothes to rights, and she hurried to do the same. God, her new coworkers could walk in any second. She needed to get her shit together here.

"Mason, I—"

He stalked out of the kitchen without a word, the towel clenched in one fist.

"Fuck," she muttered as the door swung back and forth on its two-way hinges.

Somewhere in the back of her mind, she knew they just crossed several lines. Hell, they leapt so far past the lines, they weren't even visible anymore.

She let her sort-of boss spank her. And fuck her without protection.

In the kitchen, for fuck's sake. On the very same counter holding the ingredients for her scones.

Talk about a health code violation.

Given his reaction at the end, he also clearly knew the whole thing was fucked with a capital F.

That didn't stop her from loving every goddamn second of it.

When she was absolutely sure Mason wasn't coming back, she reached around with both hands, rubbing at her still-throbbing ass. Unable to help herself, she squeezed, closing her eyes at the sharp spike of exquisite pain.

In that moment, Addison was absolutely certain of two things.

One, Mason St. John was an asshole of the first order who she needed to avoid like the motherfucking plague.

And two, she wanted to fuck him again so badly she could hardly even see straight.

CHAPTER 4
Mason

W hat in the actual fuck.

Mason bolted through the lobby and out the front door, glad Zach never came in this early. He didn't want to explain his sudden flight from the Manor to anyone.

He just spanked and fucked a goddamn employee.

Without any sort of prior agreement or discussion of limits.

For fuck's sake, he didn't even use a condom.

Jesus fucking Christ, they were absolutely getting sued. As if Jonathan wasn't already out of patience with him. He'd undoubtedly murder Mason at the earliest opportunity.

The worst part? He didn't even fully regret it. He knew he should be on the phone with Jonathan this very instant explaining what happened and working on a mitigation plan. But he couldn't get the way she called him sir out of his mind. Her plea to keep fucking her.

Hell, it wasn't even a plea. It was a demand.

His cock got so hard it fucking hurt. He had to get out of here before he marched right back in there and started over at the beginning.

Running the rest of the way, Mason slid behind the wheel of his BMW M5, throwing the used hand towel onto the passenger side floor with a snarl. Fucking hell, what was wrong with him? Starting the ignition, he reversed out of the spot without even checking the backup camera. No one would be there. This was his time to be alone. To decompress. To use the predawn stillness to read or meditate, preparing himself for the day ahead. In seven years at the Manor, he never saw another soul up and about at this ridiculously early hour.

Until Addison.

He groaned and slammed his head back against the headrest. What the hell was this girl doing to him? He'd known her for one fucking day.

Flipping on his high beams, he turned onto the winding, tree-lined road that led to downtown Fairford. The coffee shop in town opened at five. He'd get his double espresso there. Maybe while he drank it, he could figure out what the fuck to do next, because he was spiraling out of control.

And Mason never lost fucking control.

He drove way too fast, and he damn well knew it, but the way his blood surged through his veins, he couldn't stop himself. His body demanded more adrenaline, and if it couldn't get it with Addison, it would find another way.

"Because hitting a deer will help," he ground out, glaring through the windshield. Fuck, if it was a moose, it would total his car and probably kill him in the process.

And yet he pushed down harder on the accelerator, flying down one of the road's few straight stretches, his hands digging into the leather-wrapped steering wheel hard enough for the stitching to leave impressions in his skin.

God, he wanted to grip Addison like this—hold her down with enough force to leave fingerprint bruises as he slid into her sweet pussy. Hear her moan his name, beg him to fuck her as hard as he could, and call him Master—

"Fuck!" he screamed as loud as he could, needing to let out the frustration before he exploded.

He and the others had built an incredible life for themselves at the Manor. All it would take was one sexual assault lawsuit to bring the whole thing crumbling down. He'd potentially ruined all their fucking lives because . . . what? A sassy baker gave him the finger? After a lifetime of ironclad control, he let some woman he didn't even know be his downfall.

Loosening his grip on the steering wheel by sheer force of will, he made himself take several slow breaths. When he reached something in the general vicinity of calm, he lifted his foot, waiting until the car traveled at a more reasonable speed before returning it to the accelerator.

He had to figure this shit out. Talk to Jonathan, maybe even Aiden and Leo. Make a plan together to fix this before it turned into a PR nightmare.

Glancing down at the car's display, he tapped on the phone icon. Jonathan's name sat right at the top of his favorites list. The man would be aggravated to be woken at such a terrible hour, but he'd be even more pissed if he found out Mason waited on something of this magnitude.

With a sigh, he stretched a finger out toward Jonathan's name.

The steering wheel jerked in his other hand as the wheels lost traction, skidding across a patch of ice. "*Shit*," he forced out between clenched teeth, gripping the wheel with both hands and lifting his foot from the accelerator. As the car continued sliding toward the side of the road at alarming speed, he wrenched the steering wheel in the direction of the skid, desperate to regain control before it was too late.

As the trunk of a giant tree got closer and closer, he finally felt the car regain traction. At the last second, he spun the steering wheel in the opposite direction and pumped the brake.

The car slid to a stop mere inches from the tree.

"Christ," he whispered, every muscle in his body tense, his eyes as wide as they could go. Slumping back against the seat, he closed them and concentrated on breathing. Inhale for five, exhale for five. He focused on the count, the rise and fall of his chest, the feeling of his feet on the floor, his hands on his lap, the back of his head against the headrest.

Slowly, painstakingly, his heartbeat returned to normal. When at last he felt calm, he opened his eyes.

The tree loomed in front of him, even closer than he realized. He stared at the rough, icy bark, the color washed out in the harsh light of his high beams, only an inch or two from the front bumper of his car. If he'd still been going ninety . . .

Jesus. He'd probably be dead.

His heart pounded against his ribs again at the thought. He had no idea how much time passed before he managed to put his car in reverse and move back onto the road. It could've been seconds or minutes. All he knew was he needed to return to the Manor.

After making a U-turn in the middle of the road, he started back the way he came, sticking to the speed limit and analyzing the asphalt for any more black ice. He didn't stop white knuckling the steering wheel until he parked back in the Manor lot.

With a few slow, deep breaths, he climbed out of the car and headed inside. Though his feet wanted to take him anywhere else, he forced them to carry him across the lobby, through the dining room, and to the swinging door.

Addison froze when he entered, staring at him like a deer in headlights. None of the food littering the kitchen island while he fucked her remained. She had a wad of paper towels in one hand and a bottle of cleaner in the other. Moving his gaze up to her eyes, he opened his mouth and closed it, not yet sure what to say.

She didn't give him the chance to figure it out. "Are you okay?"

The genuine concern in her voice shocked him. So much so that all he managed was an incredibly debonair and articulate, "Huh?"

Dropping the towels and cleaner to the countertop, she crossed the kitchen, staring up into his face with a frown. "You look pale, and your pupils are dilated." Her hand darted up to touch his forehead, then to rest briefly against his cheek, surprising him yet again. "You feel clammy. Come over here and sit down."

Before he knew what was happening, she tugged him to a round, marble-topped table in the corner by the back door. Pulling out one of the gray upholstered chairs, she pushed down on his shoulder until he sat, then bustled around the kitchen at top speed. Only a few minutes passed before two steaming mugs of tea sat atop the table, and she dropped into the chair across from him, trying to hide her wince.

"I didn't know how you took it," she said, gesturing to the cream, milk, and assorted types of sugar in the middle of the table.

He drank coffee normally, the stronger the better. He could see how his usual double espresso would maybe be a shit idea at the moment, though. "This is perfect," he told her, blowing on the tea and taking a tiny, scalding sip. "Thank you."

With a little smile, she added a single sugar cube to her own cup, stirring it in with a teaspoon. "The Brits think tea is the answer to every problem, right? Seemed like it was worth a try."

He did his best to return the smile, though he knew it came out more like a grimace. "It certainly can't hurt."

They sipped their tea in silence for a while, both pulling pained faces the first several times, until the liquid finally cooled to a reasonable temperature. Addison waited until after her first proper gulp of tea before asking, "What's wrong? I hope this isn't because of what happened between us."

For a moment, he considered changing the subject. He wasn't really one to talk to others when things went wrong in his life—particularly not to near strangers. The earnestness in her eyes, combined with the warmth of the cup between his hands, changed his mind. "I almost crashed my car into a tree about fifteen minutes ago."

"Oh my God," she whispered. Her eyes were so wide, he could see the whites all the way around her irises. "Are you okay?"

"No damage to me or the car," he assured her. "I guess I'm just still coming down off the adrenaline rush."

She slumped back in her chair, a hand over her heart. "Fuck me, that must've been terrifying. What happened?"

Again, he hesitated. It wasn't any of her business how he got himself into that mess. But for the second time, he found the words spilling out of him before long. "I was upset and driving like an idiot," he admitted. "I've lived in New England long enough to know better."

"Ice?" Addison asked, sympathy in her green-blue eyes.

Mason nodded. "Luckily, I slowed down right before I hit the ice. If I hadn't . . ." They shuddered at the exact same time. "I don't even want to think about what would've happened."

"I'm sorry I upset you that much." Her voice was so soft, so small, and she stared down at the half-empty cup between her hands.

"I was upset at myself, not you," he assured her.

Only her eyes lifted, the rest of her locked in place.

"What I did before—I shouldn't have ever—I mean, without even discussing . . ." He let the jagged sentence trail off, unable to organize his thoughts into proper words.

One corner of her mouth lifted into the tiniest hint of a smile. "You can't possibly tell me you didn't enjoy yourself."

He let out something halfway between a sigh and a dark chuckle. "I'm not gauche enough to tell that lie."

"Then aside from having to start my scones over from scratch," she said with a little, one-shouldered shrug, "I fail to see a problem here."

Mason studied her face for several seconds, searching for any sign of a lie. She simply watched him with near indifference as she continued sipping her Earl Grey.

"I see," Mason said at last.

Apparently he didn't need to call Jonathan after all.

"Thanks for the orgasm," Addison said, pushing back her chair and standing. "But I'm afraid I'm really far behind now, so I'm going to have to ask you to please leave."

Mason blinked up at her for several seconds. This wasn't going at all how he expected. Either he'd seriously misjudged her, or something simply didn't add up here.

Until he figured out the answer to that question, best to err on the side that didn't get him sued. "Sorry about your scones," he said, standing and straightening his jacket with stiff movements. "I'll get out of your hair." With that, he walked serenely out of the kitchen, back straight and head held high.

Inside, he was reeling. Did she seriously just thank him for the orgasm? In the same tone one might use to thank him for passing the salt?

He didn't know whether to be impressed or insulted.

No, fuck that. He definitely felt insulted.

The urge to spank her again burned through him, but he couldn't do a damn thing about it. He had to keep his hands off her from now on. They might be able to survive one round of hate sex without collateral damage, but he knew better than to play with fire.

And Addison Walker was a five-alarm blaze.

CHAPTER 5

Addison

As far as New Year's Eve parties went, this qualified as the fanciest one Addison ever attended. She even sort of counted as one of the hosts, as she volunteered to help decorate when her shift ended at noon. The sight of three people carrying boxes of decorations through the lobby made her long to make new friends—or at least a few acquaintances outside the kitchen staff.

She didn't know much about Olivia, Zach, or Nell yet, and they knew even less about her. Even so, Olivia had welcomed her help with open arms. Quite literally . . . the hug had been startling but nice. Together, they'd transformed the parlor into a party paradise.

Strings of twinkling fairy lights covered the white walls, and more lights in the shape of spherical starbursts hung from hooks in the ceiling. Addison and Zach had blown up about a thousand champagne and ivory hued balloons, forming them into ten-foot-tall columns that stretched from floor to ceiling in the parlor's four corners.

At the same time, Olivia and Nell set up silk-draped banquet tables along the whole back wall, which now held platters of hors d'oeuvres prepared by Gabriel and his dinner crew. A three-tier champagne fountain completed the spread, along with a terrifyingly fragile looking pyramid of real crystal champagne coupes.

As Addison nibbled on her fifth brie and fig puff pastry, she took another glance around the room. It made her mind spin that she went from a tiny, two-room apartment in NYC to this in only a matter of days. The men all wore suits that probably cost more than six months' rent at her old place. The women, equally stunning in a variety of dresses and gowns, ranged in style from high-end escort chic all the way up to elegant, diamond draped socialite.

Even Addison wore a stunning 1920s style beaded gown that was without doubt the most fashionable—and probably most expensive— thing she'd ever worn. She found the black and gold garment in a storage room down the hall from her bedroom, complete with matching gold heels. After they had finished setting up the decorations, Zach urged her to dig through the racks of clothes and borrow whatever she liked.

She had a feeling it wouldn't be hard to get used to living like this.

Before she could head back to the little gathering of kitchen staff in one corner, Olivia and Zach sauntered up to her arm-in-arm. Olivia had the stem of her champagne glass gently pinched between two fingers, while Zach gripped his so tight it was a wonder it didn't snap off.

"Zach has something very important he wants to say," Olivia said, glancing sidelong at her unsteady companion with an amused twinkle in her eyes.

"A toast," Zach said, hoisting his glass into the air. Some of the ridiculously expensive champagne sloshed over the rim onto his fingers. "To the newest member of the Fairford Manor family."

Addison doubted he'd be quite so exuberant in his welcome if he hadn't visited the champagne fountain a dozen times that evening, but it made her smile just the same. "Thank you," she said, lifting her own glass and taking a tiny sip of the fizzy liquid. Though she indulged in plenty of the food, she still nursed her first glass of champagne. Getting plastered on her second day of work wouldn't exactly make the right impression, even if she was the only sober person in the room.

When you fuck a partner on day one, sacrifices must be made.

"It takes a little getting used to, doesn't it?" Olivia asked, swinging Zach around so the three of them stood shoulder to shoulder.

"Absolutely. I've never seen anything quite like this." It wasn't just the decorations or the food or the two thousand dollars of champagne they probably wouldn't even finish. Her gaze darted around nonstop, zeroing in on all the confident displays of sexuality throughout the room.

Two bare-bottomed spankings had been doled out since the party started, one over Rafe's knee, the other to a woman draped over the arm of the sofa. A sub in nothing but high-end lingerie and heels wore a thick leather collar, the other end of her leash wrapped loosely around Camden's hand. Earlier, Olivia and Nell announced a fellatio contest to see which woman could get her Dom to come in her mouth the fastest. All five guests in attendance participated with vigor and a complete lack of shame.

The winner got a five-hundred-dollar Amazon gift card.

Everywhere Addison looked, people were kissing, touching, groping, and finger-fucking . . . it turned her on just as much as it overwhelmed her.

Even Olivia wore a thin, white-gold collar around her neck—something Addison couldn't imagine having the confidence to do. At a place this like, maybe, but Olivia mentioned earlier that she couldn't take it off. Not unless Aiden chose to unlock it for her. Most probably saw nothing more than a necklace, but what if people figured it out? *Not-kinky* people who would judge the hell out of her?

Realizing she was staring, she dragged her gaze up to Olivia's kind blue eyes. She didn't seem to notice anything amiss, thank God. "Which one is Aiden?" Addison asked, hoping to get the conversation back on track.

"That one." With a dreamy look, Olivia pointed toward a gorgeous man with a gentle smile and a healthy dose of sexy stubble.

Aiden had his arm wrapped possessively around the shoulders of a redhead on the escort chic–end of the night's fashion spectrum. Her black sequined dress didn't even manage to cover her whole ass, plunging so dramatically in the front and back that it hardly covered anything.

Not that Addison could talk. Her own dress had a slit up the front so high she didn't dare sit down.

Ignoring the room full of people, Aiden slid his hand down the redhead's back and yanked the skirt of the skintight dress up, exposing her ass. Jesus, she was completely bare underneath, not wearing so much as a thong.

The woman had five perfectly parallel lines across her ass cheeks, each a deep crimson color against her pale skin. After a moment, Addison realized they must be cane marks. Aiden began kneading the woman's right ass cheek right in front of everyone—including his own fiancée. Rather than look mortified, the redhead threw her head back in apparent ecstasy.

Addison didn't know if her own skin heated with secondhand embarrassment, lust, or a combo of the two. No matter what she did, she couldn't tear her gaze away from Aiden and his guest. "Do you mind if I ask you a, umm . . . personal question?" she said, her voice coming out high and breathy.

"You want to know how I share without getting jealous?" Olivia guessed. She said it so calmly, like she hadn't a care in the world.

Gulping, Addison managed a stiff nod.

"That one's easy," Zach said, slurring the last two words together. "They get off on watching each other fool around."

Addison looked to the beautiful black-haired woman beside her for confirmation. The lust filling Olivia's eyes was undeniable, and she let out a small whimper when Aiden smacked the redhead's ass with a loud *crack*.

Wishing it wasn't so damn hot in the parlor, Addison downed the rest of her champagne in three gulps.

"All right everyone," one of the other Doms called out as he stepped into the middle of the room. "Less than a minute to go until midnight." From a combo of introductions and overheard snatches of conversation, she'd figured out who the other four were. By the process of elimination, this one must be Jonathan. The head honcho himself. A gorgeous woman with light brown skin and wavy black hair down to her waist hung on his arm, looking up at him like she was the luckiest girl in the world.

Several people pulled out their phones to check the time, and Zach pulled out an antique pocket watch of all things.

"Ten!" Almost everyone in the room said it together. "Nine! Eight! Seven!"

Addison looked around the parlor, realizing for the first time that everyone else was paired off. Well, except for Rafe, his sub of the week, and Nell. The three of them had been entwined in some combo or another since the party started.

"Six! Five! Four!"

Even the others in attendance from the kitchen stood in a cluster, Gabriel and his sous chef Sienna facing Luca and Kendra. Eric, the final member of the dinner staff, had gone home to celebrate with his husband, leaving them an odd number.

"Three! Two! One!"

Her gaze moved again of its own accord, searching for Mason in the crowd. He stood half a head above the next tallest man in the room, making him easy to find.

"Happy New Year!" the partygoers shouted together. But Addison stayed silent as everyone kissed around her. Even Zach and Olivia gave each other a chaste peck on the lips.

Heart pounding against her ribs, she watched Mason cup the cheeks of a woman who looked like a Scandinavian supermodel, stooping down to give her a deep, sensual kiss. The pair seemed to meld together until she couldn't tell where his perfect black suit ended and her slinky black dress began.

When he buried his hands in the woman's sleek, white-blond hair, Addison found herself weaving between couples to get to the doorway. She made it halfway down the back hall before she really even thought about what she was doing.

Good lord, she couldn't have embarrassed herself more if she tried. What the fuck was she thinking, causing a scene like that, fleeing the room like a jilted girlfriend? She had exactly zero claim on Mason. Hell, she hardly even liked the guy.

Since fucking her made him so mad he almost wrapped his car around a tree, the feeling must be mutual.

It had to be that everyone had someone to kiss except her. Merely the anxiety of being the new girl and feeling left out. Nothing else made any sense.

Too mortified to return to the party, she headed for the kitchen, turning on lights as she went. Maybe a nice cup of tea would calm her nerves. With any luck, everyone else was too drunk and occupied to notice her abrupt departure.

Addison started across the kitchen, the clicks of her heels on the tile floor echoing in the empty room. She only managed a handful of steps before the kitchen door burst open behind her. She spun around to find Mason hurrying into the room, his intense blue eyes boring into her, his mouth tilted into a hard frown.

Addison did her best to smile, though she feared it looked more like a grimace. "Can I help you with something?"

Ignoring her question, he asked, "What's wrong?"

Mind racing for a way to get out of this with her dignity intact, she wet her lips before answering. "Who said anything's wrong?"

"You ran out of the party like the room was on fire."

Her cheeks burned with shame, but she refused to look away from him. "I didn't run. I needed to check on something, so I walked over here to do it."

Mason tilted his head to one side. "What are you checking?"

"Why do you care?" she fired back.

With a little shrug, he said, "Because I don't believe you."

Her mouth fell open. The fucking audacity of this man. "I was afraid I left one of the ovens on earlier, so I came to check." She fought the urge to cringe at the terrible lie.

"Unless I'm mistaken," he said in the most infuriatingly superior voice she'd ever heard, "five other people have worked in here since your shift ended. Are you seriously going to look me in the eye and tell me you thought five people missed an oven being on for over twelve hours?"

She glared at him for all she was worth. "Obviously I lied because I want you to leave me the fuck alone," she ground out. "Why don't you take the hint?"

Mason's brows drew together into a harsh V. "I guess we're fighting again."

"I wasn't aware we ever stopped," Addison snapped back. God, what was it about this man that got her hackles up? She willed her temper to chill the fuck out. "Can you please just back off?"

Crossing his arms, he planted his feet at shoulder width, making it clear as day he had no intention of going anywhere. "Tell me what's bothering you, and I'll leave."

"For fuck's sake," she muttered. He blocked the door to the dining room, so she spun around and stormed out the back door instead.

Very. Bad. Fucking. Idea.

Within seconds, her breath came in faltering bursts, each one forming a tiny white cloud in the freezing cold. Darkness stretched out before her like an empty void.

Fuck. She couldn't go out there. Who knew what lurked in the garden or the wilderness beyond? She only made it a couple steps from the kitchen door and already she was on the edge of a panic attack.

Whirling back around, she reached for the door, but her fingers froze around the brass knob. Mason had followed her, and he stood only steps away now.

Fuck it. She could walk around the outside of the house and go through the front. Most of the lights were still on because of the party, so as long as she didn't stray too far, she'd be fine. Probably.

God, this was so fucking stupid.

Hugging herself as tightly as she could, she ran as fast as her heels allowed. She was an icicle before the door even banged open behind her, her sleeveless dress and strappy heels not exactly appropriate cold-weather gear.

Hypothermia seemed a superior idea to slinking back inside with her tail between her legs, though. Trying to ignore the rush of footsteps on the flagstone patio behind her, she kept right on going.

"Addison, don't be fucking stupid," Mason practically growled as he caught up to her. "It's two degrees out."

"Don't call me stupid." She could think it about herself, but fuck him for daring to say it out loud.

He made a low sound of frustration. "Okay, fine, this isn't stupid at all. But please be advised the groundskeepers didn't shovel around this side of the house the last time it snowed, and you're wearing heels. Kindly consider your health and safety and come back inside." Sarcasm dripped from every word.

Fuck, fuck, fuck. How could she get out of this without completely losing face? Lifting her chin, she demanded, "Go away and I will."

"Damnit, I'm just trying to help you."

Gesturing around at the dark, frigid night, she said, "You're doing a real bang-up job so far."

That was a mistake. Before she could entwine her arms back over her stomach, a violent shiver ran through her body, making her stumble in the stupid gold heels.

And of course, Mason caught her. As if her mortification wasn't already bad enough.

His fingertips dug into her bare upper arms as he wrenched her around to face him. "Tell me why you're acting like this. Now." The anger and superiority were gone. Same with that hint of entitlement, like he thought she owed him whatever he wanted from her.

No, this was completely different. This was the full force of his Dom persona—the hard command in his voice, the cold fury in his eyes, the fierce tilt of his frown.

Addison was absolutely helpless against it.

"It sucked being the only person in the room without someone to kiss, okay?" Too embarrassed to look him in the eye, she stared at his lips instead. His perfect, stupid lips. "Now will you leave me alone? *Please?*"

Mason stared down at her for a full five seconds. Addison never looked up, but her heart beat so loudly she was sure he could hear it. Then slowly, ever so slowly, he lowered his lips until they nearly brushed against hers.

Her whole body stiffened, and for a fleeting moment she considered shoving him away. They both knew yesterday's fuckfest was a mistake.

That wasn't what she really wanted, and she damn well knew it.

When his tongue ran along the seam of her lips, she parted for him without hesitation. Moving his hands to her back, he pulled her flush against his body as he claimed her mouth, kissing her absolutely fucking senseless.

The kiss ended just as abruptly as it started, and he steadied her when she almost toppled over again. She suspected she had literal stars in her eyes as she blinked up at him, like some kind of cartoon character.

"Next time," he said, removing his suit jacket with so much force, she was surprised a seam didn't pop, "be a good girl and ask for what you want." He thrust the jacket into her hands. "Don't freeze to death."

Addison stood frozen as he stalked back toward the house, so rigid his arms didn't even swing as he moved. Fixated as she was on his retreating form, she jumped when the kitchen door slammed behind him.

Her teeth chattered as she slid her bare arms into the jacket. The marigold silk lining wrapped her in Mason's body heat, and she couldn't help but close her eyes and sigh as it enveloped her. Jesus fuck, it smelled just like him. Smoky and spicy—like cedarwood and cardamom, with the most delicious hint of leather.

With her lips still tingling and her skin pulsing where he'd gripped her, she knew they weren't done with each other.

Not even fucking close.

CHAPTER 6

Mason

The next four days dragged by. Four days during which Mason managed to avoid Addison completely. The fact that they didn't so much as glimpse one another across the lobby or down one of the Manor's long hallways made him suspect she was trying to avoid him, too.

The guests finished clearing out over an hour ago, and the bulk of the staff followed suit shortly after. Only housekeeping remained, deep cleaning the mansion from the dungeon up through the guest suites on the second floor.

And, of course, Addison. The one person currently living at the Manor full time. Even the groundskeepers and housekeeping staff commuted in from the surrounding area—which was the main reason barely any locals protested when they opened their kinky little resort. Morality issues usually become more of a gray area when your top-notch wages and benefits give a massive boost to the local economy.

Mason lingered in the lobby, sitting at the reception desk and leafing through his next guest's file over and over. It had been at least an hour since he read any of the words. His eyes wouldn't even focus on the pages anymore.

For about the thousandth time, he glanced across the empty lobby, watching the doorway to the back hall for any sign of movement. Addison had to come out of the kitchen eventually. When she did, Mason would be waiting.

He hadn't stopped thinking about that kiss all week. And every-thing in the kitchen the day before . . . Jesus Christ, he wanted to get his hands on her again. Not a great mindset to be in while with his guest. The *what-if* hanging over his head was fucking with his work now. Completely unacceptable. Time to do something about it.

When she still didn't appear after another fifteen minutes, Mason took matters into his own hands. Returning the file to the neat stack on the corner of the desk, he stood and buttoned his jacket. The hard soles of his leather Oxfords clicked against the white and gray marble tiles as he crossed the lobby.

His heart beat way too fast as he made his way through the dining room. The women he'd been with these last seven years all applied to be with him. Every single one was ecstatic to be chosen, leaving no room for mystery or uncertainty.

Addison on the other hand . . . she could turn him down flat. He hadn't been faced with such a prospect in years, and he didn't like the way it made his skin feel too tight.

Pausing outside the kitchen door, he straightened his tie and dried his sweaty palms on the front of his slacks. With a final deep breath, he pushed the door open.

The kitchen practically sparkled with the light pouring through the windows, every single surface cleaned to a perfect gleam. As for the Manor's newest staff member, she was nowhere to be seen.

"What the fuck," Mason muttered under his breath, circling around the kitchen to check the pantry, then both sides of the walk-in cool-er/freezer combo.

Nothing.

Had she snuck out the back door and walked around the outside of the house to the parking lot? But the snow still hadn't been shoveled, and she had no way of knowing he was waiting for her in the lobby. Not unless someone warned her, and why would anyone do that? No one else knew about everything going on between them, at least as far as he knew.

Perhaps she decided to relax in one of the other rooms down the hall. With the guests gone, the study, game room, and parlor would all be empty and available to her, perhaps for the first time since she moved in.

He was just about to go check when a flash of blond hair caught his eye through one of the windows. Moving up to the dishwashing station along the back wall, he peered through the glass.

Addison was crouched down at the far edge of the patio, clearing snow out of a patch of garden with oven mitts on her hands. One corner of his mouth ticked up at the thought of what Gabriel would do if he saw her treating his kitchen equipment that way.

Once her little circle of dirt was clear, she reached into both pockets of her apron, then spread handfuls of nuts and what looked like dried cherries on the ground. Straightening, she wiped her hands on the apron as she glanced around the garden, examining various bushes and hedges. Her lips moved, but he couldn't hear her through the windows.

After about a minute of this, she started across the patio toward the kitchen door. For a brief moment, he considered rushing over to the pantry. He could pretend he came to grab a snack for the road and hadn't been watching her. Ultimately, though, his curiosity got the better of him.

Staring down as she came through the door, Addison stomped her feet on the mat to get the snow off. "Eat up, Alexander," she called out into the garden. It wasn't until she closed the door that she finally noticed him, freezing with her hand still on the doorknob.

"Who's Alexander?" he asked.

Her eyes narrowed, and he had to resist the urge to clench his jaw. Why was it that every goddamn thing he said to this woman pissed her off?

Even more importantly, why did that make him want to fuck her even more?

"Don't make fun of me," she snapped, tossing the dirty oven mitts into a white rattan hamper between the door and the break table, followed immediately by her apron.

That time, he did clench his jaw, hard enough to make his face hurt. "I'm not making fun of you. I saw you spreading some food out there,

49

and then you said something to Alexander on your way in. It's perfectly natural to be curious."

Frowning, she regarded him for several seconds, clearly unsure if she could trust him. In the end, some of the tension drained out of her shoulders. "I saw a cardinal out in the garden. One of his legs is broken —or maybe it used to be and didn't heal right? I can't really tell, but it sticks straight out to the side."

Addison sounded so sad when she said it, his chest literally ached. "He can land with just one leg?" he asked.

"Yeah, and he hops around," she said, using two fingers in the shape of an upside-down L to demonstrate. "I thought it might be harder for him than the other birds to find food, especially in the winter." She gave him a self-conscious smile.

In his mind, she had zero things to be self-conscious about. When she saw an injured bird, she not only hurried to give it some food. She even named it. He couldn't remember the last time he was this utterly charmed by another human being. After all, charm wasn't usually the goal in his line of work.

"Alexander is a perfect name for a cardinal," he said, surprised by the warmth in his own voice.

She peered at him warily for a few more seconds. When he didn't burst out laughing or start mocking her, the last of the tension eased out of her muscles, and she looked truly relaxed for perhaps the first time since he met her. With a little smile, she said, "I assume you want your jacket back? I'll have to run upstairs. It's in my room."

"No," he answered, then hurried to add, "I mean yes, I do want it back eventually. But that's not why I'm here."

Her smile grew a little wider, and her hazel eyes sparked with interest. "Oh? Is there something else you want?"

It was now or never. "You," he said simply, loving the way her full lips formed a perfect O of surprise. "I want you, and I'm tired of pretending I don't."

The smile she gave him then sent a jolt straight to his cock. "You told me to ask for what I want," she said, closing the distance between them with agonizingly slow steps. Flattening her hands against his chest, she looked up into his eyes, her lips slightly parted. "So that's what I'm doing. I want to fuck you again, Mason."

What little restraint he had left fizzled away. Burying his hands in her hair, he held her still as he kissed her, devouring her tiny moans and sighs, memorizing the feel of her. Her hands fisted around his lapels as she arched into him, and he released a moan of his own as her soft stomach pressed against his cock.

It was almost impossible to break the kiss, but he made himself do it. If they kept going much longer, he'd fuck her right here in the kitchen again, and that's not what he wanted. Not this time.

"We need to set some rules," Mason said between gasps for breath. "Number one, nothing else can happen between us in this house."

Eyebrows shooting upward, she released her grip on his lapels as if they burned her. "Why?" she asked, taking a tiny step backward.

"Because when I'm in the Manor, I need to be able to concentrate on my work," he said, finally wresting back control over his breathing. "If I'm constantly thinking about sneaking in here or up to your room, I won't be able to give my guests the attention they deserve."

Pleasure brightened her eyes. "Have you been thinking about this since Monday?"

One corner of his mouth twitched. "Have you?"

"Maybe," she said with a lazy shrug. "I'll admit I've been thinking it would probably be best if we kept fucking until we got it out of our systems."

"That leads us to rule number two," Mason said, pleased she'd been as distracted as him. "What are you looking for exactly? I'm not touching you again until we both know exactly what the rules and boundaries are."

She pursed her lips as she considered his question. Christ, her mouth mesmerized him. He couldn't wait to see those perfect red lips around his cock.

"What are my options?" she asked.

"Well," he said, drawing out the word. "If you prefer, we can just fuck until we *get it out of our systems*, as you said. Or, depending on how you felt about the spanking I gave you the other day, we can do more."

Her whole face lit up, drawing him in like a beacon. Lust made her voice low and sensuous when she said, "More. Please more."

Thank fucking God.

"Then here's what we're going to do. I'll get you a copy of our application from Zach's office. You can fill out the part about your hard and soft limits. When you're ready, head to my house." He pulled his cell from his pocket, tapping the screen to create a new contact. "Put your number in here, and I'll text you the address."

Worry lurked in her eyes as she took the phone and entered her number. "There's one problem," she said as she handed the phone back to him. "I don't have a car."

He blinked at her for a few seconds. "How did you get here?"

"Gabriel hired a driver with a van to bring me and all my stuff." She regarded him with a sardonic half-smile. "And yes, I was made very well aware before I came that we're eight miles from the nearest town. I know how stranded I am."

"That doesn't bother you?"

Some of the bravado slipped from her expression. "It's certainly going to take some getting used to. Especially on Saturday nights, when I'm the only one here." She shuddered, her voice strained when she added, "God, I was terrified last weekend. I turned on every single light in the house. But I don't have much of a choice. I don't have a license. I never even learned how to drive."

"How is that possible?" He looked her up and down. "You're what, thirty-three? Thirty-four?"

"Thirty-eight," she said, throwing him a flirty look. "Thank you for the compliment."

He snorted. "You do realize that makes it even worse?"

She only shrugged. "I've lived in Manhattan since I was eight. We always took the subway or cabs if it was too far to walk. My granny didn't have a car either."

Interesting. That made it sound like her grandmother raised her, not her parents. Filing that information away for later, he returned his focus to the problem at hand. "Okay, new plan. You pack an overnight bag and meet me in the parking lot. You can fill out the application on the way."

Her grin turned downright giddy, and she practically ran across the kitchen. "See you in five," she called as she disappeared into the dining room.

He watched the door as it swung back and forth, going over the past several minutes in his head. Part of him felt fairly sure this was a terrible idea—that rather than get her out of his system, additional fucking would only make him desperate for more.

But as embarrassing as it was to admit, he knew his cock was very much calling the shots. This was happening whether he wanted it to or not.

He might as well enjoy every goddamn second.

CHAPTER 7

Addison

Since Mason's car probably cost over a hundred grand, Addison wasn't exactly surprised when he pointed at the most expensive looking house around and said, "That's where we're headed." She remembered seeing it on her drive up from New York. It stood out from all the other mountainside homes.

While most of the others looked like extravagant log cabins, Mason went for a more modern vibe—all glass and steel and gray stone.

"Wow," she said as she climbed out of the silver sedan. "It's even bigger than I thought."

"That's what she said," Mason said under his breath.

Addison spun around to face him, her mouth hanging open. "Did you just . . . make a joke?"

Shoulders slumping slightly, he frowned at her. "Was it not funny?" He sounded as disappointed as he looked. "People always tell me I don't have a sense of humor."

"No," she rushed to tell him. "It was great. Perfect timing. I was just surprised. You don't really seem like the kind of person to tell those kinds of jokes."

He ran a hand through his hair, no longer looking her directly in the eye. "To be honest, I'm not. Camden says things like that all the time, and everyone always laughs, so I was—" He paused, giving a self-conscious half-shrug. "A lot of what he said at the party made you laugh."

Addison didn't know whether to laugh or frown. It was actually a solid joke, but he wore the attempt at humor like an ill-fitting suit. She didn't like the idea of him trying to mold himself into something he wasn't. Particularly not if he did it for her benefit.

The idea of him watching her at the party though . . . that didn't bother her at all.

"For the record," she said, moving around to his side of the car, running her hands up his crisp, white shirt from his stomach to his chest. "If Camden asked me to come to his house, I would've said no." Sure, the guy was hot as fuck, but it was Mason's intensity that drew her to him.

The uncertainty seemed to melt away from his deep blue eyes. He brushed a hand along her temple and up into her hair. With a few quick tugs, he pulled her hair tie out, letting her long, messy locks tumble across her shoulders.

"Oh God." A hint of a blush heated her cheeks as she laughed. "I'm such a mess. You didn't give me enough time to shower after my shift."

Unperturbed, he ran his hand through her hair, his fingertips grazing her scalp and making goosebumps rise on her arms. "It doesn't matter; you're always beautiful." His eyes crinkled at the corners. "Even with cream cheese frosting on your forehead."

Her hands flew to her face, rubbing at her skin to banish the offending frosting. Lord, how embarrassing. "Clearly, I need to buy a mirror for my room."

Taking her by the wrists, Mason forced her hands down and behind her back. "How about this," he said, leaning in to give her a slow, soft kiss that left her breathless. "Why don't you take a shower and do whatever you need to feel comfortable. Then we'll get started."

"Perfect," Addison breathed out, going up on her toes for another kiss. She groaned when he released her and backed away.

"Shower first," he scolded, but there was no anger in his eyes. Only pure lust. "Then I promise, I'll give you everything you need."

A lot of time had passed since her last relationship with a real Dom.

For the last seven years, the closest she got were the men at Luciana's, who she essentially paid to do whatever she told them to do to her. None of it was real, and sex was strictly off the table. Hell, no one even got naked. Those scenes were only about the release submission and pain gave her.

She'd have to get used to following a whole different set of rules again.

"Ugh, fine," she said, going to the trunk to get her overnight bag. Mason popped it open for her and grabbed his duffel bag—the black kind with two handles and a zipper, like FBI agents used to carry around stacks of ransom money, or an arsenal.

Retrieving her partially completed application from the back seat, Mason led her up the gray stone steps to the front door. He unlocked it and strode into the house without a word or a backward glance. Only a few inches over five feet, she had to take two steps for every one of his. The man was easily six-three or six-four, positively drool-worthy in those dark suits perfectly tailored to his long, lean frame. And that ass . . .

Addison was so focused on the spectacular view that she almost plowed right into him when he came to an abrupt stop. "Sorry," she said, wincing when her bag swung into his leg.

Eyebrows slightly raised, Mason looked down at her with a small frown, but he didn't comment. "The guest bathroom is in here," he said, gesturing toward a closed door. "Feel free to use whatever you need." Not waiting for a response, he stalked off deeper into the house, already flipping through her application.

A shiver of excitement rushed through her as she watched him go. Everything she'd experienced with this man in the last week pointed to exactly one thing: Mason St. John had more intensity in a single, arched eyebrow than everyone else she'd ever scened with added together. She had no idea what he had in store for her, but good God almighty, she couldn't wait to find out.

She hurried into the bathroom, checking the vanity and a small closet for toiletries. A treasure trove of high-end products and styling tools waited for her, making her wonder how many women he brought up here.

Except Gabriel made a comment the other day that the Doms couldn't take their clients off property.

So who did all this stuff belong to?

Her stomach twisted as she used the hair and skincare products—each and every one clearly belonging to a woman. The unease only grew after her shower, when she dug through the vanity drawer holding a hair dryer, curling iron, and straightener, all in matching black and pink. Using another woman's products made her feel dirtier than before the shower.

She'd planned to leave the bathroom in nothing but her sexiest lingerie, but guilt had her so nauseated by the time she dried and curled her hair, she couldn't follow through. Pulling on leggings and an oversized white sweater, she padded out of the bathroom on bare feet.

Mason was nowhere to be seen, so she took the opportunity to look around properly for the first time. Aside from the bathroom and one other room hidden behind a closed door—the guest room, presumably—most of the first floor was a huge open space. A living room filled with contemporary Scandinavian furniture, all in light wood and even lighter fabrics. To one side, a long, utilitarian dining room table, its eight matching chairs so perfectly arranged she suspected he placed them around the table using a ruler.

Then, best of all, the kitchen, its marble-topped island so enormous it was a baker's dream. There wasn't a kitchen like that to be found in Manhattan—at least not outside the penthouses and brownstones she'd never be able to afford.

"Focus," Addison muttered, tearing her gaze away from the island and heading for the stairs. She wasn't here to bake. And frankly, unless Mason told her what she needed to hear, she'd never see that kitchen or this house again.

The stairs were a ridiculous modern design that seemed to float in midair. They looked cool as hell, she had to admit, but they made her feel like she was one minor misstep away from breaking her neck. She made her way up slowly, white knuckling the slender metal railing the whole time.

The second floor was much more segmented than the first with a wide hallway running the length of the house, nothing but floor-to-ceiling windows to one side, four closed doors along the other. At the end of the hall, a few steps led to another glass wall, this one with a wide-open glass door. Addison headed that way, examining the artwork hanging on the wall between the doors as she went.

Mason's eclectic taste in art intrigued her. The first painting—an abstract piece that may or may not have represented a snowy field and a blue sky—fit with the modern, minimalist theme of the house. But the second framed piece was a large painting of flowers in a riot of colors, the paints thick and textured, clearly applied with a palette knife instead of a brush. She could stare at the chaotic swirls and gashes of color for hours and still find something new to fascinate her.

The third painting? Either a real Renoir or a startlingly accurate reproduction. A framed poster of a very similar piece hung over the fireplace at her granny's from the day Addison arrived in Manhattan until two weeks after she died. She couldn't afford the rent on the Upper East Side three-bedroom and had to sell what she could and donate the rest before moving in with Kate.

Addison stared at the painting for almost a minute, rubbing at the ache in her chest. Her granny had loved art more than anything and dragged a young Addison along to every art museum in the boroughs. Now that she was older, she wished she appreciated all those trips instead of resenting them, longing for an afternoon zoning out in front of the TV instead.

She'd give up television for the rest of her life if it meant one more trip to the Met with Mary Walker by her side, spouting facts and trivia like a walking, talking art history textbook.

A soft sound at the end of the hall pulled her out of her memories, and she looked back toward the open door. She was close enough now to get a good look at the room beyond. The square room jutted out from the side of the house, the glass walls giving perfect panoramic views of the Green Mountains. Only a long white sofa, a matching ottoman, and a single end table broke up the large, airy space.

Mason stood at the far window wall with his back to her—hands in pockets, suit jacket gone, and sleeves rolled up to the elbows. She found herself staring at the whipcord muscles of his forearms, remembering the strength of those arms, the feeling of his large hands when he held her, kissed her, spanked her. She clenched her thighs together and took a slow, deep breath.

She wanted this man so much she shook with need.

But she needed answers even more.

"Mason?" she said as she climbed the short flight of stairs into the room.

He turned at the sound, the desire in his eyes sending a scorching heat through her. Fucking hell, he'd even loosened his tie. How could she possibly stay strong and ask questions when he looked so unbelievably sexy? So relaxed and beautiful, but still ready to devour her?

Some of the intensity left his eyes as he looked at her, taking in her clothing before studying her expression with a slight frown. "Is something wrong?"

"I need to know something before we go any further." She tried to sound neutral rather than accusatory, but the way his frown deepened, she may not have succeeded.

"Ask me anything."

Heat flooded her cheeks, but she couldn't back down now. With a deep breath, she forced the words out. "Are you married?"

His eyebrows lifted almost imperceptibly. "I beg your pardon?"

"Or in a relationship? I obviously know about the women at the Manor, and I don't care about that, but if you're also in a committed relationship, I don't think I can—I mean, I wouldn't want to . . ." The sentence trailed off as her mind spun, unable to gain any traction.

Mason studied her for the longest, most excruciating ten seconds of her life. When he finally spoke, his voice was as controlled and neutral as she'd failed to be. "Where is this coming from?"

"The bathroom downstairs," she said, face so hot she must be red as a tomato. "All that stuff in there obviously belongs to a woman."

Understanding filled his eyes, though the rest of his expression remained unchanged. "No, I'm not married. And the last relationship I would refer to as committed ended more than eight years ago."

It was Addison's turn to frown. Maybe Gabriel was wrong about taking guests off property. Or perhaps as one of the founders, Mason didn't think the rules applied to him.

Seeming to read her thoughts, Mason said, "I've never brought a guest here either. That all belongs to Olivia."

"Olivia?" Her voice came out quite a bit louder than intended. "Olivia Adams?" God, was he was admitting to having an affair with his business partner's fiancée? How fucked up would that be?

And what a fucked-up position it would put her in, having to either keep the secret or potentially destroy a relationship.

Mason shook his head, a knowing look in his lapis lazuli eyes. "A few of us get together sometimes on Saturday nights to unwind between guests. We almost always meet here because my house is closest to the Manor. But Aiden and Olivia live over an hour away, so they usually sleep over rather than drive home in the middle of the night."

Addison felt an intense desire to disappear into a puff of smoke, never to be seen or heard from again. Instead, she forced her shoulders back and looked him in the eye. "I'm sorry for assuming the worst." Cringing, she added, "Twice."

"It's all right." His voice sounded so gentle and soft. Crossing the room, Mason brushed his fingertips over her cheeks and up into her hair. "You have nothing to be sorry for. I like knowing you wouldn't be part of an affair. It makes me respect you more."

Relief flooded through her, and she buried her face against his chest. "Thank you," she muttered, her voice muffled by his shirt. "Thank God I was wrong. It would've killed me to walk away from you."

With a low hum of satisfaction, Mason buried his hands deeper in her hair. "You're not going anywhere. Not until I'm through with you." He took a deep breath, then made a soft sound of frustration. "Though I'm going to have to insist you make a list of the products you usually use, so I can have them here before we do this again. I want you smelling like orange blossoms again, not smelling like Olivia."

A laugh bubbled up out of her. Pulling away enough to look up into his eyes, she asked, "We're doing this again?" Her voice came out softer than she intended, and more than a little unsure.

An icy fire burned in his eyes. "I don't have a clue how long it'll take to get you out of my system, Addison. But I do know it'll be a lot longer than a single weekend."

She felt those words in her throbbing clit and empty pussy.

Squeezing her thighs together, she held her breath, waiting to see what he would do next.

"Are you ready to begin?" he asked, voice low and full of promises.

"Yes."

Mason lifted a hand, wrapping it around her throat but not squeezing. "First, I need to teach you what I'll expect of you." He moved toward her, the sudden pressure against her windpipe pushing her backward with each step he took. When they reached the center of the room, he lifted her arms above her head, pulling the sweater off with a single swift tug.

Gaze darting to the glass walls surrounding her, she had to resist the urge to cross her arms over her breasts. When she glanced at Mason again, he watched her with the slightest downward tilt of his lips, the merest hint of a line between his dark brows.

"What is it?" he asked.

"Nothing," she said, attempting to smile.

The line between his brows deepened. "That's the one free lie you get to tell me. After this, you'll be punished accordingly. Do you understand?"

Addison gulped, knowing she should be terrified of the cool fury in his eyes. But damn if that didn't make her wet as the fucking ocean. "Yes."

"Good. Now answer my question."

"The windows," she said, making a vague, sweeping motion toward the walls. "Won't people be able to see us?"

The line disappeared, and he cocked his head to one side. "Is that a problem? You marked exhibitionism as a four on your application."

Fairford Manor's official application included a seven-page checklist of potential sexual and BDSM related acts. That was the part Mason instructed her to fill out on the way to his house, rating every item on that list from one to five. Some things, like sharing with other men, had gotten a one—in other words, something she had no interest in ever trying. Others received an enthusiastic five, such as spanking or face fucking.

A four meant *Have tried and enjoyed, or am very interested in trying*, or something along those lines.

The fact that he remembered her exact rating for a single category out of dozens only mildly surprised her.

"I did," she agreed. "But this wasn't what I had in mind. Anyone could be down on that road. I don't want a minivan full of kids to look up here and get a whole new education, if you know what I mean."

His lips pursed, but there was no annoyance in his eyes. In fact, they seemed to sparkle with amusement. "Understood," he said after a few seconds. "Fortunately, you can't see into the house during the day."

"Too much light reflecting off the glass?" she said, thinking of the millions of windows and glass-sided skyscrapers in New York City.

"Indeed. Even at night, they'd need binoculars to see anything of interest from the road or the handful of buildings with line of sight to my house." He settled his hands on her hips, his fingers dipping beneath the waistband of her leggings. "You're safe here. I give you my word."

She had to admit, it would be magical to fuck in this room— surrounded by the glass with the Green Mountains spread out around her, covered in a blanket of snow. Smiling, she said, "I trust you."

With a satisfied nod, Mason whisked her pants down her legs and away. Folding her clothes with the swiftness and precision of a veteran retail worker, he placed them in a neat pile on the floor.

When at last she stood before him in nothing but her favorite lingerie set—matching panties and bra of black mesh, embroidered with black roses and thorny stems—he commanded, "Kneel."

She descended less gracefully than she would've liked, doing her best to hide a wince when her knees hit the rigid loops of the wool rug. Without another word of instruction, he circled the ottoman and settled onto the sofa, moving the black bag to the floor at his feet.

One by one, he pulled items out of the duffel and laid them in front of her in a neat row. The last item stayed in his hand, mostly hidden from view until he once again stood in front of her.

A black collar, the leather an inch wide with beautiful greenish-blue stitching and a shining silver buckle and matching O-ring.

None of her past experiences prepared her for the reality of being collared for the first time. Addison lacked the words to explain the feeling that crashed through her body like a tidal wave.

All she knew was she wanted to feel it again, as often as she could.

"A collar is a very personal thing," Mason said as his slender fingers undid the buckle. "Not with the guests at the Manor, perhaps. Everything that goes on there is fleeting. Transactional."

Addison closed her eyes and gulped when the impossibly soft leather pressed against her throat.

"But this, what we're doing here . . . I don't want anything about this to be fleeting." After fastening the buckle, he arranged her hair over her shoulders, running his fingers through the thick curls until they fell exactly as he wanted them. Then he got to work on the rest of her body, tilting her chin just so, pushing her shoulders back, spreading her legs a little wider. She let him manipulate her like a doll, keeping her eyelids clamped shut and focusing on every single touch—the glorious heat of skin on skin.

When he finally stepped back, she blinked open her eyes, watching him as he surveyed his work. "I chose this collar specifically for you," he said, brushing a thumb along her cheekbone. "The stitching matches your eyes. No one has worn this collar before you, and no one will ever wear it after. It's ours—a symbol of your willing submission to me, and it'll never mean anything else."

God, she wished she could read something, *anything*, in his expression. But he rarely showed any sort of emotion at all, except in his eyes, and she needed a lot more time before she had any chance of truly understanding what went on in those blue depths. "Do I please you?" she asked, needing to know the answer.

"Everything about you pleases me, Addison." His voice was soft, little more than a whisper.

Sweet lord, she never felt more beautiful in her life. It buoyed her, making the muscles in her back ache a little less, the rough wool of the rug no longer digging quite so painfully into her skin. She almost felt like she was floating.

Clearing his throat, he continued in a stronger voice. "Now be a good girl and listen. As already agreed, when we're at the Manor, we're colleagues, nothing more. But when you're in this house, you will wear my collar and call me either Master or Sir—your choice. You belong to me when you're here. Completely. There are no breaks. We'll never reach the end of a scene and then carry about our day.

From now on, from the moment you step through the front door to the moment you leave back through it, you're mine to do with as I please."

Holy fucking fuck. If she didn't figure out how to breathe soon, she was going to pass out.

"However." He stared into her eyes, ensuring he held her complete attention. As if she'd ever be able to concentrate again after what he just said. "The decision about if and when you come here, and when you leave, rests entirely with you. I will never force you. I will never coerce you. My hand may hold the whip, but you hold all the power. Do you have any questions?"

Forcing the haze of lust to stop clouding her mind, she considered everything he said. Giving the laden ottoman a pointed look, she asked, "If something is too much for me, how am I supposed to get up and walk out if I'm restrained?"

"I apologize," Mason said, his even tone not matching the intensity in his eyes. "I realize I didn't explain that as well as I should have. It doesn't have to be all or nothing. If something makes you uncomfortable or goes too far, use your safeword. We can adjust and continue until you're ready for me to take you back to the Manor, or an hour before check-in on Sunday evening, whichever happens first."

Relief flooding through her, she let out a small sigh. The way he described things, it had sounded like she wouldn't have any sort of safeword at all. Like she would need to endure whatever he chose to do to her, or admit defeat and go home unsatisfied.

But this . . . this sounded like all her darkest, most delicious fantasies come to life.

"Would you like to choose your own safeword?" Mason asked.

Her mind instantly went to the bright red feathers of the injured bird she saw that afternoon. "Cardinal."

The hard features of his intense Dom look slipped for a moment, but he hid the rare show of mirth instantly. "Cardinal it is. Do you understand and agree to these rules?" She opened her mouth, but before more than a syllable came out, he added, "Including proper form of address?"

There wasn't any chance in the world she'd say no. "Yes, Master."

Her eyes widened as soon as the word slipped out. She'd intended to stick with sir, but something about master just felt so fucking right.

When the air left his lungs on a harsh exhale, his eyes boring into hers, it solidified her decision. "I like the sound of that in your voice."

Blushing, she admitted, "So do I, Master."

One corner of his mouth lifted into the merest shadow of a smile. "Then let's begin."

CHAPTER 8

Mason

From the moment Addison slammed a door in his face, Mason wanted to take her over his knee. He spent the last week fantasizing about it far more than he'd ever admit to another soul, and he refused to rush it now that the moment had arrived.

Her gaze tracked him as he made his way leisurely around the ottoman, picking up his half-empty duffel bag and moving it over by the door. Then he settled on the sofa and surveyed the tools of his craft laid out before him. Where to begin.

Making his selection, he met her gaze and ordered, "Crawl to me."

Her whole body flushed with excited pleasure as she tipped forward onto hands and knees. Addison kept her back arched slightly as she crawled, her eyes locked on him the whole way. Christ, she was stunning. Her full lips in a slight pout begged him to kiss her senseless. Her breasts looked like they were mere seconds from tumbling out of her sexy little bra, one large, rosy nipple already peeking over the edge of the sheer fabric.

And of course, the flare of her hips and that perfect fucking ass. It was made for spanking. He had no doubt about that.

When she finally knelt up at his feet, he hooked a finger through the O-ring on the front of her collar. Not pulling her toward him, but holding her still. Letting her know he was in charge of everything she did, up to and including when and where she could move. "I'm going to punish you now. I think we both know you've earned a long, hard spanking."

Disappointment flashed through her eyes, there one second and hidden the next. Clearly, she had other activities in mind. "As you wish, Master." Though she tried to hide it, there was a trace of displeasure in her voice, too.

"You thought perhaps we'd begin with something a little more fun?"

Her gaze skittered away, and for a moment, he suspected she intended to lie to him again. But he heard the truth in her words when she said, "I'm all for spanking, and obviously I'll do whatever you tell me. I just . . . I didn't realize we'd start with an actual punishment."

He watched her closely, noting the slight tensing of her muscles, her hands wringing in her lap, the furrowing of her brow. The way she sucked her lips between her teeth, trying to stop herself from saying more. "Look at me."

It took a few seconds, but she managed to meet his gaze.

"Do you think you deserve a punishment?"

"I—I don't know?" At the last second, she turned it into a question.

"You refused to accept my apology, slammed a door in my face like a spoiled brat, then caused a scene and nearly froze to death on New Year's in a fit of jealousy." Her eyes grew wider and wider with each word. "And you very rudely called me an asshole and flipped me off, but since I already spanked you for that, it won't be included on your list of transgressions today."

She swallowed again, the soft skin of her throat shifting beneath the collar. Every inch of her mesmerized him.

"Do you agree that a punishment has been earned?"

"I acted like an idiot at the party," she said, genuine shame in her voice. "I can admit that now."

When she didn't continue, he arched his brows. "Is that all you have to say?"

She pursed her lips together, but it didn't hide the way one corner lifted into a mischievous half smile. "To be honest," she said with a little shrug, "I'm not sorry for slamming a door in your face."

This day kept getting better and better. Mason loved a challenge.

"By the time we're done, you will be," he promised, leaning forward to grab an anal plug and a small bottle of lube from the ottoman. He held them out for her examination, a thrill of excitement coursing through him when her eyes rounded again. If she wanted to make things worse for herself, far be it from him to argue. "You put anal plugs as a three, and anal sex as a two on your application. I'd like you to explain why you chose those ratings."

Blood rushed up her neck and spread across her cheeks. She was adorable when embarrassed. "I don't enjoy anal," she said, drawing out the word *enjoy* for a solid two seconds. "It doesn't feel good to me, but I'm not against it for, well, you know."

Taking hold of her chin with his free hand, he squeezed only hard enough to properly get her attention. "Look at me," he ordered again.

Her gaze shot to his. This close, and with the sunlight pouring through the windows, he could see every speck of gold in her hazel eyes.

"There's no reason to be embarrassed," he told her, keeping his voice as matter-of-fact as possible. "I need you to explain what you mean as clearly as you can so I know how best to take care of you."

She blinked, blinked again, and then answered in a low, hesitant voice. "I don't like anal for pleasure. But for punishment . . ." She faltered, but found her voice again after a few seconds. "When I'm spinning out of control and I can't force myself to be good, make the right decisions, do the things I know I need to do . . ." Forcing out a shuddering breath, she finished with, "It makes me feel like a good girl again. It makes everything make sense."

He loosened his grip on her chin. "Good girl," he said, sliding his hand down to rest over her collar. "Thank you for telling me."

All the tension melted out of her body, even with the plug still clutched in his other hand. "You're welcome, Master."

Enough delays. It was time to get truly started. Moving his hands out of her way, Mason ordered, "Place yourself over my lap."

He sat perfectly still as she climbed onto the sofa and draped her perfect little body over his thighs. Only once she settled on the cushions did he set the plug aside and make slight adjustments, getting her ass exactly where he wanted it. Slipping his fingers beneath the waistband of her panties, he drew them slowly down to her upper thighs, dragging his nails lightly against her pale skin. She shivered as goosebumps sprang up everywhere he touched.

"Bad little girls who don't feel sorry when they misbehave deserve extra punishment," he said, voice hard as steel. Spreading her ass cheeks wide, he squeezed the bottle.

Addison yelped as the cool liquid hit her sensitive skin, but didn't attempt to pull away. Even when he ran his hand up and down her folds, spreading the lubricant around and coating his fingers, she stayed perfectly still.

Until she didn't.

She bucked like a filly trying to throw her rider when he plunged a finger into her ass.

"Be still," he said, giving her bottom two swift spanks. "You know you've earned this."

A high, frustrated groan drifted out of her, and she buried her face in her arms, going limp over his lap.

"Good girl." Mason started pumping one finger in and out of her, then added a second, preparing her for the spade-shaped plug. When even her tight ring of muscle relaxed, he knew she was ready.

Coating the silicon plug generously, he pressed the tip against her asshole. "Open," he ordered when her cheeks clenched together. "Don't fight it."

Another keening moan, but she did as he said, and the plug started to disappear inside of her. "Please," she begged, choking on the word, sounding near to tears. "*Please* don't."

"Only one word will make me stop," he reminded her, pushing the plug deeper still. "You know what it is."

She stretched her arms out, wrapped her fingers around the edge of the sofa cushion, and squeezed as hard as she could. But she didn't say her safeword.

Pleasure surged through him, making his already hard cock throb. Such a good girl. Some submissives loved to have their assholes filled and punished and fucked, like Olivia. It was always a pleasure to scene with an anal slut, but this . . .

Addison's struggle made this a million times better. The fact that she would endure it, would suffer for him, made him feel like a fucking god.

"Do you deserve to be punished?" Mason asked when at last the plug settled into place.

It took her two tries to get out, "Yes, Master."

"Does the plug help you remember what a bad girl you've been?"

Another whimper. "Yes, Master."

He brought his hand down five times in the center of each cheek, hard enough to make her cry out. Waiting for her to settle back down, he rubbed a gentle hand across her punished flesh until she relaxed.

Without warning, he started back up, ten hard smacks on each cheek this time. By the time he finished, her skin glowed a soft pink. He examined the rosy color, comparing it to her usual fair complexion. Excellent. He had her exactly where he wanted her.

He couldn't fucking wait for her ass to be red hot and throbbing beneath his hand.

"That will do for a warm-up."

Her soft sound of distress was like music to his ears.

Stretching out one long arm, Mason wrapped his fingers around the handle of the paddle he'd placed on the ottoman. For their first scene, he didn't want anything too severe—a medium-sized paddle coated in black leather, eight small holes evenly spaced across the rounded business end. This paddle was designed to sting rather than truly punish.

"This is going to hurt," he assured her, letting the paddle rest across the center of her ass. "I know you can be a good girl and take it."

"Please remove the plug, Master," she said, a whimper threaded through each word. "Please. I'll take whatever else you want, but please take it out first."

Mason frowned down at the sub draped over his lap. "We've already discussed this. I have nothing more to say on the matter."

She squirmed for a few seconds, her ass clenching and unclenching. With a hefty sigh, she settled down and murmured, "Yes, Master."

With that, he raised the paddle and slammed it back down, hard enough that she jerked and cried out. He did it without any sort of warning on purpose, wanting to see her reaction.

A warm, soothing sense of pride spread out from his chest when she didn't try to pull away from him, cover her bottom, or even protest. She merely got herself back into the proper position and waited.

"Good girl," he murmured, then got right back into it, landing hard strokes around different parts of her ass and thighs with such quick succession that she stopped breathing partway through.

Mason drew the paddle away, waiting for her to draw in a slow, ragged breath, then another. Before she truly caught her breath, he went again, longer this time, pushing her further. He kept this up for some time, changing the location and the level of force of each stroke at random, varying the lengths of her reprieves.

Most of the Doms he knew—and certainly the others at the Manor —tended to be more systematic. Hell, Rafe even liked to make patterns whenever he used a cane. There was a time and place for that kind of punishment.

Not now . . . not with Addison.

Mason had long since discovered that the submissives who placed themselves in his hands were much more open, more honest, if he stayed unpredictable.

He wanted her honesty.

For reasons he couldn't explain, he wanted all of her. More than he ever wanted any sub he worked with.

After several minutes of this, she started to cry. Not the deep, wracking sobs of a person in a great deal of pain. That wasn't the goal of this exercise. No, her tears were those of a woman overwhelmed by both the thoughts swirling in her mind and the confusing sensations coursing through her body.

Soft, quiet, and utterly beautiful.

"Lovely," he said, brushing tears from her upturned cheek with his thumb. "You've been such a good girl, Addison. You've earned a reward."

Placing the paddle aside, he took his time removing the plug, easing it carefully out of her. Even with his attempted gentleness, every muscle in her body tensed up, her hands again forming tight fists around the edge of the sofa cushion.

"Thank you, Master," she said, sagging with relief as the widest part came free. "Thank you so much."

Setting the plug aside, he let his hand rest on her bottom, loving the warm red color and the heat of her skin. He found himself imagining how she would look and act and feel the first time she earned a severe punishment. He couldn't wait for that day. "Since you took your punishment so well," he said, gently rubbing her disciplined flesh, "I'm going to give you a choice. You can come on my hand right here, and then I'll fuck you."

She shivered. It almost made him smile.

"Or I can fuck you right away, and you can come with my cock buried deep inside you."

"Oh my God," she breathed out, clenching her thighs together, shaking with anticipation. "The second one. Please."

Mason had a feeling they were going to get along just fine.

Helping her up as he gained his own feet, he slid her panties the rest of the way down her slender legs. Her sexy little bra joined them on the floor, leaving her totally bared to him at last.

He swept his gaze over her, drinking her in. "Lovely," he whispered again, holding onto his self-control as much as he could. No matter how much he wanted to bend her over and drive himself into her, he would take his time. Do this right.

Bending down, he plucked the leather cuffs from his row of equipment. "Turn and place your hands at the small of your back," he ordered, swiftly trapping her wrists in the cuffs when she complied. Then Mason wrapped her golden hair around his fist, sighing softly as she arched her neck back. She was all soft, curving lines, so graceful and petite and perfect. The top of her head only came to his chest, and when he marched her around to the end of the sofa, bending her over the arm, her toes barely touched the floor.

Fuck, he loved how tiny she was. Though he was the tallest Dom at the Manor, he was also significantly slimmer than the other four, his muscles running more toward the wiry end of the scale. Rafe and Camden could probably bench press him with their bulging muscles, and he saw the way guests looked at them. Drool practically ran down their chins.

He wasn't jealous, exactly, but he relished towering over Addison. He loved thinking how easily he could overpower her, even though he had enough wisdom to know how fucked up that sounded. Perhaps that part of men's brains hadn't changed much from the days of cavemen—at least not in men with his particular tastes.

Was it some form of toxic masculinity that made him feel like the biggest, strongest man in the whole fucking world when he had this tiny woman at his mercy?

If so, in this moment, he didn't give a flying fuck.

Mason pressed against her, grinding the bulge in his slacks against her bared pussy. "You've been so well-behaved. Such a good little girl." His cock jerked at her needy whimper.

Stepping away, he shed his clothing, placing them in a neat pile beside hers. Then he grabbed a long length of black silk, folded into a neat square, from his dwindling supplies on the ottoman.

The silk tumbled down from either side of his palm as he moved up beside her. "I don't want you to do or think about anything as I fuck you," he told her, his voice rougher than normal. "I only what you to feel, Addison. Do you understand?"

Turning her head to one side, she looked at him. Her eyes went wide when she saw what he held in his hand. "Y-yes, Master." Her voice trembled, and it made him want to kiss her so intensely that the rest of her would tremble, too.

Mason pulled her upright by her hair, delighting in her soft hiss of pain. He arranged her hair and tied the blindfold in place with meticulous, practiced movements. To his absolute delight, her whole body did start trembling as he bent her back into place over the sofa arm.

Fucking a naughty girl with a freshly punished ass had been one of his favorite pastimes for as long as he knew such a thing existed.

But this—to fuck this woman who had embarrassed him, denied him, insulted and irritated him . . .

Christ. He wasn't ashamed to admit he wanted to fuck her into the ground. Take all his confusion and frustration of the last week out on her pussy.

Finally get back to a place where part of his life made sense again.

Rolling on a condom, Mason moved into place behind her, lining his cock up with her wet heat. "Now be a good girl and take every single inch," he ground out, shoving his hips forward.

He expected her to moan or gasp or cry out at the sudden, full intrusion. But she didn't utter even the tiniest of sounds or move so much as a single muscle.

What the hell?

Her pussy was certainly wet enough, so there was no doubt in his mind that she was as turned on as he was. And after all, he gave her a choice. She asked him to fuck her.

Frowning, he pulled back and tilted his hips forward again. Slower this time. Softer, so it barely made a sound when his hips bumped up against her ass. Perhaps the sudden force of it had startled her. He could build up to that. Help her body and mind be truly ready before he fucked her the way he wanted to.

She remained stark still, her shoulders hunched, her face pressed firmly against the cushion. Something was wrong. *Very* wrong.

Pulling out entirely, Mason leaned over her tensed body, wrapping his hands around her upper arms. "Addison?" He started to haul her upright, intent on removing the cuffs and blindfold so they could talk properly.

Addison threw her head back so fucking fast, he didn't have time to dodge. Her skull cracked against his nose, and he shouted more from shock than actual pain. She crashed back down against the sofa when his hands flew to his face, gently prodding and assessing for damage.

That lasted for about half a fucking second.

Then she kicked and writhed, catching him once in the shin, almost slamming a heel into his groin. "Jesus!" he shouted, leaping out of range at the last possible second. What in the ever-loving fuck was going on?

"Let me out! Let me the fuck out!" She jerked so violently she almost rolled right off the sofa and onto the floor.

"Addison." He said it soothingly at first as he rushed in to catch her. When that didn't do a damn thing, and she kept shrieking that he let her out, he tried his sternest Dom voice instead. "*Addison.* I can't help you until you calm yourself. Be still."

75

His words had no effect whatsoever. She continued to thrash around as he knelt beside the sofa, half-holding her while he tried to undo the cuffs—right up until the blindfold slid off her eyes.

All the fight went out of her the moment he caught a glimpse of one hazel eye.

Her gaze locked with his for the space of five frozen heartbeats, and then she burst into tears.

It took Mason half a second to form a new plan. With swift movements, he yanked the blindfold the rest of the way off, tossing it over his shoulder. The cuffs followed mere moments later.

Lifting the limp, sobbing woman into his arms, he cradled her against his chest as he carried her from the room.

CHAPTER 9

Addison

"I'm sorry."

"You have literally nothing to be sorry for."

"I ruined everything."

"You didn't ru—"

"Did I hurt you?"

"Addison, you didn't ruin anything."

"Did. I. Hurt. You?"

A sigh. "No. My nose isn't broken."

God, she wished she could fucking die. "I almost broke your nose?"

When she started to cry again, he pulled her tighter against his chest, fitting his body along hers so their skin touched in a thousand different places. "Shh. You clearly didn't do that on purpose. You have nothing to be sorry for."

As if him saying it could make the feelings go away—could take the shame away.

Why the fuck didn't she rate blindfolds as a one? She should've known what would happen. She'd slept with a nightlight in her room for the last three decades, for fuck's sake. The clues were fucking there.

It simply hadn't occurred to her that a blindfold would have the same effect as a completely dark room. It always seemed so sexy in books and movies. And after all, the room beyond the blindfold had been flooded with sunlight. It wasn't the same thing.

The moment the silk covered her eyes, it sure felt the same. She was six years old, trapped, afraid, and alone. The memories flooded her mind, completely overpowering her.

"That's it," Mason said, gently stroking her hair as her tears dried up again. "It's okay. Everything's okay."

"Why are you being so nice to me?" She hated how accusatory her voice sounded.

If he noticed, he didn't react. "Because you deserve it."

She didn't know why his kindness bothered her so much. Maybe because it felt sort of like pity? Why else would someone who hated her for the last week suddenly be so sweet and caring. "I went crazy and almost broke your fucking nose," she snapped, pulling away enough to glare at him. "Why the fuck would I deserve it?"

Propping himself up with one elbow on the bed, he frowned down at her. "I don't know what happened in your life," he said, cupping her cheek. "And you don't have to tell me anything if you don't want to." His thumb stroked up and down, the touch featherlight. "But I'm absolutely certain you're not crazy."

She yanked her head back from his touch. "Oh, you don't think so?" God, she sounded so angry. So fucking *mean*. Why did she react this way when he was being overwhelmingly kind? She hated it, but she couldn't stop it. "What would you call it then?"

He took a few slow breaths, clearly trying to rein in his own temper in the face of hers. "I'm not an expert." His voice stayed perfectly steady and calm. "But my best guess would be PTSD."

Addison opened her mouth to argue some more, but no words came out. Hiding her face in a pillow, she started crying again.

"I'm here," he whispered, wrapping her up in his embrace again. "You're not alone. You don't have to do this alone."

That was the thing, though. She'd always done this alone. Oh, her granny took her in and patiently waited for Addison to feel safe enough to start dismantling the walls she'd built around herself. Shared her passion for art, and nurtured Addison's newfound obsession with cooking. Got her a nightlight when she screamed and cried in her bedroom at night.

But she never asked why the darkness terrified her so.

Others had loved and been there for her in one way or another in the last thirty years. Kate, who had been her best friend since seventh grade. The few other friends from her school days she still texted or met up with now and again. She even connected with a couple people from the restaurants she worked in before the café—friendships forged in fire. And of course, Lola.

Nearly all had asked why her grandmother raised her and not her parents, but they all seemed genuinely relieved when she changed the subject. They clearly asked because it was the polite thing to do, but knew they were better off not knowing all the gritty details.

Mason wouldn't be any different. Why on earth would he? He didn't even like her outside of what she could provide for him sexually. She had a feeling this would be the last weekend he invited her to his house.

God, she really hated herself sometimes. Couldn't she have one good thing in her life without somehow fucking it up?

Sitting up, she scooted awkwardly to the edge of the mattress. Her clothes would be nice, but she didn't even know where in the house she was anymore—only that it was clearly his bedroom. Keeping her back to him, she searched for the appropriate thing to say. "Well, uh, thank you. For, you know . . . helping me."

She cringed. Could she have sounded more idiotic? Thank God he couldn't see her face, because her blush made everything even worse.

Her only choice was to plow on ahead. "Anyway, I don't know if you're done with me now, or if you still want to fuck, or what. Just let me know what's good for you. I'm fine with whatever." It came out in the same tone she'd use to order fast food at a drive through.

Mason stayed silent for so long, she finally risked a glance over her shoulder. He sat propped against the headboard, watching her with slightly narrowed eyes, his lips pressed into a tight line.

She considered the best expression for a moment, ultimately going with mild confusion. "What?" she asked, keeping her voice light.

"I don't know what you're doing right now," he answered slowly, the line between his brows deepening. "But I don't like it."

Yeah, she was done. Reaching up, she fiddled with the buckle on the collar until she got it loose. "I'm ready to go home."

Dropping the collar on the bed, she stood and went to search for her clothes, using every last ounce of her strength to keep her spine straight until she passed out of his sight.

Mistakes were made.

Not that Addison would admit that to anyone but herself.

For the last five days, she'd been kicking herself for screwing everything up on Saturday. Would it really have been that hard to give him a teeny tiny little glimpse into her past? It wouldn't have taken much—just enough vague info to understand what happened with the blindfold so they could get back to the fucking.

God, the weekend she could've had. Her body pined for those lost spankings and orgasms. Straight-up fucking *pined* for them. Like the wife of a sailor when her husband went off to sea for two years.

How absurdly dramatic.

Clenching her thighs together, she closed her eyes and took a few deep breaths. She had a date with her vibrator the second she got up to her room after this shift.

"You okay, Addison?"

She opened her eyes to find Kendra watching her with a furrowed brow. The junior member of the breakfast and lunch staff had enthusiastically welcomed Addison to the kitchen. She delighted in no longer being the only woman around in the mornings.

Addison liked the younger woman. A lot, in fact. It would be a while before their friendship hit a talk-about-how-you-wish-you-fucked-your-boss-more-this-weekend level, though. "I think I feel a migraine coming on," she lied. "I'll probably go lie down as soon as I finish this cake."

"Ugh, migraines are the worst." Every inch of her screamed genuine sympathy, from her eyes to her posture to her clenched hands. "Do you want me to finish it for you?"

"That's so sweet," Addison said with a grateful smile. "But I'm almost done. They'll start coming down for lunch soon, and I'm sure you've got enough on your plate as it is."

Kendra looked like she wanted to object, but Luca said, "If you leave your dishes by the washing station, Kendra can take care of them after lunch if she wants. Right now, I really need her back over here before something burns."

Wishing she'd picked a different lie, Addison made a shooing motion. "Go. I promise I'm fine."

"Okay." With a reluctant frown, Kendra turned back toward the stove. "Seriously, though, leave your dishes," she called over her shoulder. "I owe you one anyway for making that focaccia for me yesterday."

Addison had to repress a laugh. "That's literally my job."

"Staying late because I didn't give you enough notice isn't."

It had been twenty minutes, if that. "I didn't really—"

"No more arguing," Luca said, the edge of a command in his voice. "I can't handle the distraction right now. Just let Kendra do it."

Guilt clawed at her chest, but she couldn't do anything about it now. Silently promising to do their dishes later in the week, she finished icing the ten-layer Smith Island cake Gabriel would serve with dinner tonight. After moving it to the walk-in, she stacked her dirty dishes as neatly as she could near the industrial dishwasher, then wiped down her workspace. It would have to do.

Only one thing left before her date with the hot pink Rabbit waiting in her nightstand drawer. Slipping into the cavernous pantry, she grabbed a handful of mixed nuts and headed out the back door. Alexander might not even be finding the offerings she left every day, but she would keep doing it anyway, just in case.

The door barely swung closed behind her when she stopped in her tracks. A white vinyl post rose out of the ground, right where she always left her assortment of nuts, seeds, or dried fruit. At the top stood an elaborate wooden bird feeder with multiple levels.

Addison stared at the feeder for several seconds, her brain doing a sort of record scratch. As she watched, a female cardinal and a chickadee flitted over from the nearby hedges, grabbed some food, and flew right back into the boxwoods.

The cold finally snapped her out of her stupor. Tossing the mixed nuts onto the patio for critters to find later, she rushed back into the kitchen. "Hey, did you guys see who put that bird feeder out there?" She tried to sound vaguely curious, and not like her heart was about to burst out of her chest.

"Hmm?" Luca said, tossing something in the pan and not looking up.

Kendra glanced her way, but only long enough to shrug. "I didn't notice it. Maybe ask Zach? He sees *everything*."

The way she said it made Addison smile—like Zach was the Great and Powerful Oz. "Thanks again," she said, tossing her apron in the hamper and heading off to find the receptionist.

Luckily, he made the task incredibly easy by being at his desk. He looked up as she crossed the lobby, gracing her with a smile that made his green eyes sparkle. Addison made up her mind then and there to put some legit effort into befriending the man. Something about him made her feel better about herself when she was around him. As if his obvious goodness somehow rubbed off on her.

"What can I do for you this fine morning?" Zach asked, putting his feet up on his desk. He wore a silver-gray suit and vest today, his bow tie gray-and-white floral on a charcoal background. The guy quite possibly held the record for the world's largest supply of vests and bow ties, and was too adorable for words.

"Is it still morning?" she asked, leaning her elbows on the reception counter.

Zach glanced at his computer screen. "For six more minutes." He flashed another smile. "What's up?"

"I'm hoping you can satisfy my curiosity about something." She pitched her voice in what she hoped was a fun, conspiratorial way.

He immediately took the bait. Dropping his feet back to the floor, he leaned toward her and fake-whispered, "Are we spying on someone? I love spying on people."

That made her laugh. "So I've heard. A bird feeder mysteriously appeared outside the kitchen last night. I want to know how it got there."

For a moment, she worried he'd lose interest. A bird feeder wasn't nearly as exciting or salacious as what he normally saw on the security cameras. But then his eyebrows arched upward. "Where you leave the birds food every day?"

She lifted her own brows. "Wow, they weren't kidding. You do see everything."

With a smug smile, Zach blew air on his nails and buffed them against his chest. "Naturally." He grabbed his mouse and got to work, the ghost of a smirk hovering around his lips. "Do you have any suspects?"

An image of Mason, stark naked and stretched out on his bed as he comforted her flashed through her mind. "I might."

That only made him smirk harder. "Okay, keep your secrets."

Addison knew the instant he found the answer. His whole expression changed—the sparkle gone from his eyes, his mouth a straight, emotionless line. Motioning her around the counter, he said, "We have our culprit." Bland disinterest replaced the usual warmth in his voice.

What on earth was that about? She wished she knew Zach well enough to ask, but they'd only spoken a handful of times since the New Year's Eve party.

Keeping her own expression neutral, she circled around to look at his screen. Her heart skipped a beat as she watched a video of Mason slamming a post hole digger repeatedly into the hard ground, his black suit rendering him half-invisible in the darkness. Zach fast forwarded several minutes to when Mason laid the tool aside in favor of the vinyl post, bird feeder already attached.

"Well." Zach sounded almost bored now. "There you have it. Mason St. John has taken a sudden interest in birds."

"Apparently," Addison said, her chest unbearably tight. If she felt like being honest with herself, she knew it the second she saw the feeder out in the garden. The same way she knew Mason was responsible for the gorgeous, full-length mirror that appeared in her room while she worked Monday morning. There would be no more embarrassing frosting incidents in her future.

Her gaze stayed glued to the video until Zach closed the laptop, snapping the screen down so hard the sound made her jump. Picking up the computer, he tucked it under his arm as he stood. "I hope that was helpful. Now if you'll excuse me, I need to make some phone calls." He walked into the little office behind the reception desk, shoving the door closed behind him without ever glancing back.

Weird as fuck? Absolutely.

Something she was remotely capable of figuring out right now? Not even a little bit.

With a final regretful look at Zach's closed door, she headed up to the third floor. She could only deal with one bizarre turn of events at a time, and Mason had to be her priority.

Mind spinning the whole way, she tried to figure out the best way forward. Searching the mansion for Mason definitely wouldn't work. He made it abundantly clear his focus needed to be on his guests during the week.

Except apparently at 4:26 in the morning. Then he could install an absurdly fancy bird feeder to provide for the injured cardinal she wanted to befriend like some sort of kinky Disney princess.

So she could either wait and see what happened, or find another way to be proactive.

By the time she arrived at her room, she had made up her mind. She didn't need to pour her heart out or prostate herself at his feet, begging for forgiveness, but she could still apologize.

Closing her bedroom door behind her, she leaned against it and fished her phone out of her pocket. She pulled up the text thread with Mason, if she could even call it that. A solitary message floated within the gray bubble at the top of the screen.

This is Mason St. John.

She stared blankly at her phone for almost a minute as she composed message after message in her head. Finally, she typed out, *I'm sorry about*

Saturday. I'd like to talk when you have the time and hit the blue send arrow.

Before she could close the window, three dots appeared in their little speech bubble. They hovered there for several seconds, then disappeared.

Again, three dots, this time only for a moment.

And then nothing.

Well then. That was just fucking great.

Tossing her phone onto the bed, she stripped down and plodded into her en suite bathroom. Less than a minute later, she stood under the too-hot spray of the shower, eyes closed as water cascaded over her.

Images flashed through her mind. Mason stalking across the kitchen, cold fury radiating off every inch of him. The exact movement of his lips every time he said *good girl*. The look on his face as he lowered a collar toward her throat for the first time.

It wasn't long before her mind turned to even dirtier things. The way the muscles in his butt moved when he walked. She wanted to wrap her legs around him and dig her heels into that tight ass as he drove into her.

And it was a goddamn tragedy she barely got to see his cock on Saturday. Even so, she could picture it perfectly, and she salivated at the thought. She imagined herself on her knees, Mason looming over her like a god as he pushed his cock down her throat.

Good lord, if she didn't come soon, she would explode.

Stretching up on her toes, she grabbed the handheld showerhead, twisting the dial around until it emitted a narrow, intense stream. They might say this setting was for massages or something, but everyone knew that was bullshit. This setting was for the ladies.

Spreading her legs wide, she used her free hand to expose her clit, positioning the showerhead so the water made perfect contact. Fuck, it felt good. She moved the showerhead in the tiniest of circles as she remembered when Mason bent her over the countertop, ripping down her pants and panties to spank her with a wooden spoon.

The muscles in her lower abdomen started to cramp, so she lifted one foot up onto the low corner shelf she used when she shaved her legs. Leaning against the shower wall, she aimed the water stream at her clit and got back to her fantasy. Mason fucked her against the counter with bruising force, his hips sending a new burst of pain through her each time they slammed against her recently punished ass.

She wanted that again. She wanted it so badly she couldn't even think straight anymore. Only her pleasure mattered in this moment.

The illusion shattered when someone banged their fist against her bedroom door. "Fuck!" she said, dropping the showerhead. It hit the wall with a loud *bang*, the water whipping around until gravity finally settled the showerhead into place.

The pounding came again, even louder this time. Lamenting the almost-orgasm, she turned off the water and grabbed a towel. Drying off only enough to avoid trailing water all along her bedroom floor, she wrapped the towel around her body.

"This better be fucking important," she grumbled as she stomped toward the door. Like, the-building-is-on-fire-so-everybody-out important. Or else someone just made a new worst enemy.

Undoing the bolt, she threw open the door with a huff.

Mason froze on the other side, his fist raised to knock again.

CHAPTER 10

Mason

S weet. Motherfucking. Jesus.

It took every ounce of self-control Mason had to keep from ripping that towel off, bending Addison over the nearest piece of furniture, and fucking her until neither of them could see straight.

He clenched his jaw so damn tight it gave him a headache.

"Oh!" Addison said, her belligerent expression morphing into one of surprise. "I thought you couldn't come see me when you're with a guest?"

Mason realized his hand still hovered an inch from where her closed door had been. Dropping his arm to his side, he said, "My guest is still asleep. Once she wakes up, I probably won't have another free minute until tomorrow. I didn't want to wait."

"Right. Good." She clutched her towel a little tighter around her body. Not that it did anything to hide her spectacular curves. "Do you want to come in?"

Do. Not. Fuck. Her. Against. The. Wall. Mason repeated those words over and over in his head, desperate for his cock to listen to his brain. But it was a losing battle when she stood there in a thin layer of Turkish cotton, hair dripping down her shoulders and between her breasts.

"Why don't you put on some clothes first," he suggested, knowing his control would crumble the moment he stepped over the threshold. "Then we can talk."

"Right," she said again. "One sec." For the second time, she slammed her door in his face.

Fisting a hand in his hair, Mason screwed his eyes shut and tried to calm his body. Coming up here was a mistake. That was fucking obvious now.

Too late. He had to make the best of it.

By the time Addison reopened her door, he stood serenely in the hall, hands in his trouser pockets.

"Come on in," she said, stepping out of his way and holding the door.

"Thank you." He hated the formality of the conversation. He'd fucked this woman, had her naked across his lap, and wrapped his collar around her throat. How did they go from that level of intimacy to . . . *this*?

Mason settled on one of the armchairs over by her gabled windows. After a moment of indecision, she folded herself onto the other chair, tucking her legs up under her. Picking at her fingernails while she stared at her hands, she let several seconds tick by before clearing her throat. "Thank you for the bird feeder. That was an extremely kind thing to do."

Though he usually didn't feel a need to celebrate his successes, Mason repressed the urge to pump a triumphant fist in the air. He had no problem admitting his sole purpose in installing that bird feeder was to get her to talk to him again. Thank Christ she appreciated it, rather than being furious at his obvious scheming.

"I know how important Alexander is to you," he said, trying to soften his usual businesslike tone, but it didn't sound any different to his ears.

Fuck, he sucked at this.

It earned him a small smile, though, and she finally met his gaze. "I didn't mean . . . when you said . . . I couldn't . . ." She let the sentence trail off with a frustrated groan. Then, taking a deep breath, she blurted, "I think you're right about the PTSD thing." She slumped back in her chair. "God, why was that so hard to say?"

Mason stretched his arm across the space between them, wrapping his hand around one of hers. "It took a lot of bravery to say that. Give yourself the credit you deserve."

She stared at their joined hands for a long time before responding. "I freaked out when you said it the other day, and I'm sorry. I'm sorry about all of it. I know I should've used my safeword, but I just . . . panicked." She sighed, then straightened her shoulders, giving him a hopeful look. "I'd like to try again this weekend if you're interested."

"I can't," he said, wishing it wasn't true.

"Oh." She watched him with an unreadable expression, and he wondered if perhaps she expected him to say more. "Right. Of course. Sorry." She started to slip her hand out of his.

Mason's fingers instinctively tightened. No more misunderstandings. No more pulling away. Something drew him to this woman, and goddamnit, he would figure out what it was once and for all. "I don't mean I can't ever. I'll have most weekends free during the rest of your trial period. Well, except the end of February—I'm traveling to Chile that last week."

"Oh!" she said again, relief flashing in her eyes. "That sounds amazing. I've never been on a plane. Even if I could afford it, I'm too afraid." She gave an overly dramatic shudder, and he couldn't help noticing her breasts shaking beneath her thin cotton top. That little minx didn't bother putting on a bra when she got dressed.

He dragged his gaze back up to her eyes. "I hope you get over your fear of flying someday. There's an awful lot of world you'll never get to see if you don't. As for this weekend, I found out about an hour ago that I'll be attending a last-minute wedding on Saturday."

"Sounds like someone's pregnant." She gave him a look that was half jesting, half nervous. As though she wasn't sure how he'd react to the comment, and wished she could take it back.

Mason didn't see why. It was a perfectly logical assumption. "I don't think so, but I'll admit I didn't ask." He'd spent most of his morning in the dungeon, restocking all the spanking and sex toys. Housekeeping sterilized everything after each use, but Mason generally put it all back where it belonged. Otherwise, he always had trouble finding things when he needed them. He was organizing a selection of paddles by size and severity when Aiden tracked him down with the invite. "Aiden and Olivia went to her friend's wedding in Boston last weekend and apparently caught wedding fever. Neither of them mentioned a single plan the whole year they were engaged, but now they can't wait another second."

To his surprise, Addison's eyes softened, and she gave him a sappy grin. "That's so romantic."

Was it? He was happy for his friends, certainly. But like everyone else at the Manor, he'd been part of more than one whispered conversation about why the pair seemed to lose all interest in marriage as soon as they got engaged. To him, this sudden turn of events seemed more hormonal than anything else. Like when your friends have a baby, and suddenly the chemicals in your brain tell you to have one too.

He chose not to say any of that out loud, however.

"How about Sunday morning?" he proposed, watching her carefully. If she'd rather wait another week, he didn't want her agreeing out of obligation. "I know it's your one day to sleep in, so if you'd rather—"

"No. I don't need to sleep."

Their gazes locked for a second, and they both chuckled. "I'm not sure that's true," he teased.

"I don't need to sleep *in*," she clarified with a smile so impossibly sweet, he wanted to devour her. "I'll be up early anyway. I'd rather be with you."

That simple statement made his chest swell with pride. "Then I'll be here when the sun rises," he promised. "Come to the parlor whenever you're ready. I'll be waiting for you." With that, he stood, helping her up out of her chair. If his guest wasn't already awake, she would be soon. He really needed to get back.

"Until Sunday, then?" she said, giving him a shy, hopeful look.

In answer, he cupped her face in his hands, brushing back her still-damp hair. Her eyes fluttered closed as he lowered his lips to hers.

He took his time with her today, tasting and exploring, studying the little sounds she made. She tasted like sugar and chocolate, and he wanted this moment to freeze in time so he could savor her forever.

If only.

Pulling away, he planted a soft kiss on her forehead. "Be a good girl until then," he said, then hurried out of the room while he still could.

As soon as they entered his house on Sunday morning, Mason turned and pointed to a small table by the door. Only the black leather collar with green-blue stitching rested atop it. "Leave your clothes there and put on your collar," he instructed. "That's the first thing I want you to do whenever you come into this house. You need to always be naked and available to me while you're here."

She squirmed in a deeply satisfying way. The command clearly spoke to the most submissive parts of her. "Yes, Master."

"Come upstairs when you're ready. I'll be waiting in the same place as last week." Mason moved deeper into the house, resisting the urge to turn around and make sure she did as he instructed. If not, she would be punished accordingly. Either outcome worked for him.

He only had one goal for today: to help her grow more comfortable with him. He could accomplish that with pleasure or pain.

If only they had the whole weekend together. Not that he would trade yesterday's wedding for anything. Whatever their reasons for finally tying the knot, the wedding was absolutely fucking beautiful. A tiny affair in a heated tent outside Aiden and Olivia's cabin, with only their little Manor family present.

Addison even volunteered to help Gabriel and Sienna prepare the food, making five different types of bread, and baking and decorating several dozen mini cupcakes. That she would do all that in her free time, for the sole purpose of helping two people she barely knew? It shifted his perspective on humanity the tiniest bit.

It also made him want to give her the best orgasms of her life.

Only a few minutes passed before Addison met him upstairs in what he thought of as his observation deck. He turned from the window when he heard her soft footfalls behind him.

Addison stood just inside the doorway, staring at an antique pine armoire he bought and had delivered a few days ago. The simple cabinet was made in Sweden in the mid-1800s, and still bore the original faded white paint. As soon as he saw the auction listing, he knew it would fit his purposes perfectly.

"Don't worry," he said, a dark promise in his voice. "You'll find out what's in there soon enough."

Her gaze snapped over to him, a smile toying at the edges of her mouth. "Yes, Master."

"Jesus Christ, you're beautiful," he murmured, sweeping his gaze up her perfect body.

She flushed all over at the compliment but didn't say anything more. Her hands fidgeted at her sides.

"Talk to me," he said, doing his best to make it sound like a request, not an order. "Tell me what you're thinking." He needed much more insight into this woman's mind if he wanted any chance of things going better than last time.

Her brow furrowed. "I don't know what you want me to say," she admitted after several seconds.

He desperately wanted to move closer—to hold her. He wanted to run soft kisses along the lines in her forehead until they smoothed away.

Instinct told him that wasn't what she needed right now, so he forced himself to stay across the room, giving her space while she processed. "I just need to know where your head is so I can make sure I give you exactly what you need."

Her lips pressed into a tight line. With any other sub, he'd give her a nice long spanking to loosen her tongue. Or perhaps keep that mouth open wide with his cock between her lips.

With Addison, he attempted to smile. "There's no right or wrong answer. You can be thinking how beautiful the view is, or that you wish it was warmer in here. That I cut a fine figure in this suit, but you like me even more naked." That startled a smile out of her. "Hell, you can be thinking about the tuna fish sandwich you plan to eat for lunch tomorrow."

She laughed—*everyone who said he didn't have a sense of humor could fuck right off*—and the tension eased out of her shoulders. "I do make a damn good tuna fish sandwich," she said, still smiling.

"I look forward to trying it someday." He moved casually to the sofa, taking a seat and gesturing toward the cushion beside him.

"May I kneel, Master?" she asked, voice tentative but eyes hopeful. "I think it'll help."

"Of course." He waited patiently as she moved to his side, trying to hide a wince as she knelt on the rug. He'd chosen the rug intentionally, loving how the stiff wool fibers would feel under a submissive's knees if he ever met someone he wanted to bring home. It pleased him that the decision he made almost seven years ago finally bore fruit.

Addison took her time getting situated, arranging her body into almost the exact position he put her in last weekend. Even her hair fell across her shoulders the way he liked. That she remembered so much after a single interaction—that she would put this level of effort into pleasing him with the tiniest of details . . .

It left him momentarily breathless.

"Like this, Master?" Her voice sounded like the sweetest song.

Leaning forward, he made minor adjustments, tilting her chin to the most pleasing angle, pushing her shoulders back the tiniest bit. "You're perfect." The words came out rougher than he intended.

That earned another small smile from her. "You sure know how to make a girl feel beautiful."

"You should feel beautiful." He ran a reverent hand through her honey blond hair, straight today, but as silky as he remembered. "Every second of every goddamn day."

Her breath left her on a sigh. "I'm thinking about what happened last time," she said, no trace of her earlier fear in her voice or expression.

"Understandable." He waited patiently for her to continue.

"I'm ashamed of how I acted."

Shaking his head slightly, he said, "You had no control over what happened."

"Maybe." She didn't sound like she really believed it. "I know how much the dark scares me, though. It was stupid to put anything but a one for blindfolds. I don't know what the fuck I was thinking."

His mouth almost dropped open, but he stopped it at the last second. A fear of the dark? That's what sent her into such a fit of terror?

There had to be way more to the story than that. A simple fear wouldn't have garnered that level of reaction—or compelled her to literally line the Manor's third floor with nightlights. Though now that he knew she put them there, he was glad he never got around to asking housekeeping to get rid of them.

He wanted to ask for more details. To dig into the *why*. But it was clear in her eyes she had no intention of discussing it, at least not yet. Instead, he settled for, "It doesn't sound like you ever wore a blindfold before last week, so there wasn't a way for you to know. It was still out of your control."

"Even if that is true, I was in total control of how I treated you after, in your bedroom. I'm . . . not like that. Not usually." She cringed. "Though I guess my behavior these last couple weeks doesn't give you much proof of that."

One corner of his mouth twisted into a wry smile. "Neither of us have been on our best behavior."

Amusement flashed in her eyes. "When you said that thing about Cinnabon . . . oh my God, I seriously wanted to strangle you with my bare hands." She sighed, the humor draining out of her as quickly as it appeared. "My granny taught me how to bake after some . . . not great things happened in my life. It's been like a lifeline to me ever since. Moreso than it probably should be."

Mason ran a hand through his hair, only holding her gaze by sheer force of will. Talk about ashamed. "I'm sorry. I genuinely had nothing against you or your food. It's just that a lot of things have changed at the Manor recently. Things I maybe should've expected, but every single one of them still somehow managed to shock the hell out of me. I haven't handled any of it very well, to be honest. Jonathan's been about ready to strangle me for months now." Hell, Rafe might actually kill him if he dared say anything about Nell again. "Your arrival was just the cherry on top of the sundae."

"What things?" she asked, sympathy filling her voice now. "Like Aiden and Olivia getting together?"

How had this turned into him talking about his feelings? He almost steered the conversation back into more comfortable territory, but stopped himself at the last second. He supposed he shouldn't expect her to talk about her issues if he couldn't be bothered to do the same. Maybe this would help her open up.

"That's when everything started to change," he said, slumping back against the sofa. "And I fucking hate it."

Her eyes widened, but she didn't say anything. It took him a moment to realize how bad that sounded.

"Don't get me wrong—Olivia is wonderful. I don't hate her or their relationship. I fucking love how happy they both are. I just . . ." Letting the sentence trail off, he tried to find the perfect words. This wasn't something he'd managed to articulate yet, even in his own mind. "At first, I convinced myself I was upset because her presence might cause issues with some of the guests. I thought they might not want to spend an absolute fortune to be with a man in a committed relationship."

"Has he had fewer guests since they got together?" she asked.

"The opposite, actually. As soon as it got out on our subreddit that Aiden was taken, applications addressed specifically to him started pouring in. I think some women see it as a challenge. Others just like the fantasy of the forbidden fruit."

Her laugh bewitched him. How could he feel such a simple sound in the depths of his heart?

"The Manor has a subreddit?" she asked, still smiling.

Mason rolled his eyes. "That was all Zach. I thought the idea was absurd when he proposed it, but that shows what I know about marketing." He sighed. "I guess I just didn't want things to change, even for the better."

"Not unless the change was under your control."

The words hit him like a sucker punch to the gut, despite the kindness with which she said them. Was that it? The reason at the core of all his recent frustrations—that no one asked his permission, or even his opinion, before turning his world back upside down?

"I'm sorry if that was out of line," Addison whispered.

He looked down to find her studying his face with a worried little frown. "Not at all," he assured her. "You just gave me a lot to think about."

Aiden and Olivia. Rafe and Nell, who might even be leaving Vermont altogether. Fuck, he didn't even want to think about what they'd do if that happened. If Zach was right about their plans, the hole Rafe would leave at the Manor would be astronomical.

Then came the woman kneeling at his feet. A change he neither anticipated nor wanted—and one he tried to stop for the sole purpose of wresting back some control over the impetus of his life.

If he had succeeded in convincing the others to send her away . . .

The very idea sat like a leaden weight in the center of his chest.

Maybe some changes could be good. Even if he didn't choose them for himself.

"What about you?" he asked. "It seems like your whole life just changed."

Her gaze skittered away, landing in the vicinity of the doorway. "Every time I get comfortable, it all gets ripped away. It's happened so many times, I've just sort of learned to roll with it at this point."

Questions raced through his mind, but he didn't want to push her too far too fast. "Do you want to talk about it?"

She glanced at him for only a moment. "Not really."

Nodding, he said, "All right. Do you give me your word you'll tell me right away if anything else I do is a trigger for you?"

"Yes, Master." She gave him a rueful smile. "Trust me, I don't want that to happen again any more than you do."

Mason cupped her cheek again, needing to touch her. "Good girl."

CHAPTER 11

Addison

I f Addison had to fill out a customer satisfaction survey about this morning so far, she'd put *way too much talking, not nearly enough fucking* in the comment box.

It wasn't like she was in this for the stimulating conversation.

Was she?

As soon as that thought ticked its way through her mind, guilt formed a deep pit in her belly. How many frenemy fuckbuddies took the time to check on their partner's mental well-being? And frankly, given how things ended last time, she should be glad they were still fuckbuddies at all.

When he asked if she wanted to talk about it—God, it felt like every single drop of her blood turned to ice. Of course she didn't want to talk about it. She never talked about it.

Her granny taught her long ago that no one wants to hear you whine about how unfair your life is. At best, they'll pity you and walk on eggshells around you. At worst? They'll decide you're too much work and stop returning your calls.

Time to do what she'd learned to do as a teenager—shove all that shit into a box in the back of her mind and pretend everything was fine.

As long as they stayed in well-lit rooms, she failed to see how anything could go wrong this time.

Standing, Mason hooked a single finger through the O-ring in her collar, his knuckle pressing against her windpipe. When he tugged, she lifted her bottom off her heels, kneeling up as straight as she could.

Holding her there, his knuckle making it hard to draw a full breath, he brushed her hair behind her ear with his other hand. "I have something very special in mind for you," he said, gazing down at her with a look so hot it made her pussy clench. With another tug on her collar, he pulled her to her feet.

The last of her nerves drained out of her as he led her toward the largest wall of windows. Halting right in the center, he dug his phone out of his pocket and tapped on the screen several times. Before she could ask what he was doing, a soft scrape sounded above her.

Addison craned her neck back to watch as a small panel on the ceiling slid to one side. A moment later, with a gentle whir and a clink of metal on metal, a thick steel chain descended from the hidden compartment. Leather cuffs dangled from the heavy metal ring at the end.

"You . . . have a retractable chain in your ceiling." She sounded every bit as dumbstruck as she felt.

Rich people were fucking wild.

"I had it installed when the house was first built," he said, tugging on the ring, testing the chain's strength. "The idea amused me. I've never had a chance to use it until now."

A thrill ran through her.

"You like that, don't you?" Mason mused, studying her face. "That you'll be the first."

She couldn't hold back a smile. "Yes, Master."

He responded with what she started to think of as his backward smile—basically the opposite of when someone's mouth smiles, but their eyes stay hard and cold. His eyes held a smile the rest of his face failed to produce.

Without another word, he took her right wrist, lifting her arm above her head to buckle it into the cuff. Her left wrist came next, and he hooked the cuff around it with swift, confident movements. A few taps on his phone screen lifted her arms even higher, until she had to stretch her spine to keep from going up on her toes.

Walking a slow circle around her, Mason examined every inch of her body. When he made it back to her front, he traced a fingertip around one nipple, then pinched the sensitive bud between two fingers.

Closing her eyes, she arched her back, focusing on the exquisite pain.

"Beautiful," he said, and she swallowed a gasp as he did the same to the other nipple. "You were born to be chained like this, Addison. To be ruled and possessed."

She almost cried out when he let go. Eyes flying open, she watched him walk across the room, pulling an old-fashioned skeleton key from his pocket and fitting it into the keyhole on the new piece of furniture.

The lock turned with a soft *click*, and Mason pulled open the two large doors. The enormous antique cabinet sported three shelves, each one packed with kinky paraphernalia. Her eyes widened as she took in paddles, straps, crops, a terrifying assortment of plugs, and cuffs and restraints of every kind.

"Master?"

"Yes?" He didn't turn to look at her.

"That cabinet wasn't there the other day."

Mason stilled for a moment, then went back to running his fingers across a cluster of crops as he considered his options. "Was there supposed to be a question in that?"

"Well," she said slowly, trying to decide what she really wanted to know. "I guess I was wondering when it got here."

Picking up a brown leather crop, he examined the wide loop on the business end, then wrapped a firm hand around the smooth handle with its brass fittings. He swished it once through the air before testing the flexibility of the rod between his hands.

Seeming satisfied, he turned to face her at last. "On Thursday," he answered, his tone businesslike. "A friend of mine bought it for me at an auction in London and had it shipped here."

Good God, Addison didn't even want to think about what that had cost.

He regarded her for several seconds, head tilted slightly to one side. "Is there a problem?"

"No, Master," she hurried to say.

His lips thinned. "Remember what I said about lying."

"That's not a lie, Master. I promise." She didn't have a problem with the sudden appearance of a giant old cabinet full of sex and bondage gear. Quite the opposite—her arousal literally dripped down the inside of her thighs.

Mason prowled back across the room with the grace and pent-up strength of a panther, the crop trailing at his side. Tracing the leather tip around her breasts, he ordered, "Tell me what's going on in your head."

She was powerless against that commanding tone. "I'm the only woman you ever brought here," she said, resisting the urge to squirm away from the leather loop as it brushed across her belly. "And I told you I was never coming back."

"Ahh." With two quick flicks of his wrist, the leather hit one aching nipple, then the other, leaving behind a biting pain. "Well." He leaned in, soothing one punished nipple with his tongue. Kissing his way across to her other breast, he once again chased away the sting with the wet heat of his mouth. "Let's just say I wanted to be prepared in case you changed your mind."

Her gaze drifted over to the still open cupboard. "All that is for me?"

"If we're lucky."

A shudder of desire crashed through her, forcing a low moan from her throat.

"Would you like that?" Mason asked, trailing the leather tip along her skin again as he moved behind her. "Would you like me to systematically work through it all with you? Would it make your sweet pussy wet for me to know that I chose each and every item on those shelves with you in mind?"

Before she could even think of an answer, the crop struck, landing again and again on her ass. She hissed as the pain grew, the strokes continuing to fall until she was sure every inch of her bottom glowed a rosy pink.

God, it felt so good. And it wasn't even close to enough pain.

"Please, Master," she whimpered.

"More?"

"If it's also what you wish, Master."

His hum of satisfaction filled her with pride. "Good girl." With that, he started back up with the crop.

The strokes fell in an erratic way, sometimes several in quick succession, other times with long pauses. They landed on her ass, breasts, stomach, upper and inner thighs in no pattern she could discern. Just when she thought she knew what would come next, everything changed again.

Once and only once, he brought the crop up between her legs. She screamed at the blinding pain.

By the time he tossed the crop aside, tears slid down her cheeks in a constant stream.

"You're such a good girl," Mason said, cupping her face with his hands, wiping the wetness from her cheeks with gentle brushes of his thumbs.

"Did I p-please you, Master?" she asked, her voice catching partway through as she struggled to control her tears.

His eyes told her all she needed to know. "You're fucking perfect."

A sense of calm spread out from her center, washing over her entire body. She was his perfect, good girl. She could handle anything as long as she knew that.

"Open," Mason ordered, tapping two fingers against her lips. As soon as she did, he slid those two fingers into her mouth, pressing them against her tongue. "Suck. Get them nice and wet, little one."

She followed his instruction with relish, swirling her tongue around his long, beautiful fingers, hoping this meant what she thought it meant.

Desire built in her chest when he lowered his hand, positioning it between her legs. That was quickly replaced by confusion when he froze in place, his fingertips hovering just over her clit, not quite touching.

"If you want to come, you're going to have to work for it."

She stared into his eyes for a few seconds, not yet comprehending. When it hit her what he meant, a blush turned her already heated skin into a raging bonfire.

"Show me," Mason said, the power in his voice making her weak in the knees. "Show me how much you want it."

Good God, how could something be so mortifying and so fucking hot at the same time? Closing her eyes, she tentatively shifted her hips, sliding her clit against his fingertips. A tiny whimper escaped her.

"You're going to have to do better than that." He sounded almost disappointed. "If you don't want to come, we can move on."

No fucking way. Embarrassment could fuck right off when there were orgasms to be had.

Screwing her eyes shut even tighter, she started to properly move. Rocking her hips back and forth, sliding her clit over his wet fingers at a constant pace. Lowering her body as far as the chain allowed, desperate for more pressure.

"That's it," Mason said, his voice like liquid smoke. "Writhe for me. Show me what a little slut you are."

Jesus, Mary, and Joseph, those words had a direct line to her pussy. "I need you inside me." It came out high and wheedling—nothing like her normal voice.

"Finish what you started," he commanded. "Only good girls who do what they're told get what they want."

Fuck, fuck, fuck, she was so damn close. If only he would lift his fingers the tiniest bit, or lower the chain.

She knew that wouldn't happen, so she did everything else she could. Her breath came in harsh pants as she bucked and twisted, desperate for as much sensation as she could take from him.

"Such a good girl," he murmured, and at last, he lifted his fingers higher.

Her orgasm crashed through her almost instantly, the explosion so fast and intense that tears leaked from the corners of her eyes. Head thrown back, she stared up the length of the chain as her whole body thrashed with pleasure.

When the final shudders passed through her at last, he dipped his fingers into her achingly empty pussy, then brought them up to his mouth. He closed his eyes as he tasted her for the first time, sheer ecstasy in every line of his face. "I could lick you for hours," he ground out, groaning, eyes still closed.

Um, yes please.

His eyes slid open, the inferno blazing in them hot enough to burn her. "We can try that later. For now, it's time for my pleasure."

Retrieving his phone from his pocket, he tapped the screen a few times. Before she knew what was happening, the chain started to coil back up into the ceiling, her wrists still attached to it.

"Hey!" she shouted, eyes widening with panic. "Stop! I—"

The mechanism halted abruptly, leaving her dangling with only the very tips of her toes brushing against the floor.

Circling around her, Mason pressed his body against hers from top to bottom. "Did you just try to give me an order?" he breathed against her ear.

"I—" She stopped herself before a lie spilled from her lips. Mason had made it abundantly clear what would happen if she ever lied to him again.

"Mmm," he murmured, running his hands down her sides with a tortuous, featherlight touch. When the muscles in her lower abdomen spasmed, he froze for a moment, then did it even more slowly. "Are you ticklish, Ms. Walker?"

She did *not* like the barely restrained glee in those words. Not one fucking bit.

"Please," she said, choosing not to answer his question. "I did everything you said. You said good girls get what they want."

Wrapping her hair around his fist, he yanked her head back, leaning over her to kiss her exposed throat just above the collar. "So I did," he whispered against her skin, kissing her again, his tongue darting out to taste her.

Addison closed her eyes, giving herself over to the sensations running riot in her body. The post-orgasmic leaden feeling in her muscles and the tingling across the surface of her skin. The prickle in her scalp as he tightened his hold on her hair. The lingering burn from the riding crop lashing her skin. The ache in her shoulders as she dangled mercilessly from the ceiling. The hot, wet kisses that set off a flurry of butterflies in her stomach.

God, it was too much. She didn't know how much longer she could last without his cock buried deep inside her.

When he snaked his free hand around her, giving her nipple a ruthless twist, her desperate cry finally did the trick. Releasing her, he shed his own clothing in a matter of seconds, tossing them on the sofa without folding them. He stood in front of her in all his naked glory, the shallow, V-shaped grooves between his hips and groin making her literally salivate.

And his cock . . . sweet fuck, it was even better than she remembered. Long and thick, jutting out from his hips in the most inviting way, pre-come glistening in the sunlight.

Her tongue darted out to wet her lips as she imagined him pushing his length into her mouth. She'd fall to her knees right now and beg for the privilege if he didn't have her cuffed to the chain.

Before she got too carried away, Mason grabbed her ass with both hands, hoisting her up and pressing her back against the window. Relief flooded through her as most of the pressure left her shoulders. She wrapped her legs around him and dug her heels into his spectacular ass.

Pinning her against the glass, he pulled back only enough to line his cock up with her entrance. Then he surged forward, his whole length filling her with a single hard stroke.

Addison threw her head back against the window and screamed. Too much. Way too much.

But also not nearly enough.

"Harder," she pleaded, wishing the chain had enough slack to wrap her arms around his neck. How she longed to dig her fingernails into his skin.

With a fierce growl, Mason did as she asked, fucking her with so much force, a tiny part of her brain feared the window might crack. Not that she gave a flying fuck. She couldn't fall anyway with the chain connecting her to the ceiling. It would be worth being fucked right through the glass as long as it kept feeling this fucking good.

"You're mine." He pressed a possessive hand against her throat, pushing hard enough to steal her breath. "You're fucking *mine.*"

"Please, Master," she panted back. "I'm so close. Please let me come again."

His answering snarl almost sent her over the edge. One hand holding her to the glass by the throat, the other digging into her hip, he fucked her with abandon, rolling his hips at the end of each thrust so his pelvis ground against her clit.

So. Fucking. Good.

Her second orgasm hit her like a fucking train, tearing through her body with so much force she felt sure she'd fly apart. Her clenching pussy dragged him to completion with her, his jagged breaths filling her ears as he spasmed and jerked through his own orgasm.

She was dead. Literally fucking dead. That was the only logical explanation for the way she seemed to float in nothingness, no physical form left to anchor her to the Earth.

For a fleeting moment, she considered trying to claw her way back.

Fuck it. If she really had been fucked to death, what a way to go.

CHAPTER 12

Mason

I t took almost an hour for Addison to come back to him. He loved sending his submissives into subspace, but he took extra pride in it this time . . . with her. He had to explain what happened to her when she finally came back to herself. Knowing he was the first person to ever send her into that state of trancelike euphoria made him feel like a fucking king.

As if his ego needed that boost.

They were down in his living room now, relaxing until it was time to return to the Manor. The view was better upstairs, but the soft rug down here would be much more comfortable for her. He sat reading in his favorite chair—a midcentury piece with a simple beechwood frame and ivory cushions, the wooden arms perfectly shaped to nestle his long arms. Addison sat at his feet with her head resting against his thigh, legs once again curled up under her, still wearing nothing but her collar. Every now and then, she gave a soft sigh as he stroked her hair.

He'd never imagined himself doing something so . . . domestic.

"Master?" came Addison's tentative voice.

"Yes, little one?"

"I—I want to explain," she said, the words halting and soft. "About what happened last weekend."

Putting aside his book, he gave her his full attention. "I'm happy to listen to anything you want to tell me," he said. "As long as it's because you're ready, not only because you think I want you to."

"I—I think I am?" She sure as hell didn't sound certain. "I mean, you *do* want me to, don't you? You keep asking, and I want to please you."

Mason rubbed his fingertips in gentle circles across her scalp, hoping to put her at ease. "I want to know you. Understand as much about you as I can. But I only want to know what you want to share. This isn't obligatory."

She remained silent for well over a minute as she turned that over in her mind. Continuing to rub soothing circles into her hair, he waited patiently for her to make a decision.

"I'm afraid," she admitted at last.

"Of what specifically?"

Huffing out a harsh breath, she said, "That you won't like hearing what I have to say. You're my Dom, not my therapist."

His fingers stilled for a moment, until he made a conscious effort to get them moving again. So much frustration filled those simple words. "Has that happened to you before?" he asked. "Did you try to talk to someone, but they didn't want to hear it?"

Her shoulders hunched forward, which was all the answer he needed.

"That's not going to happen with me," he assured her. "I give you my word."

Addison fell silent again, and he didn't press the matter. She would talk if and when she felt ready, and that was more than good enough for him.

At long last, she took a deep breath and said, "I got taken away from my mom when I was six."

He remembered her comment about being raised by her grandmother, so that didn't surprise him. "What happened?"

"My granny told me Mom died of a drug overdose while I was living with my second foster family, but I don't remember anything about that to be honest." Her voice sounded so incredibly small. "I just remember being alone a lot. Alone and hungry."

Mason swallowed as he tried to figure out how to reply to that. "You went to foster homes first?" he asked, his mind drawing a complete blank on what to say to the rest of it. "Why didn't you go straight to your grandmother's?"

"I think it takes a lot of extra time and paperwork to transfer kids across state lines. And I guess it also took them a while to track her down?" She sounded like she didn't entirely believe it. "I requested a copy of my file when I turned eighteen, and it said I had no known relatives for a while. Pretty sure they didn't look too hard outside of New Mexico, though. It was the early nineties, so it's not like everything was online and easy like it is now. And I apparently didn't even know my last name when they came to get me, let alone who my dad or grandparents were."

Mason couldn't remember another time in his life when he was this stunned. Words completely failed him.

"Anyway." She let out a sigh that seemed to carry the weight of the world. "The official reason they put down in my file for taking me away was severe neglect. Apparently, my mom left me home by myself when she went out of town with her boyfriend. Five days after she left, a neighbor heard me moving around in the apartment and called the police."

Jesus Christ. "I'm so sorry that happened to you." It seemed like such a deeply inadequate thing to say, but he had no idea what would be better.

Craning her neck, she looked up into his eyes, her own filled with worry. "If you want me to stop, I will."

Mason cupped her face with one hand, brushing his thumb along her cheekbone. "You're not going to frighten me away. I'm here to listen to anything you want to tell me. Anything."

Her eyes glistened with unshed tears as she settled her cheek back against his thigh. "The first foster home they put me in was . . ." She trailed off, taking several seconds to gather her thoughts before continuing. "It was fucking horrible." Gasping, she turned again, panic in her eyes. "I'm sorry for swearing, Master."

He had absolutely no idea why, but her fear in that moment broke his fucking heart. "It's okay." Hauling her onto his lap, he tucked her head up under his chin. "For the rest of this conversation, you can say whatever the fuck you want."

Addison snuggled into his chest, fiddling with one of the buttons on his shirt for a bit before she kept going. "My first foster parents were Mr. and Mrs. Dabrowski, in a part of Santa Fe I'd never been to. I remember I was so fucking scared in the car on the way there. They explained what was happening to me, I'm sure, but I was fucking six. I didn't understand."

Mason kissed her hair, wishing he could somehow go back in time and protect her. So many kids went through this around the world, every goddamn day . . .

He fucking hated humanity sometimes.

"When we got there, I was actually kind of excited. There were five other foster kids there, with one room for the girls and one for the boys. I used to be alone all the time. Now there were lots of other kids around and lots of toys." For a second, she actually smiled. "They even had bunk beds. I'd seen them on TV, but never in real life. What kid doesn't love bunk beds, right?"

"Did you get top bunk?"

"No, I didn't have seniority," she said, continuing to twist his button in between her fingers. "It was still fucking cool."

Mason understood how six-year-old Addison felt on a visceral level. He'd begged his parents to give him a bunk bed for Christmas the year he turned eight. He'd recently attended a sleepover with a friend who had one, and he still remembered so clearly the thrill of climbing up to the top bunk and feeling like he was on top of the world.

That Christmas wasn't the first one to disappoint him.

It was absolutely the last one he allowed to break his heart.

"So at first, I think maybe everything is going to get better, right?" Disdain filled her voice, as if she resented her former self for believing that. "I missed my mom, cause as awful as I now know she was, she was the only thing I knew. Even so, this place seemed like paradise compared to what I was used to."

"Seemed," Mason repeated.

"Yeah, seemed." She sighed. "I always took care of myself, you know? My mom left me home alone for hours at a time on the best days.

And this wasn't the first time she abandoned me for several days in a row. I knew how to make myself a bowl of cereal, how to put a frozen dinner in the microwave—that sort of thing. It was either that or go hungry. Now I was in this place that had so much fucking food. I'd never seen that much food outside of a store. God, I must've looked like those kids in Willy Wonka when they first see the room made out of candy."

He had a feeling he knew where this was going. "Your foster parents didn't want you getting food for yourself?"

"Mrs. Dabrowski completely lost her shit when she found me eating cereal without permission." A hard shudder passed through her little body, and he held her even closer. "Fuck, I still can't eat Cheerios. It's been over thirty years, but even thinking about it makes my heart beat out of my fucking chest."

Burying her face in his shirt, she took several deep breaths, and he held her as she trembled.

"My mom never screamed at me," she said after a while, voice choked with tears. "Never punished me. She just ignored me most of the time. When Mrs. Dabrowski grabbed me and screamed all those awful things in my face and shook me . . . God, I was so terrified. I had no fucking clue what was happening."

It was Mason's turn to breathe deeply—to attempt to slow his heartrate. Nothing in this world disgusted and infuriated him more than people who abused children. The fact that child abusers existed at all was the main reason he stopped believing in God more than a decade ago. What the fuck kind of deity would let that happen to the most innocent?

"Then she put me in the hole."

Every muscle in Mason's body went rigid. "What?" Horror filled the word. "Do you mean an actual hole?" His imagination ran wild with images of a tiny, blond child trapped at the bottom of a deep, dark pit.

"I think they called it that because of prisons," she said nervously, her eyes shifting up toward his face. "Like what they call solitary confinement?"

That calmed him down, but only by the absolute tiniest of margins.

Dread filled his chest, making him feel almost sick. "I get the feeling this wasn't simply a time out."

She started to tremble again, so he cradled her against him with gentle arms, waiting patiently for her to be ready. "It was a little closet down in the basement," she whispered. "With a lock on the outside and no lights. When the door was shut, you couldn't even see your hand in front of your face."

"Jesus fucking Christ." He couldn't think of anything else to say.

He'd put a blindfold on this woman. *A fucking blindfold.* If he'd known, if he had even a tiny little clue . . .

"All that food, and there was never enough to eat there. Fucking never. All six of us were skin and bones, but the Dabrowskis would yell at us all the time about how greedy we were, how we were eating them out of house and home, how the state didn't pay them enough and we were such a burden. Anytime we got in trouble, even for the tiniest things, it was straight back to the hole." A hard edge entered her voice when she said, "God, I still hate them so much."

Her story made Mason so fucking angry, his hands shook. "Where the fuck was your caseworker? How did they let that happen?"

She shrugged. "It was 1992. Foster care was so different back then. I was just another drug addict's kid. No one gave a shit about me."

Mason made up his mind to research the foster care system as much as he could. He'd find charities and other ways to help. Not just in New Mexico where she grew up or here in Vermont, but all over the country. He had considerable resources at his disposal, and he would fucking use them. "If shit like that is still going on—" He was too angry to even finish the sentence.

"From everything I've read—and trust me, I've looked into this a lot —the system has gotten a lot better since then. It takes a lot more for foster parents to get licensed than it used to, and they check on the kids a lot more." Her tone very clearly said, *They fucking better.* "Kids still fall through the cracks, but it's nothing like it used to be."

"Thank fuck for that," he murmured, trying to regain control over his emotions. He needed to stay calm if he had any chance of helping her.

"Anyway. It wasn't all bad. The other kids looked out for me as much as they could. They taught me how to steal food and hide the evidence." A tear made a slow, solitary track down her cheek. Addison wiped it away with the back of her hand. "The oldest boy, Ricky, used to take the blame for the younger kids when he could. He'd sneak us food if we were sent to bed without dinner." Her lips held the memory of a smile. "He always called me Addy."

At least she didn't have to go through it alone. He had to take some comfort in that. "Are you still in touch with Ricky?"

A sad little shake of the head. "I don't even know his last name. I got moved to a new home about a year and a half later, and I never saw any of those kids again."

"You'd think they'd let you stay in touch." Why pile even more heartbreak onto a kid who already dealt with so much? "At least talk on the phone or write letters or something."

"I would've liked that," she said, a slight catch in her voice again. "I always wondered what happened to him. I really hope his life turned out well and he's happy."

"Was your next home better?"

Addison shrugged again. "Yes and no. They didn't mistreat me. I was the only kid there, but there was a playground down the street, so I got to play with other kids a lot. They were always really nice to me. They even talked about adopting me for a while."

"But?"

One corner of her mouth twisted into a sardonic smile. "There's always a but, isn't there?" She sighed. "I'd picked up some . . . less than entirely desirable behaviors at the Dabrowskis' house. I was only seven when I moved there. It's not like I could just flip a switch and turn them off."

"Full grown adults can't just flip a switch," he assured her. "That's not remotely how brains work."

"Well, I wish someone told Mr. and Mrs. Boyle that. Almost a year after I moved in, I heard them talking about me when they thought I was up in my room. They must've found some food wrappers I hid under the sofa. They weren't even mad. They were just . . ." Her lips pursed as she considered the best way to describe it. "They were just *done*. So done with me. They didn't understand why I couldn't just behave the way they wanted me to and be good all the time when they were so nice and gave me nice things and didn't mistreat me. They must've thought I was completely nuts. I left that home less than a month later."

"They wanted to be saviors of a cute little girl so they could feel good about themselves," Mason said through clenched teeth. "As soon as it got hard, they bailed. What a fucked-up thing to do to a kid."

She pondered his words for a while. "That's interesting. I never considered that." Her tone and expression gave no clue of how she felt about it. "It all worked out, though. After that, I moved in with my granny. I lived with her until she passed away almost two years ago."

"Your entire voice changed when you mentioned her," he said softly, kissing the top of her head again. "She must have been an incredible woman."

"Incredible," she repeated, and he could hear the smile in her voice. "That's the perfect word to describe Mary Walker. Though she was a hard woman in a lot of ways. Absolutely hated talking about my mom or the foster homes. She flat-out told me when I was thirteen that the reason no one wanted to be my friend was because I talked about sad shit all the time."

Mason froze. Jesus, how could he even respond to that?

"Probably would've been better to put me in therapy, but I mean, it was the nineties. I can't be too mad at her. And I guess she was right, because as soon as I stopped talking about it, I made some friends. Including Kate, who's my best friend to this day."

"I'm glad it worked out, but it couldn't have been easy."

She sighed again, and this time it sounded almost wistful. "No. It was way better than anything else that came before, though. Granny may not have liked talking, but she showed me how to heal. When she saw how fucked up my relationship with food was, how fixated I was on it, she didn't yell at me. Didn't say I was crazy or kick me out. She taught me how to cook."

So many pieces fell into place in that moment. "No wonder you grew up to be a professional baker."

"From the moment she taught me how to make biscuits when I was eight years old, it's all I ever wanted to be."

"Where was your dad through all of this? They must've found him too, right?"

When her shoulders slumped forward, he wished he hadn't asked. "I never found out who he is."

"Did you try one of those ancestry things? See if you could find out that way?" He'd seen so many stories about people finding estranged parents or half siblings they never knew existed. Hell, they even found the Golden State Killer because of those companies.

"I've thought about it a lot. I even ordered a DNA kit once, but I couldn't make myself mail it back in."

Regret filled every facet of her voice. It made him desperate to do anything to help her. "Why not?" he asked gently. "It doesn't sound like you simply changed your mind."

"I don't know." One shoulder lifted in a halfhearted shrug. "While Granny was still alive, I thought it would be like a slap in the face to her, you know? That she took me in, raised me, gave me literally everything, but I still wanted to go off and find some mythical parent figure I never even knew."

That made a lot of sense. He imagined how an adoptive parent might feel to find out the child they loved and raised all their lives started searching for their bio parents. It had to hurt like hell, even if most parents probably wouldn't admit it. "What about after she passed?"

"I don't know," she said again. "I took the test. I got the package ready to send in. But I couldn't stop thinking about what I'd do when I got my results."

Mason frowned. "What do you mean?"

"Well, it's not like I could tell anyone. There wasn't a single person in my life who knew I had no idea who my dad was." Her soft groan made it clear how much this still frustrated her. "I'd have to keep it a secret from everyone I knew. I wouldn't have anyone to help me reach out or go with me to meet him. And I knew for damn sure I wouldn't be able to do it all by myself. So what was the point?"

"Am I the only one you told about this?" he couldn't help asking, some of his surprise making its way into his voice despite his best efforts. Obviously, she listened to her grandmother's advice to make friends in middle school, but it never occurred to him she still followed it to this day.

She tilted her head just enough to meet his gaze. "Is that bad?"

"Not at all," he assured her. "I just . . . I'm honored you trust me enough to tell me."

A blush colored her cheeks, and she dipped her chin, hiding her eyes once more. "You're the first person to ask more than once."

How many times could she break his heart in one day? "Well," Mason said, making up his mind in an instant. "Now you have me."

She went still as a statue carved into marble. Several seconds passed before she whispered, "I do?"

"I'm sure it won't be the same as having Kate or your grandmother help you," he said hesitantly, not sure how to gauge her reaction. "But if you want my help, you have it."

Addison stayed frozen for a few more agonizing seconds. Then she twisted around in his lap, throwing her arms around his neck and covering his face in rapid kisses.

At first, Mason had absolutely zero idea what to do. Nothing like this had ever happened to him before—not even close. As she continued planting gleeful kisses all over his face, he realized there was only one thing he could possibly do.

He laughed.

Addison jerked back, planting her hands on his shoulders and locking her elbows.

"What?" he asked, his brows drawing together.

"I've just never heard you laugh before." The shock morphed into a teasing smile. "Not like that. I didn't even know you knew how."

He pursed his lips, trying to hide a half-smile. "I only pull it out for special occasions."

"Well, I'm glad I made the cut." She smirked at him. "Don't worry. I won't let it go to my head, Master."

CHAPTER 13

Addison

F our weeks and three days. That's how much time had passed since they mailed in her DNA test.

Well, since Mason mailed in her test. Once again, she managed to prepare the saliva sample and box it up on her own. When the time came to add it to the outgoing mail tray on the reception desk, she chickened out. For three days, the sample sat in her room, until Mason came to fetch her on Saturday morning. Seeing it sitting on top of her dresser, he grabbed it without a word, and dropped it in the tray as they passed through the lobby.

That kindness was why she found herself in the kitchen right now. It was that in-between time, after Kendra and Luca left for the day, but before Gabriel, Sienna, and Eric arrived for the dinner shift. In other words, the perfect time to bake Mason a batch of alfajores—delectable dulce de leche cookies that would get him in the right mood for his trip to South America next week.

God, she hoped her results would be in before he left. Since she'd never have the guts to look at the results herself, they'd created a new email address just for this, using it to register her ancestry account. Mason promised to go through the results and deliver the news, good or bad, as soon as the notification arrived.

The website said she'd have her results in three to four weeks. Which meant she'd been freaking the fuck out for almost a week and a half at this point.

Well. Not the whole week and a half. The weekend she just spent at Mason's didn't leave much room in her brain for worry.

Jesus, Mary, and Joseph, that man could fuck. He tied her to his bed for hours on Saturday, spread wide and completely at his mercy. The things he did to every goddamn inch of her body . . .

The things he did with his tongue.

"I know that look," said a conspiratorial voice to her left.

Addison whipped around, sloshing raw egg over the sides of the eggshell halves in her hands. She looked down in surprise, shocked to find the partially separated egg there. It wasn't like her to get distracted while baking.

"Oh yeah, I *definitely* know that look," Olivia said with a laugh. "Here, let me help." Crossing the kitchen quickly, she grabbed a wad of paper towels and dabbed at the dripping mess on Addison's hands.

"Thanks," Addison said, willing her blush to go away. "Sorry about that. I must've been daydreaming."

Olivia's grin could only be described as sly. "About anyone in particular?" she asked, voice all innocence.

The stark contrast made Addison laugh. "Oh, I don't think so," she said with a secretive smile of her own. "Just generic daydreaming, really."

"Generic daydreaming," Olivia repeated, her sapphire eyes positively sparkling. "My favorite kind."

"It keeps the mystery alive, you know?"

Olivia leaned back against the huge island in the center of the kitchen. "How long have you been staring out that window while holding a cracked egg, exactly?" she asked, arching her eyebrows in a clear challenge.

"I'm afraid I'm not at liberty to say," Addison said, a barely restrained laugh threaded through the words. Tossing the ruined egg into the trash, she grabbed a new one and started over.

"Mm-hmm." Olivia crossed her arms and pursed her lips disapprovingly, but that mischievous twinkle stayed in her eyes. "I think you may have seriously underestimated my dedication to finding out Manor gossip."

Addison couldn't hold back her laughter anymore. "How about a wager then?" she said with a grin. "You have twenty-four hours to figure it out. Loser buys the winner drinks in town Friday night."

"Oh, you are *on*," Olivia said, tossing her black curls over her shoulder. "I hope you're not a sore loser, cause you're going d—."

"Unless you're flying down to Brazil to pick the coffee beans yourself," Zach said as he came strolling through the kitchen door, "I don't see what's—" He froze when he saw the two women standing together, a dark look burning in his eyes. In the blink of an eye, he was back to normal, smirk and all. "Never mind. I see exactly what's taking you so long."

Addison raised a hand to wave at him, only belatedly realizing she still held the new eggshell. More raw egg dripped down onto her sleeve. "Fuck," she muttered, tossing the second egg into the trash with the first. "That's twice."

"More generic daydreaming?" Olivia joked.

"What's this now?" Zach asked as Addison cleaned the new batch of slime off her clothes and skin.

Olivia gave him a crafty grin. "You wouldn't happen to know who our new baker is sneaking around the Manor with, would you? She bet me I couldn't figure it out."

Zach's answering snort sounded more derisive than amused. "I'd hardly call it sneaking around." His tone wasn't any kinder.

This wasn't the first time Addison got the idea he didn't approve of her relationship with Mason. He'd made a handful of not-exactly-complimentary comments in the past few weeks.

If relationship was even the right word.

Maybe that was the problem. Maybe he didn't approve of her casually fucking one of the Doms, distracting him from his work. Zach certainly seemed dedicated to making the Manor run like a well-oiled machine.

Seemingly oblivious to Zach's discontent, Olivia rolled her eyes sky high. "Of course you know. With the way you watch the security cameras all day, I should've guessed." She planted her hands on her hips, mock-glaring at her friend. "You're not going to tell me, are you?"

Gaze darting over to Addison, Zach frowned. But half a second later, he flounced over to the espresso machine, his customary cocky smirk firmly back in place. "That feels like cheating," he said, placing a tiny white cup under the dispenser and pushing several buttons on the complicated machine. "Do your own dirty work."

"Traitor," Olivia grumbled, but she didn't seem upset in the least.

Zach started to snipe back, but the kitchen door flew open with such force it banged against the wall. All three of them whirled around as Mason stalked through the doorway.

"To what do we owe this thrilling entrance?" Zach said, arching an eyebrow at the Dom. He held up his small white cup. "In need of your next double espresso?"

Mason hardly even glanced at Zach before his eyes found Addison. As soon as their gazes met, she knew.

The results.

Not only were they in. Mason already knew what they were.

"Oh. My. Fucking. God." Olivia's exclamation drew every eye in the room. She looked like Christmas arrived ten months early. "It's Mason. Ho-ly shit."

Mason gave her the kind of Dom look that brought Addison to her knees. "What on earth are you going on about?"

Olivia practically jumped up and down in her excitement. She wasn't kidding about the gossip obsession. "You two are one hundred percent fucking, aren't you?"

The look on Mason's face would've been bland on anyone else. But the minute widening of the eyes, the way his lips parted the tiniest bit—on him, it was an expression of utmost shock.

Addison couldn't help herself. She burst out laughing.

Her laughter died off abruptly when Zach walked out of the room without another word. He didn't even take his espresso.

"What's his problem?" Olivia muttered, a troubled frown replacing her look of manic glee. She started to say more, but then seemed to notice that Mason clearly wanted her to follow Zach out of the room.

Her eyes narrowed in the most joyfully scheming way. "Oh, do you want to be alone? I'll give you two some privacy then."

"Did . . . did she just skip out of the room?" Mason sounded dumbfounded.

Though her heart pounded against her ribs as she both longed for and dreaded the news Mason brought, she had to smile. "She did. I think she's happy cause she just won a bet."

With a shake of the head, he said, "Whatever you say." Slowly, he turned away from the door, facing Addison again.

She studied his eyes, his mouth, his hands. The tilt of his brows and the slope of his shoulders. Searching for any clue of what the results might be.

He was so unreadable to her.

Fuck, she could hardly even breathe.

"I read the results," he said at last, his voice as steady and unrelenting as an empty blue sky.

"What do they say?" Nerves made her throat so tight, she hardly got the words out. "Do you know who my dad is?"

Looking her right in the eyes with such intense kindness that her heart pounded for a different reason entirely, he said softly, "Yes. I know."

Downtown Fairford had a single pub called O'Shea's or O'Brien's or some other generic Irish name, the inside decorated with a stereotypical Irish theme. Lots of dark wood and emerald green, Celtic designs carved into the front of the bar, old metal advertisements for Guiness and Jameson—the whole shebang.

Addison checked the cocktail napkin under her untouched glass of water. O'Leary's. That's right.

"We're back!" Olivia announced as she and Nell scooted up to their table, plunking down another trio of tequila shots and a small dish of lime wedges.

"Hang on a second," Addison said, laughing. "You said you were just going to the bathroom."

Nell grinned. "We had to pass the bar on the way back anyway. Don't worry, this round's on us." Winking, she shoved one of the shot glasses in Addison's direction before lifting another. "To the ladies of Fairford Manor."

"To the queens of the Manor," Olivia corrected, donning a hilarious attempt at a regal expression. "Forever may we reign."

Laughing, Addison hoisted her fourth shot of the evening into the air. "Forever may we reign," she echoed, knocking back the shot and swallowing it in a single gulp. "*Fuck.*" Coughing, she sucked on her lime, not that it helped too much. "That fucking burns."

Nell, who had decided at the last second to tag along on their little outing, smirked at her. "The more you drink, the less it'll burn. Want me to go grab round number five?"

"Oh God, you two are definitely trying to get me drunk, aren't you?" Addison answered with another laugh. "Do you realize how old I am? If we drink much more, it'll take me days to recover."

Giggling, Olivia leaned in and stage-whispered, "And you know what Aiden and Rafe will do to us when we have to call them for a ride. They both told us not to drink too much tonight. It'll take a week to recover from that."

"Oh no, a spanking," Nell said, her grin positively devilish. "Don't threaten me with a good time." All three of them cracked up at that, laughing so loud they got a few glances from the surrounding tables. "Yeah, we definitely need another round." Nell bounced off to the bar.

"What about Mason?" Olivia asked, leaning in and whispering conspiratorially. "Do you think he'll spank you when he finds out?"

Addison's face flooded with heat. "I don't think—I mean, we don't exactly—"

"I'm not trying to embarrass you," Olivia said, resting a hand gently on her forearm. "I'm sorry."

"No, it's okay." She didn't want the other women to think she was a prude when she was anything but. "I'm not embarrassed. I'm just not sure he'd care. We're not really together, you know? We're just fucking when we have the time."

Olivia arched her eyebrows. "Uh huh. And that's why Gabriel told me Mason forced him to give you next week off so you two could go away together? Cause you're just fucking when you find the time?"

Oh God, as if she wasn't already mortified enough about that. "Forced" was almost too nice a word for it—Mason straight-up bullied Gabriel into giving her the time off. He'd called the head chef on Wednesday to inform him she wouldn't be in next week.

Not ask. *Inform.*

Gabriel had thrown back a slew of arguments about Mason not having authority over his kitchen staff. That she needed to clear vacation time with him in advance. And perhaps most damning, that her three-month trial period didn't even technically include vacation time.

Mason listened to all these objections in perfect silence, his expression unreadable. Then he simply said, "You got along just fine without her for seven years. You'll survive seven fucking days. She's taking the week off." He hung up without even waiting for an answer.

Gabriel informed her the next morning that her vacation time was approved, while she blushed from head to toe in abject shame.

"We're not going away together," she said as Nell finally returned to the table, not wanting the other women to think Mason was whisking her off on some extravagant vacation. "Not the way you think."

Nell's eyes widened as she realized the new topic of conversation. Handing out the shots in silence, she watched Addison with obvious fascination filling her big brown eyes.

"You aren't going to Chile with him?" Olivia asked, confused.

Shaking her head, Addison admitted, "Mason cancelled his trip."

The other two gave each other a long look that Addison couldn't read. God, she hoped they weren't judging her. She hadn't meant to ruin his plans. In fact, she tried her hardest to convince him to still go. They could always go another time. Plan it out in advance, keep it from fucking up everyone's schedules.

Mason wouldn't hear of it, though. Now that she finally knew who her father was, he didn't want her to have to wait any longer than necessary to meet him.

"So," Olivia finally said, drawing out the word. "Where are you going?"

The whole truth, or a more palatable version of it?

In years past, the answer would've been obvious. But with four shots of tequila coursing through her bloodstream, her usual boundaries looked awfully blurred.

Fuck it.

Picking up the fifth shot, she dropped it down the back of her throat, not even sucking on a lime before saying, "We're driving to New Mexico to meet my dad."

She expected them to shut down, lose interest, change the subject.

This time, it didn't happen. Shock and pleasure showed equally on their faces, and they peppered her with questions about her dad, her childhood, her life.

About her. They wanted to know *her*—the part she kept buried deep inside.

She did her best to answer every single question, truths and memories pouring out of her in a way only liquor makes possible.

Never in a million years did she imagine they'd do the same, sharing their own stories, reliving their own pain.

Olivia's abusive parents. Nell's psycho ex.

"I never thought . . ." Addison couldn't figure out how to finish the sentence. So much emotional baggage lay spread out on the table between them—still raw and bleeding, but no longer hidden in the dark. She couldn't have guessed how warm and comforting it would be to thrust all that turmoil into the light. "Thank you," she said at last. "Mason's the only other person I've ever told about any of this. I'm only starting to figure out how amazing it feels to say it all out loud."

Nell grabbed her hand, giving it a squeeze. "And that right there is why I'm going back to school to become a therapist."

God, as if these two could get any more amazing. "Thank you," Addison said again. "For everything tonight."

She had a feeling she'd found a pair of true, lifelong friends.

Addison's life felt like being in the center of a tornado, with everything whipping around her as she clung on for dear life. She still didn't know quite how it all happened, but in the space of five days, she went from not having a clue who her father was to being in the passenger seat of Mason's BMW on the way to meet him.

Steve Redford. Born in July of 1962. He had a Dennis Quaid smile and kind eyes. Apparently he never moved away from the tiny New Mexico town where he grew up, barely more than an hour from where she spent the first eight years of her life. She hadn't entirely wrapped her mind around any of that yet.

Not to mention the cancelled Chile trip, receiving special treatment from Gabriel because she was fucking one of the partners, and the fact they were driving for thirty-three hours since she was too much of a wuss to fly . . . all that would hang over her head for a long-ass time.

At the end of the day, though, she couldn't do this alone, and she damn well knew it. If Mason wanted to bend over backward to make the stars align for her, she wouldn't say no.

She would, however, do her level best to pay him back. Not necessarily for the trip expenses—he'd assured her enough times that the money had no effect on him whatsoever, and she didn't have too much pride to take the gift. But she would sure as fuck find some way to make it up to him and show him the same level of kindness he showed her.

"You're being uncharacteristically quiet," Mason said, glancing her way before returning his gaze to the road. "What's on your mind?"

She had a feeling he'd give her a spanking if she told him she still felt guilty (it would be the third such punishment in five days). So she went with the other matter weighing on her mind instead—the one she hadn't admitted out loud yet.

"Is this a mistake?"

Though his face showed no reaction, his hands tightened on the steering wheel for a few seconds.

"Shit, I'm sorry," she rushed to add. "I'm not saying I don't want to go. I know how much you gave up to make this happen for me, so please don't think I'm not grateful."

"It's all right." It came out a little too commanding to be considered entirely soothing. "I'm not mad at you. It's perfectly reasonable to feel anxious about this." When she didn't respond, he said, "Tell me what you're worried about."

She thought about that for a second. "I mean, what if he's an asshole?"

"I thought that's why we were driving down there instead of messaging him."

Mason knew perfectly well that was the reason, but it was kind of him to point it out in such a polite way. She had the option to reveal herself to relatives online—an option her dad clearly chose when he took his own ancestry test. If she did that, any blood relatives with an account would be notified, and she'd have the option to send them messages.

The notion fucking terrified her. She refused to reach out to a perfect stranger, announce she was his long-lost daughter, and just hope for the best. So they did the next best thing: stalked the shit out of him online.

Google and Facebook revealed that Steve Redford owned a bar in the tiny hamlet of Cedar Crest, New Mexico. Which apparently wasn't even technically a town, but a Census-Designated Place, whatever the fuck that meant. He was its primary bartender and could be found there almost every night. The plan was to sit at the bar, act like a vacationing couple, and strike up a conversation. Once she knew what he was like, she could decide what to do.

All of which was very much beside the point as far as she was concerned. "Well yeah, but there are levels of assholery. What if we get there, and he's literally the biggest douchebag on the face of the planet, and I wish I never found out who he was at all? Or, like, what if it turns out he's a serial killer, and he tries to murder us?"

"Statistically, I don't believe that's likely to happen." One corner of Mason's lips twitched. "Though I suppose we can't rule it out entirely."

"Okay, so that was a bad example." She held back her own smile. "Ugh, fine, no more worrying. At least not until we're in the same time zone as him. In the meantime, we might as well figure out how to enjoy this little road trip." Pulling out her phone, she began typing into a Google search. "I'll figure out all the kitschy tourist attractions along our route. I bet we can find the world's biggest ball of yarn or something."

Addison learned in that moment that Mason St. John gave the most vicious side-eye of all time. "If you so much as *think* about that again, I swear to God, I'll pull this car over and spank you right on the side of the highway."

A giggle bubbled up out of her. Oh so tempting, but she decided to be good, at least for now. Connecting her phone to the car's Bluetooth, she asked Mason several questions about his music preferences, putting on a Spotify playlist instead. At least then he wouldn't find it weird if she didn't talk.

Because in truth, finding out her dad was a major twat wasn't even her biggest worry. She just couldn't bring herself to admit the other part out loud.

What if he knew about her all along and simply wanted nothing to do with her?

CHAPTER 14

Mason

Driving across the country was not on Mason's bingo card for the year. Yet here he was, fiddling with a plastic keycard at the best hotel he could find in Cleveland, desperate to lie down after twelve hours on the road.

"I would've thought this place was absurdly fancy if I came here two months ago," Addison said as they finally stepped into their suite. "The Manor has ruined me for all other hotels."

Mason let out an amused huff. "I'm sorry this is no longer up to your standards."

"Oh, I suppose it'll do," she said, green-blue eyes sparkling with excitement as she surveyed the room.

A large sitting area stood to their right, with a sofa and three chairs in an assortment of grays and whites. They were arranged in a half circle in front of an enormous flatscreen TV. To the left, a sleek black dining table and six gray chairs sat under a dramatic faux-crystal chandelier. The corner of their king-size bed was just visible through a partially open door on the far wall.

Addison sashayed over to one of the floor-to-ceiling windows, pressing her forehead against the glass so she could look straight down.

"I never thought of Cleveland as a pretty city," she mused. "But it looks really beautiful at night."

Mason moved over to the sofa and settled down on the center cushion. Crooking a finger, he beckoned her toward him. She sauntered across the room with a saucy look in her eyes, giving a surprised burst of laughter when he grabbed her hips and pulled her down onto his lap.

God, he'd never get sick of her laugh.

"So," he murmured, pressing soft kisses along her neck. "Given what you were just doing, I guess it's safe to say your aversion to flying has nothing to do with a fear of heights."

"No," she agreed, arching her neck back, giving him better access. "Heights are fine. It's just the crashing part that terrifies me."

Pulling her shirt lower, he ghosted his lips across her collarbones, making her shiver in delight. "You're more likely to die in a car crash than a plane crash, you know." He brushed the pad of his thumb over her nipple, feeling it harden beneath her clothes.

"There you go with your statistics again," she said, the words coming out high and breathy. "The thing is, I've spent about a quarter of my life in New York City cabs. I'm not afraid of crashing in a car."

Unable to wait another moment, Mason pulled her shirt over her head, tossing it into the nearest chair. She'd dressed for comfort today instead of seduction, but even the simple baby pink bralette had his cock hardening in his slacks.

"Perhaps," he said slowly, tracing one hand up her inner thigh, stopping just shy of her pussy, "I can think of some way to incentivize you."

She tried to pull his hand farther up her leg, but he wouldn't budge an inch. Her little groan of frustration filled him with triumph. "Incentivize me how?"

"Oh, let's just say I can think of several ways to reward you for agreeing to go on your first flight." His hand moved up just enough to nudge at the seam of her yoga pants, right at the juncture of her thighs. "I'm perfectly willing to hold off until I get some assurances."

With a needy whimper, she said, "Yeah, right. Like you can restrain yourself anyway."

Mason knew his answering look was downright diabolical. He could see it reflected in the horror filling her eyes. "Challenge accepted." With that, he removed his hand from her leg entirely.

"Oh, come on." With a sound very much like a growl, she pulled her bralette off and tossed it over her shoulder. "Don't you want to fuck me, Master?" she practically purred, pressing her perfect fucking breasts against his chest and rolling her hips.

This was going to be harder than he thought.

Sliding down to the floor between his knees, Addison ran her hands up his thighs to his belt with a hungry look in her eyes. "Maybe I can incentivize you." She freed his cock from his slacks with warm, gentle hands, running her thumb along the underside from base to tip.

He resisted the urge to pump his hips forward, chasing the sweet feel of her hands when she pulled away. "Take me in your mouth," he ordered through clenched teeth.

"But . . ." She watched him through her lashes, her face the picture of angelic innocence. "I thought you didn't want me?"

His eyes narrowed to tiny slits. "If my cock isn't buried in your throat in the next ten seconds, I swear to God you won't sit down for a week."

Addison's devilish grin made him want to fuck that mouth even more. "You're sending me very mixed signals, you know."

"Enough." Taking hold of a fistful of her hair, he drew her mouth downward.

She didn't even pretend to resist. Closing her eyes, she took him into her mouth with a contented sigh, closing her lips around his girth and trying to take him deeper on her own.

"Oh, no," Mason said, tightening his grip on her hair, holding her in place. "It's too late for that. You think you can tease me like that and get away with it, little one?"

She looked staggeringly beautiful like this. Eyes closed. Lips straining to accommodate him. Utterly still with her hair trapped in his fist. This image would haunt his fantasies for the rest of his days.

"You have no control here. Now be still and let me fuck you like the little fucktoy you are. Understand?"

In answer, she twisted her tongue around his cock in a way that forced an involuntary groan from him. The little viper.

Dropping her hair, he gripped her face between both hands, yanking her down as he surged his hips forward. She gagged for a few seconds before he withdrew, then did it again. "My cock is going down your throat either way. You might as well relax and let me in. It'll be easier for you."

This wasn't the first time he'd fucked her face. He knew she could take all of him.

Still she gagged, though she kept trying her hardest, not even once attempting to pull away. If he didn't find the right angle, it didn't matter how hard either of them tried. Her eyes flew open when he pulled her off his cock completely. "Master?" she said, voice hoarse.

Mason nudged her back until he had enough room to stand. The moment he gained his feet, understanding dawned in her eyes, and she surged toward him, mouth open and ready. He stopped her with her lips only an inch from his rigid cock, looking down at her with a disappointed frown. "Who is in charge here?"

Pouting up at him, she admitted, "You are, Master."

"Then stop topping from the bottom and do as you're told."

She couldn't have looked more horrified if he screamed accusations and insults in her face. "I'm so sorry, Master. I promise I wasn't trying to do that."

It was one thing to say she'd been a naughty girl. It was another thing entirely to question her submission altogether.

"I believe you," Mason said, brushing his knuckles along her cheekbone. "I'm sorry I hurt your feelings. I know what a good girl you are, even if you're being a naughty little thing right now."

Relief washed over her face, making her practically radiate light. Utterly fucking glorious. "Thank you, Master. Am I still allowed to please you?"

"Open your mouth and try to hold still." Dark promises dripped from every word.

Her eyes drifted closed again as her mouth stretched wide. She stayed perfectly motionless, completely focused on being used for his pleasure.

She was the goddess of lovemaking. Sex personified. Beauty to a level he'd never seen before in his life.

Addison was everything. And he was fucking terrified what that meant.

Burying that whole line of thinking in the back of his mind, he took his cock in his hand, guiding it between her lips. "Take it all," he ground out, his muscles going rigid as she took him deeper and deeper. "Swallow me whole."

Oh, sweet mother of God. He threw his head back in absolute ecstasy as his cock slid deep into her throat. *So fucking tight.*

Holding her immobile between his hands again, he withdrew almost completely before pushing back in, as slowly as he could manage. She needed to get used to him before he lost his tenuous grip on control.

Twice more he managed it, pushing into her with little resistance, her neck arched just so to allow the sweet slide in and out of her throat.

What little control he had left dissipated as he began pushing into her mouth again. She was his. And goddamnit, he would use her however the fuck it pleased him best.

With a harsh growl, he pumped his hips forward with much more speed, holding her head still so he could fuck her face properly. "That's it," he said, ramping up his pace even more. "Suck your Master's cock like the good little whore you are. I know you love it when I use you for my pleasure."

Her answering moan vibrated through his cock, almost forcing him over the edge. Fuck, he was close.

Pushing in one last time, he held his cock there, cutting off her air completely. "You'll swallow every single drop, do you understand?"

Addison hummed her agreement, and as he withdrew from her mouth, she sucked so fucking hard on the tip that he couldn't hold it back anymore.

"Fuck!" he shouted, jerking and shuddering, his movements completely out of his control now. Her throat worked as he emptied himself inside her, holding her in place with a single hand in her hair. As the last wave ripped through him, his arm jerked, pulling her hair hard enough to make her cry out.

As soon as he pulled free of her, he collapsed back onto the sofa, completely boneless. "Just in case no one has ever told you this before," he got out between panting breaths, "I want to make sure you know—you're exceptional."

She ran a finger along her bottom lip, gathering up a few drops of come that escaped. Her tongue darted out, licking them off. "Thank you," she whispered, giving him a shy smile. Climbing to her feet, she slowly lowered her yoga pants and panties to the floor, stepping out of the bunched fabric before kicking it aside. With one hand, she traced a lazy finger around her nipple. The other started at her hip, inching ever so slowly toward her center.

The wicked little seductress.

"Come here." He held out a hand, turning her around and helping her down onto his lap. "You were such a good girl," he murmured in her ear, pulling her back against his chest, spreading her legs wide to either side of his. "Hold yourself open for me."

Without hesitation, she wrapped her arms around her thighs, splaying her legs as wide as she could, her heels propped against the edge of the sofa cushions. With torturous slowness, he slid two fingers into her pussy.

Addison drew in a sharp breath, closing her eyes as her head fell back against his shoulder. "Please more, Master. *Please.*"

"You're absolutely soaked for me." He easily added a third finger, pumping them in and out of her. "Did it turn you on to have my cock buried in your throat? Did you like being my little plaything?"

A delightful shiver ran through her. "Yes, Master." Her whisper was so low, he barely heard her.

He lowered his lips to her ear, making her shiver again with the heat of his breath. "That's because you're meant to be mine. You were made for me to fuck. To possess. To bring you all the pleasure you could ever imagine." Coating the pad of his thumb in her slick wetness, he began rubbing slow, soft circles over her clit.

Her moan was long and low—the most perfectly sensuous sound in the world. How desperately he wanted to claim her mouth, swallow her moans and gasps of pleasure, and take all of her for his own.

No, he had to stick to his plan, no matter what.

Instead of giving in to his own desires, he continued stoking hers, building her pleasure higher and higher, bringing her to the verge of total collapse.

Then he withdrew his hand.

It took her a few seconds to realize he wasn't merely changing hands or shifting angles. Her head swiveled from side to side as she took in his hands, both resting serenely on the sofa.

"Umm," she said, clearly at a loss. "I, uh . . . I didn't . . ." She craned her neck, trying to catch a glimpse of his expression. "Is something wrong, Master?"

"Not in the least." He tried to sound nonchalant, but it came out more like a boast. "I'm doing exactly what I told you I would."

She went utterly still for five seconds. Then she threw back her head with an annoyed groan. "Are you kidding me right now?"

"I think we've already established I don't know how to tell jokes," he said, unable to hold back a smug little smirk.

"You're not playing fair," she grumbled, letting her feet tumble over the edge of the sofa and crossing her arms. "This is pure manipulation."

"Oh, please," he said with an amused huff. "You're the one who just had my cock buried in your throat to try to manipulate me. I don't want to hear it."

She didn't have an argument against that one. "It's not fair though," she said, pushing out her lower lip in the cutest little pout. "You've probably been flying your whole life. Of course you're not afraid. I'm almost forty for God's sake. I'm too old to try new things."

"Oh, Addison," he said, running a hand slowly down her center, stopping just shy of where she wanted to be touched. "It's never too late to try new things. Fly with me. Let me show you the whole fucking world. I promise you won't regret it."

His fingers drifted lower, brushing over her clit with the lightest of touches.

"Okay!" she shouted, throwing her hands up in the air. "I'll get on a plane, I promise, but not right now. Not for this. I can't handle meeting my dad and flying for the first time all at once. It's too much. Please?"

With a triumphant smile, he shifted her down onto the sofa on her back. Kneeling up between her spread thighs, he hooked her knees over his shoulders, arching her ass up off the cushion.

"Your terms are acceptable," he said, prying her apart with his fingers, revealing her gorgeous pussy to his eyes. "Good girl." And then he dove in, swirling his tongue as deep into her cunt as he could, lapping up her sweetness.

She was every fucking bit as delicious as he remembered. He wanted to consume her. Utterly devour her. Savor every last drop.

Sweeping his tongue up her folds, he flattened it over her clit, taking his time running over it, bit by painstaking bit. Hips bucking against his face, she dug her heels painfully into his back.

"Oh my fuuu—freaking God," she said.

He smiled against her center, his five o'clock shadow scraping against her most sensitive flesh. "You're such a good girl," he said as she squirmed. Then his tongue was right back at her clit, licking and twisting, pushing her pleasure higher and higher, until every single muscle in her body was taut, ready for the explosion.

"Please!" She screamed it loud enough that anyone with an adjoining room most certainly heard her. Hell, the whole fucking floor might have heard that.

Plunging two fingers into her pussy, he pumped them in and out, laving her clit with his tongue with as much force as he could manage. Within seconds, she screamed as pleasure cascaded through her. He didn't stop until the very last shudder passed through her tight pussy, and she collapsed down onto the cushions.

"See?" Mason said, smirking down at her. "Wasn't that worth one tiny little concession?"

Throwing her arms over her eyes, she struggled to catch her breath. "Here's a helpful tip for you," she mumbled at last, her words not quite clear. "As long as you keep doing that shit with your tongue? I'll agree to just about anything you want."

CHAPTER 15
Addison

"You got us a whole house?" Addison went for the same tone she'd use to comment on the weather. *Sunny day, isn't it? Did you hear it's supposed to rain tomorrow? Oh, cool, you rented a three-bedroom house just so the two of us have somewhere to crash for eight hours? What a totally normal thing to do.*

Given his arched brows, she maybe didn't quite succeed. "I had my reasons," was all he deigned to say. Checking his phone, he punched a four-digit code into the keypad on the front door. The smart lock chimed, then whirred as the deadbolt slid out of the way.

Pushing the door open, Mason motioned for her to precede him into the brick, ranch-style home. It was a nice house, with vaulted ceilings everywhere she looked. A gas-burning fireplace and a set of comfy looking, matching leather sofas in the living room. Granite countertops and stainless-steel appliances in the kitchen, including a five-burner gas range.

With the framed nature photos on the walls and the worn books filling a bookcase in one corner, it looked a lot less like a rental property than she expected. Throw some toys around and stack a few pairs of shoes by the front door, and it would be easy enough to believe a family lived here.

Unable to stop herself, Addison imagined what her life would be like if she'd grown up in a place this like. If her mom and dad had been together, maybe even married. If she lived in one place with the same people her entire life, instead of bouncing around Santa Fe before being shipped off to her granny's in New York.

If she'd never been alone. Or terrified. Or starving.

How different would her life look right now? What kind of person would she be?

"I didn't mean to upset you," Mason said, watching her with a deep frown.

It took her a second to process what he said. "I'm not upset," she assured him, smiling. "I just got lost in my thoughts for a second there."

"Are you sure?" He studied her face, clearly not believing her smile. "If it makes you feel any better, an Airbnb in middle-of-nowhere Missouri costs way less than our hotel did last night."

That made her chuckle. "I guess that makes sense. Everything's probably cheaper in the middle of nowhere." It wasn't that she cared how he spent his money anyway. She was just already so greatly indebted to him for every single aspect of this trip, staying at a Motel 6 maybe would've assuaged her guilt a little bit.

Of course, then she'd have to feel terrible about making Mason sleep at a crappy motel.

"Do you want to see why I picked this place?" he asked, the merest hint of excitement in his voice.

"Absolutely." When he extended his hand, she took it without hesitation, letting him pull her down the hallway to the bedrooms.

Cracking open the first door, he peeked inside, then kept going a second later. When he did the same at the second door, he stopped dead in his tracks. "Okay, this is it," he said, taking both her hands, watching her with eyes that sparkled with excitement. "Are you ready?"

She couldn't have kept a grin off her face even if she wanted to. "What shenanigans are you up to? For you, this is practically giddy."

With a smile playing at his lips, he backed into the room, letting go of one of her hands to flip the light switch. "Ta-da," Mason said with a little flourish.

In that moment, Addison fell in love with him a little bit. Her heart didn't give her any choice.

The long, narrow room sported a pair of matching bunk beds pushed up against opposite walls, a scant three feet of space between them.

"We both have seniority here, which means we both get top bunk," he announced proudly, puffing out his chest a little bit.

Words completely failed her. Wrapping her arms around his neck, Addison pulled his face down low enough to kiss him, hoping to show him how profoundly grateful she was instead.

The kiss was slow and gentle—nothing like their usual frenzy. When at last they broke apart, she rested her forehead against his chest. "Thank you," she managed at last. "I can't tell you what it means to me."

He pressed his lips against the top of her head. "It means a lot to me, too. Why don't we get ready for bed? We still have almost thirteen hours to drive tomorrow, so we should get some sleep."

Twenty minutes later, Addison snuggled up under the fuzzy red-and-black plaid comforter as she stared across the narrow gap. Mason lay on his back in his own bunk, his feet sticking out between the bars at the foot of the bed—perhaps the only flaw in his otherwise glorious plan.

Not that she spent much time looking at his feet. He had the comforter folded down to his waist, revealing his bare chest. Even in the dim light of the nightlight she brought on the trip, he looked good enough to eat. God, she could stare at his beautiful body for hours.

The emergence of his favorite Prada frames when he returned from brushing his teeth only made him sexier. He was gorgeous with the contacts in, of course, but the glasses made him look like a sexy professor. An exceedingly strict professor who would gladly punish a naughty student if she required correction.

Someday, she'd build up the nerve to ask him to bring that little fantasy to life. After all, she'd been having it since the first time she spent the night at his house. Not tonight, though. She had much more important matters on her mind.

"Do you have an older brother?" she asked once they both settled in.

He rolled his head to the side, so he could see her between the bars of the black metal railing. "No, but I have a younger brother. Why do you ask?"

"What you said before," she started tentatively, hoping she wasn't reading too much into things. "About this meaning a lot to you, too. I thought maybe you had an older brother, and he never let you have top bunk."

That earned her one of his backward smiles. "Very astute."

The praise warmed her from the inside out, and she hid her smile behind her comforter. "What's the real story?"

He didn't answer at first, though he didn't look away either, so she knew the question hadn't made him angry. At least a couple minutes ticked by before he finally started talking. "I went to a sleepover when I was a kid. My friend had the coolest bunk bed I'd ever seen in my life. A twin bed on top, but a full on the bottom, with actual stairs instead of a ladder."

Addison smiled. "That sounds magical."

"It was. To eight-year-old me? It was the most magical thing in the world, and I wanted one so badly I could hardly think straight some days. Imagine the sleepovers I could've hosted with that in my room." He almost smiled as he said it, but then the light left his eyes. "Not that my parents ever let me have sleepovers anyway. But I thought maybe, with that bed . . . I don't know. Little kid logic."

"Why couldn't you have sleepovers?"

"Because Nate always had friends over, and they didn't want to deal with that many kids at once." Not even a trace of emotion colored the words. "Or at least that was the reason they always gave me."

"Nate is your little brother?" she guessed.

He nodded, but didn't speak for a long time. "Jonathan convinced me to find a therapist shortly after we founded our company. My therapist was the one who told me my mother has a narcissistic personality disorder. It explains why she felt entitled to anything and everything she ever wanted, and pitched a fit when things didn't go her way. Why she was always the victim, even when she was so obviously at fault. And Nate . . . he was her perfect golden child. The boy who could do no wrong, who deserved everything he ever wanted. My dad and I were the scapegoats."

"Like in *The Good Place*," Addison said, her heart going out to him, "with Jameela Jamil's character and her little sister."

"I love that show," Mason said, rolling onto his side and propping his head up on his hand. "Well, once I got to the end of the first season anyway. Zach harassed me for months until I finally binge watched it, and after the season finale, I was hooked." He sighed. "And yes, very much like that. But unlike Tahani, I found an exceptional therapist and eventually went no-contact with my family."

Tears pricked at the backs of her eyes. "That must've been so hard."

"The hardest part was letting go of how desperately I wanted everyone to apologize." He let out a long-suffering sigh. "My mom for obvious reasons. My dad for watching it happen and never saying a word. Nate for not sitting up one day and going wait, this is total bullshit, I've done nothing to deserve being put up on this pedestal, and he's done nothing to deserve being treated like shit." His mouth formed a grim line. "But there's no point in torturing myself while I wait for something that's never going to happen."

For the first time since entering the room, she wished they were in the same bed. She desperately wanted to hold him close—to make sure he knew he wasn't alone.

"I suppose my old therapist would say my need for control and aversion to change are coping mechanisms or trauma responses or some such thing." He sighed. "Probably true."

After a while, she said, "I guess you didn't get the bunk bed for Christmas, then."

"No. Nate did."

She sat up so fast she scraped her forehead against the ceiling. "Are you fucking kidding me?"

"Nope," he said, enunciating the *p* with a sarcastic popping sound. "I'll never forget what my mom said to me when she saw how disappointed I was. Every word is burned into my brain. *Don't be selfish, Mason. You know he needs it more than you. He's so popular, and you don't even have any friends.* Even though she knew I did. It was her fault they never came to our house."

"Tell me where she is," Addison demanded, her voice a low,

dangerous growl. "I swear to Jesus Himself, I'll punch her in the throat for you."

His answering chuckle was like a balm to her raging emotions. "I appreciate it, but don't bother. It won't change anything, and my therapist taught me how important it is to look forward, not backward."

"I'm almost afraid to ask," she said, cringing, "but what did you get for Christmas that year?"

"An N64 I never even got to play, because it ended up in Nate's room, and some clothes."

"Well." She tried to adopt a jaunty sort of tone, with moderate success. "If my trial period is extended and I'm still here at Christmas, I promise to give you something special."

As soon as the words left her mouth, she marveled at the fact she thought to say them at all. Never once had she planned to stay at Fairford Manor. From the beginning, it was always go for three months, cash out, and figure out her new life back in the city.

So why did her imagination flash images through her mind of what the Manor would look like all done up for the holidays?

Why did the idea that she probably wouldn't be there to follow through on her promise make her eyes burn?

"We should get some sleep," Mason said, settling back down on his mattress and pulling his comforter halfway up his torso. "We've got another early start tomorrow. But thank you. For listening. It really means a lot to me."

"I'm here anytime you need to talk," she said, once again wondering after the fact why her mouth was making promises the rest of her wouldn't be able to keep.

Even more than that, she wondered why she suddenly wanted to keep all those promises, no matter the cost.

Addison clung to the handle on the BMW's passenger side door. "Unlock the car."

"No." His voice held no trace of anger or dominance. It was just a simple statement of fact.

"Goddamnit, Mason, don't fuck with me right now."

His brows lifted ever so slightly. "We just spent three full days driving across the country. We didn't do that to get to the parking lot and turn around."

He sounded so calm. So perfectly reasonable. It made her want to throw something heavy at his head.

"I'm not ready to go in there. Now unlock the fucking car." Most of that came out between clenched teeth.

"Addison—"

"Don't talk to me like you think I'm crazy."

He took a slow, calming breath before trying again. "I don't think you're crazy. In fact, I think what you're feeling right now is to be expected."

She'd been gearing up to yell at him some more, but that stopped her up short. She studied his face for several seconds, searching for the trick, the catch. Coming up empty, she asked, "Then what's the problem?"

"The problem is that this feeling won't go away just by waiting until tomorrow to walk in there. In fact, it'll probably get even worse."

She glared daggers at him. "That doesn't make any sense."

"The longer you build this up in your mind, the harder it'll be."

Letting her hand unclench from around the handle, she crossed her arms over her stomach instead. She hated it when he made sense. "What if he's terrible?" she whispered, fighting to hold back tears.

"Then I'll throw some cash on the bar to cover our drinks and we'll leave." Mason walked toward her slowly, like he was afraid she might bolt or lash out if he moved too fast. "You don't even have to speak to him if you don't want. You can sit there and watch while I do the talking. That's totally up to you." He ran gentle fingers along her upper arms until her muscles slowly unclenched, and she let her arms fall to her sides.

Addison closed her eyes, taking several slow, deep breaths. "I have your word?" she demanded once she got a handle on the worst of her panic. "As long as I go in there and meet him, we can leave as soon as I want? You'll unlock the car this time?"

"You have my word."

It took nearly a full minute after that, but finally she managed a single step forward, then another.

"Good girl," Mason said, lacing his fingers through hers, lending his strength through her trembling hand. He led her toward the squat stucco building and its neon sign spelling out Frank's Bar. Though the k and second r were both out, so it actually said *Fran 's Ba*.

Run! The word cycled through her mind with increasing urgency, but she only tightened her grip on Mason's hand. Together, they stepped through the door and into her father's bar.

For a town with a population under a thousand people, it was a hopping place. Especially for a Tuesday. Most of the barstools were taken, and a small group surrounded the ancient pool table to one side.

"That's him," Mason murmured in her ear.

Addison had pointedly looked anywhere except behind the bar from the moment they entered the room. But Mason's words drew her gaze like a moth to a flame.

Steve Redford looked exactly like the pictures on the Facebook page for Frank's Bar. Kind eyes. Disarming Dennis Quaid smile. Hair just a little too long, like he never had time to get it cut.

Hell, he even had on the same faded T-shirt he wore in several of the photos, black with a salmon-pink *Frank's* embroidered over the left side of his chest.

"We should go sit down before people start looking at us," Mason said, nothing but kindness in his voice. "Let's stick to the plan and act natural."

Act natural, she thought as she strolled up to the bar on wobbly legs. That's it, just act natural and stop staring at the bartender like he's your long-lost fucking father.

Less than a minute after Mason helped her up onto her barstool, Steve moved down the bar to stand in front of them. "What can I get for you two weary travelers?" he asked with a smile.

Up close, she realized his eyes were the exact same shape and color as hers, right down to the specks of gold. Holy fucking shit, she couldn't breathe.

Reaching across to lay his hand over hers on her lap, Mason gave Steve a small smile. "How can you tell we're travelers?"

"Well, for one thing, I've lived here all my life and never laid eyes on you before." He placed two cocktail napkins on the bar, sliding one toward each of them. "And forgive me for saying so, but you don't look like the kind of people who would move to a place like this." He eyed Mason's finely tailored suit with a little chuckle.

Mason tried to match the chuckle, but it came out hollow and fake. Though Steve didn't seem to notice, so perhaps she only felt that way because she'd heard his true laugh before. "Fair enough. My girlfriend and I are on vacation. We'll be here for a few days before we move on to Arizona."

"Well, welcome to the only bar in Cedar Crest. What'll it be?"

Addison paid exactly zero attention as Mason ordered their drinks, studying the lines of her father's face, the movements of his hands, the way he walked. Searching for some additional connection. For anything else that screamed *this man provided half your DNA*.

When a drink appeared in front of her, she gulped down half of it without looking. She hardly even tasted the liquor before it burned its way down her throat.

"What are your plans while you're in the area?" Steve asked, directing the question at her this time.

Staring at him, the entire English language temporarily forgotten, she clenched her teeth so tight she couldn't even pry her jaw open.

This was a mistake. She never should've come here.

"We just want to relax and enjoy the mountains for a few days," Mason answered for her. "Get away from the world for a bit."

Steve's laugh sounded remarkably like hers, only deeper. How was that even possible? Could a laugh be genetic? "You've certainly come to the right place for that. If you want the insider scoop on the best views in the area, I'm your man."

"That would be great," Mason said. "We're planning to visit Sandia Crest tomorrow if the weather holds, but after that—"

"Hey, Steve!" a man called from the other end of the bar. "Can I get another?"

Addison's father gave them the kindest smile she'd ever seen in her fucking life, and it made her want to scream until she lost her voice. "I'll be right back," he promised before turning to fill a clean glass from one of the taps.

"I have to go," she said, her voice low and hoarse. "Now."

She slipped off her stool and all but ran for the door, not even checking to make sure Mason followed her out into the night.

CHAPTER 16
Mason

The woman beside him was a ticking timebomb. He only hoped they'd be safely back inside their rental before the clock ran all the way down.

Getting her through this would take meticulous handling on his part, and he couldn't worry about driving or keeping her safe outside—in an unfamiliar place, in the fucking dark—at the same time. She needed to be his one and only focus.

Luckily, Addison seemed almost dazed at the moment. It was like she'd completely checked out as soon as she climbed into the car.

If only he had an idea of how long it would last.

Heart thumping painfully against his ribs, he navigated the winding roads to the house he rented as fast as he dared in the dark. It had seemed like the perfect place when he chose it. A lovely little two-bedroom cottage in the center of three acres of land, surrounded by ponderosa pines and right on the border of a national forest. He thought the privacy and beauty this house offered would do a lot to make up for the complete lack of luxury hotels in the area. Best of all, it was a mere ten-minute drive from Frank's Bar.

In this moment, though, ten minutes felt like a fucking lifetime.

When they made it to the house at last, he drove right up to the covered patio, stopping only inches from the low stone wall surrounding it. She didn't move a muscle as he climbed out of the car and hurried around to her side. Even as he opened the door and unbuckled her seatbelt, she simply stared at the dashboard with a vacant look in her eyes.

"Come on, little one." He kept his voice soft, hoping it would soothe her. Lifting her out of the car, he carried her through the covered patio to the door. Unlocking it with Addison in his arms was an exercise in patience, but he didn't dare put her down. Not out here.

When at last they made it inside, he carried her straight to the bedroom, lowering her gently onto the king-size bed. Settling onto the edge of the mattress beside her, he ran his fingers through her silky hair.

"It's all right," he whispered. "I'm here. You don't have to do this alone."

"I don't need your fucking platitudes right now."

Mason jumped. He hadn't realized she was snapping out of it, but he saw a new fire burning in her eyes. "That wasn't a platitude," he said, stung at the accusation.

Knocking his hand away from her hair, she sat up against the headboard. "Oh, really? Because it sounds like the kind of shit they put on advertisements for online therapy and suicide hotlines."

"Even if that's true," Mason said, doing his absolute best to cool his rising temper, "those services save countless lives. It's not a platitude either way."

She rolled her eyes toward the ceiling. "Don't split hairs with me. You know what I mean."

"Actually, I don't, so if you'd be so kind as to explain it to me—"

"My mom didn't ever give a shit about me, abandoned me to go get high with her boyfriend, and fucking died. Alone." Her voice grew angrier and louder with every word. "The more I think about it, the surer I am the state found Steve back then, and he said he didn't want me. He's got his life and his bar, and how the fuck would I ever have fit into that? Alone." She was on the point of hysterics now. "The foster family that was supposed to take care of me locked me in the fucking dark every time I did something they didn't like. Alone. They took me away from my foster brothers and sisters and never let me see them again. Fucking alone. The family that was supposed to adopt me thought I was too crazy to love and got rid of me. Alone. Then I finally had Granny, but now she's fucking dead and I'm completely fucking alone."

"What about me?" Mason demanded.

She gave him an incredulous look. "What about you?"

"I literally just drove you across the fucking country to be here for you."

"Because you feel sorry for me." She said it like he should be ashamed of himself.

"Because I care about you," he shot back.

Her lip rose into a vicious sneer. "The only thing you care about is my willingness to keep fucking you."

"That's enough." Mason did everything in his power to find his way back to levelheadedness. He knew she didn't truly mean any of this. Fear controlled her in this moment, making her lash out irrationally.

It still fucking hurt.

"Fuck you, Mason. Fuck your rules, your orders, your fucking collar. I don't need you to save me, okay?" She shoved him off the bed, moving so fast he didn't have time to dodge or brace himself. Getting up on her knees, she glared down at where he lay sprawled on the floor. "And I sure as fuck don't need you to control me. I'm not your *little one* or your *good girl*. I'm a grown-ass adult, and I just want everyone to leave me the fuck alone."

Mason knew he glared back at her with fury burning in his eyes. Afraid of what he might do if he lost control, he stayed perfectly still, not even untangling his long legs from the uncomfortable way they landed beneath him. She didn't need his anger right now. She needed his cold, calculated precision. He'd do whatever it took to give that to her.

Hands fisted at her sides, she watched him with a look that was half triumph, half challenge. Daring him to contradict her. "What?" Another sneer. "Nothing to say?"

An icy sense of calm settled over him, like a fresh blanket of snow turning a dreary landscape into something pure and beautiful.

This was it. The exact feeling he chased within each and every scene.

Reducing a complex situation to its simplest form. Creating order out of mayhem.

Calming an entire goddamn lifetime of chaos.

He stood slowly, seeing no need to rush, keeping his gaze locked with hers the whole time. Her breathing came faster and harder as he moved, like she was gearing herself up for a fight.

Mason was done fighting. It was time for him to take charge.

Sitting on the bed, he shoved her down over his lap before she had a chance to react. She tried to push herself back up, to pull away from him, but he was so much bigger and stronger, she really didn't stand a chance.

Without a word, Mason yanked her pants and panties down, then started spanking. He didn't bother with a warmup. That would do fuck-all for her in this moment. She needed sharp, immediate pain to keep her from spiraling even more out of control.

"Get your fucking hands off me!" So much vitriol dripped from those words, he almost questioned his plan.

But no. He knew Addison Walker, and despite only knowing her for a little over two months, in some ways, he suspected he knew her better than anyone on this planet. He needed to get her into the submissive headspace by any means possible. Only then would she calm down and approach this situation with her father from a rational perspective.

Still she fought, writhing and kicking, screaming her fucking head off without reprieve. When she almost flailed right off the bed, he got an idea. "Maybe this will help you calm down," he said, shifting forward so his thighs stretched far beyond the edge of the mattress. Her torso toppled over with no bed to hold her up anymore, and she gave a shriek of surprise, her hands flying out to catch herself on the floor. Taking advantage of her moment of distraction, he trapped her legs between both of his, completely immobilizing them.

"Let. Me. *Go!*" When she attempted (and failed) to move her legs, she began flinging her hands back, trying to hit him anywhere she could reach.

It was easy enough to grab hold of her wrists, pressing them into the small of her back with one of his hands.

"I swear to fucking God, Mason—"

"Stop," he interrupted, raising his voice over hers. "Be still and listen to me. I'm giving you what you need right now. And I think you fucking know it, because you haven't used your safeword. Either say it or stop fighting me and let me help you."

Not waiting for an answer, he brought his hand down across the center of one ass cheek, immediately followed by the other, as hard as he possibly could.

Her scream was like nothing he'd ever heard from her or any other sub. Low and raw, a wail of profound loss, not of pain. The sound of utter heartbreak one might make when a person they truly love dies. Tears sprung to his own eyes just hearing it.

Finally, they were getting somewhere.

He kept going, raining down the hardest spanks he could, until each impact sent a wave of pain through his own hand, and the muscles in his arm hurt. When at last her entire bottom glowed red in the low light, her skin radiating heat, he stopped. The room was utterly silent except for the soft sounds of her crying.

Mason waited, keeping her draped over his thigh, listening as her little hiccups and sniffles grew fewer and further between. He needed some sign. Any sort of indication that she was back to herself.

"Please, Mason." Her voice came out low and scratchy. "Find a way to make this feeling go away. I'm fucking begging you."

He knew immediately what he needed to do. Pulling her up to her feet, he led her to the foot of the bed, bending her over the padded footboard.

A single sob ripped its way out of her throat. "Make it go away. I can't stand it. I feel like I'm about to fucking explode." She didn't fight him at all, laying limply on the bed like a lifeless ragdoll.

With no choice but to leave her there, Mason crossed the house with long, swift strides. Grabbing his duffel bag from their pile of luggage by the door, he hurried back to the master bedroom.

She'd stayed exactly where he left her, not seeming to have moved a muscle. Dropping his bag on top of the dresser, he rummaged around inside until he found what he needed. He stood behind her a moment later, so close his pants brushed against her swollen, punished flesh.

"Make it go away." A whispered plea this time. "*Please.*" Then she sucked in a sharp breath as he forced two lubed fingers into her ass.

"Is this what you need?" Mason asked, pushing, not relenting until he buried the digits inside her.

Her answering whimper told him all he needed to know. He wouldn't even have to restrain her.

He took his time preparing her, knowing how she hated this, how much pain it caused. But also remembering what she'd said when he asked about the rating she gave to anal sex on her application.

"I don't like anal for pleasure. But for punishment . . . when I'm spinning out of control and I can't force myself to be good, make the right decisions, do the things I know I need to do . . . it makes me feel like a good girl again. It makes everything make sense."

She whimpered again when he withdrew his fingers, the muscles in her back and shoulders bunching as she tensed. Burying her face in the quilt, she waited without another sound, but every single inch of her lithe little body trembled.

Tossing his belt aside, Mason shoved his clothes haphazardly out of the way, coating his cock in a healthy layer of lubricant. Carelessness here wouldn't give her what her mind and body needed right now.

He moved in behind her, spreading her ass cheeks wide with his fingers. Lining the tip of his cock up with her waiting hole, he asked, "Addison, have you been out of control and acting completely out of character?"

"Yes, Master." The quilt muffled the words.

"And do you need me to fuck you in the ass, so you come back to yourself, and remember how to be a good girl again?"

A shudder ran through her. "Yes, Master. Please don't make me wait. I hate myself so much right now, I can't stand it."

Without another word, he shifted his hips forward. His baser instincts urged him to slam into her hard and fast, forcing his way past the ring of muscle trying desperately to keep him out. Keeping a firm grip on his control, he inched into her so goddamned slowly that his own muscles began shaking from the strain of it.

The wail that drifted out of her when he finally got the head past her tight ring was equal parts pain and despair. It slashed at his chest with jagged claws, the sound nearly powerful enough to rip his heart out of his fucking chest. Jesus Christ, this woman had experienced more heartache than any one person should ever have to endure. It made him want to gather her against his chest and never let her go.

That thought would have to wait until he had the time and mental energy to analyze it. For now, he redoubled his focus on taking care of this sweet, wounded creature before him. Gathering all his resolve, he continued pushing forward until his hips pressed gently against her bottom.

"You're being such a good girl," he said, voice shaking as the effort of restraint weighed on him. "When this is over, it'll all be in the past. You can start fresh."

"Do you promise?"

"I promise."

Her hands fisted in the quilt. "Then fuck me as hard as you can. If this is my penance, make it real. Please, Master."

She didn't need to ask him twice. A sound halfway between a growl and a shout burst out of him, and his tightly wound control sprung free with explosive energy.

"*Fuck!*" Addison screamed as he pulled most of the way out and slammed back into her, his hips slapping against her punished ass.

Grabbing a fistful of her hair, Mason yanked her head back with enough force to pull her torso halfway off the bed. "What have I told you about watching your fucking language?" he ground out, slamming into her again.

"I'm sorry, Master. It won't happen again."

Releasing her golden hair, he returned his concentration to punishing her ass. It was so fucking perfect. Round and soft and beautiful, meant for spanking and fucking.

As he neared his completion, Addison turned her head, pressing her cheek against the quilt. Her eyes were closed, but not screwed shut in pain or concentration. No, everything about her looked gentle, peaceful, so she appeared to be sleeping. Her lips held the barest trace of a smile.

"Addison?"

"Yes, Master?" Her voice came out soft and serene. Almost like she was in a trance.

His cock jerked, and he nearly came. Sweet fucking Jesus. She was the most singularly marvelous creature he'd ever known.

Pulling out of her completely, he grabbed hold of his cock, pumping his hand with so much force he could hardly see straight. Mere seconds passed before jets of hot come landed upon her back and swollen, crimson bottom.

He didn't stop until every last drop painted her skin. Only then did he come fully back to himself.

Picking up his discarded shirt, he gently wiped her skin clean. Then he lifted her up and led her toward the head of the bed, lying down with his arms around her, her back pressed to his chest.

Addison breathed out a contented sigh. "Thank you. I . . . God, I really needed that. I'm sorry about before."

"You don't need to be sorry," he told her. "That was your penance, right? Is that what you said?"

She nodded.

"That means it's done and over with. The only thing that matters now is what happens next. Do you know what you want to do?"

A long time passed in complete silence. After a while, he thought she may have even fallen asleep. But then she said in an unsure, almost questioning voice, "We should go back to the bar tomorrow."

"If that's what you want, I think it would be wise." Mason tightened his arms around her for a moment, giving her a comforting squeeze. "I'll still be there with you the whole time. You're not alone."

"No," she said after a moment. Pure wonder filled her voice, making his heart swell with pride. "I guess I'm not."

Their second visit to Frank's Bar already exceeded his expectations. For one thing, Addison got out of the car and walked inside as soon as they parked. For another, when Steve asked her what she was having tonight, she answered, "A Jack and Ginger, please," without so much as a tremor in her voice.

"You're doing great," Mason whispered, squeezing her thigh.

She squirmed dramatically on the hard barstool. "The throbbing in my ass is helping center me," she whispered back with a little smirk.

He pressed his lips together to hide a smile. "Whatever works."

"Here you are," Steve said, returning with a drink in each hand. "A Jack and Ginger for the lady, and scotch neat for you, sir."

Mumbling her thanks, Addison picked up her drink, taking a huge gulp. He considered suggesting she slow down, but perhaps a little liquid courage wouldn't go amiss here.

"Where are you visiting from?" Steve asked, looking between the two of them with a genial smile. "You ran off last night before I had a chance to ask."

Another smaller gulp, and Addison answered, "Vermont."

"I always wanted to travel up that way." Steve poured a beer and placed it in front of a man a couple stools down from them. The guy must be a regular, because Mason didn't hear him order. "I've seen pictures of New England in the fall, but I'm sure that's nothing compared to the real thing."

Mason gave her thigh another gentle squeeze when she didn't respond. *You can do this.*

With a shaky breath, she managed to say, "I've actually only been in Vermont for a couple months, so I haven't gotten to see fall there, yet."

"Hopefully I'll make it out there someday," Steve said with an almost wistful smile. "I've never been east of the Mississippi. Pretty sad for a man my age, wouldn't you say?" He gave a self-deprecating chuckle.

When Addison faltered, Mason picked up the conversation, wanting to keep her father here and engaged as long as possible. "It's never too late, right?" he said with a small smile. "How long have you lived in New Mexico?"

"Since the day I was born," Steve answered, a note of pride in his voice. "And I've spent half my life right here." He patted the smooth, lacquered wood of the bar with both hands. "My granddaddy built this place with his bare hands. I was here every day after school sweeping floors and washing glasses. When I got old enough, I started tending bar. And when ol' Frank was ready to retire, he handed me the keys and said he knew the place was in the right hands. Proudest day of my life."

The story had a practiced quality, like he'd told it over and over through the years, changing and refining the wording until it was perfect. Addison obviously loved it though. She stared at her father with an emotion he couldn't quite name, though the closest he could get was adoration. Too much sadness lurked in her eyes for the word to fit entirely.

"So the bar is like home to you," she said after a moment. The word *home* came out rougher than the rest.

"This bar is more home to me than anywhere else has ever been," he agreed.

Addison forced out a nervous laugh. "Your wife and family must love to hear you say that."

With a laugh of his own, Steve held up his left hand, wiggling his ring-free fingers. "Never married," he said. "Probably for the best. People always say I'm married to this place. Wouldn't want my woman getting jealous."

She tilted her head slightly to one side. "No kids?"

Some of the mirth drained out of his eyes, though he did his best to hide it. "Sadly, that wasn't in the cards for me either."

"Sadly," she repeated, no inflection in her voice. She'd gone very still. "Sad because you have no one to take over for you when you retire?"

Steve blinked at her for a couple seconds, taken aback by the question, or perhaps by her sudden change in tone. "I'll admit, it makes me sad to think of this place leaving my family." He shrugged. "But mostly I'm just sad because I think I would've liked being a dad."

Picking up her drink, Addison moved the straw aside and emptied the glass in three large gulps. "If you'll excuse me," she said with a polite nod, then headed toward the ladies' room.

Mason and Steve watched her go, neither moving or saying a word until the bathroom door closed behind her. "Your girlfriend all right?" Steve asked, clearing away her empty glass.

He considered the best way to answer that question. Dissemble and change the subject? Straight-up lie?

In the end, he said, "I'm not sure. Do you mind if I go check on her?"

"Pretty sure she's the only one in there," Steve said. "Go ahead."

Throwing a couple of twenties on the bar, Mason followed in Addison's footsteps, weaving his way through small, round tables and scuffed wooden chairs. When he reached the bathroom door, he knocked before entering, pushing it open slowly in case Steve had missed another woman heading in.

The main part of the bathroom stood completely empty, and only the handicap stall door was closed. Mason waited until the door completely shut behind him before speaking. "It's me," he said, taking extra care to make his voice soft and gentle. "Are you okay, little one?"

A hiccupping sob drifted out of the one closed stall.

"Oh, Addison." He moved up to the door. "Let me in."

After a few seconds, the lock scraped back, and he pushed the door open. Addison leaned against the off-white subway tile along the back wall, arms wrapped tightly around herself, tears pouring down her beautiful face while she tried to remain as silent as possible.

"It's all right," Mason said, pulling her into his arms, holding her as close as he possibly could. "You don't have to hold it back. You're allowed to cry."

As if his words opened a dam, she began to sob in earnest, each new wail or gasp like a tiny pinprick to his heart.

"That's it," he murmured into her hair. "Let it out."

He hated this so fucking much. In a scene, he knew exactly how to handle a woman's tears, but this . . .

Her pain was like a physical thing, ripping her up from the inside out. He wanted to soothe her, heal her. Take it away. All he could do was stand in her presence, letting her agony slice into him, too. Death by a thousand papercuts.

"I think I'm gonna be sick," she said, lurching away from him. As she doubled over the porcelain bowl, he gathered her hair as quickly as he could, holding it out of the way as she vomited into the toilet.

Unsure what to say, Mason rubbed gentle circles on her back. He felt so fucking useless.

She stayed hunched over the toilet for almost a minute, unsure she was done. As the seconds ticked by, her sobs turned into silent tears, before finally drying up altogether. When she straightened at last, she wiped the tears from her cheeks with her fingers, then swiped the back of her hand over her mouth.

"I'm sorry," she said, voice a hoarse whisper. "That was . . ." She screwed up her lips as she searched for the right word. "More dramatic than I would've preferred."

"You have nothing to be sorry for," he assured her. "That was a lot to take in. I can only imagine what you're feeling right now."

Addison's lower lip wobbled, but she managed to hold back any additional tears. "He wanted to be a dad." Her voice was so incredibly small. "He would've wanted me."

Pulling her back to him, Mason held her close, one hand between her shoulder blades, the other on the back of her head. "I'm sorry."

"My life would've been completely different," she whispered into his shirt. "If my mom hadn't . . . if she'd told literally *anyone* about him, I could've . . ." The sentence trailed off, and she didn't even try to speak again.

Not sure what else to do, Mason held her close, staying silent as she processed everything she learned tonight. The one thing he knew for sure was that he would move fucking mountains to ensure she never felt this kind of pain.

Never again.

"I don't really like surprises," Mason grumbled as he followed the GPS on his car's display.

Addison tsked. "It's literally a nineteen-minute drive from the house. You can give up control for nineteen whole minutes. It'll be good for you."

For a moment, he considered pulling the car over and giving her a quick spanking. Maybe even dragging her smug ass into the national forest that ran along the road, finding a fallen log or some such thing to bend her over, and giving her a quick fuck to show her who was in control.

But she seemed so giddy when she asked if he would drive her somewhere secret—literally bouncing up on her toes. Given how hard the last two nights were for her, he had to give her this.

After they got back to the house last night, Addison went right to bed, not even changing out of her leggings and sweater. All she managed to do before collapsing onto the mattress was kick her sneakers off her feet.

Mason lay on the bed beside her for hours as she slept last night, staring up at the exposed beams on the ceiling. His chest ached far too much for sleep to be a remote possibility, not to mention the swirl of confused thoughts in his head.

For the life of him, he couldn't figure out why.

Pre-dawn light filtered through the gap in the curtain before he finally made up his mind. The only logical conclusion was that he had developed feelings for Addison. What those feelings were, exactly, he didn't quite know, but he could think of no other reason why her pain would cause him to experience pain. Why her future happiness mattered to him more than his own.

He had to figure out his next move, and fast.

For now, though, he thought perhaps he could get by with a triple espresso. Something to look forward to after this little surprise of hers.

"There it is," Addison said, pointing excitedly at a small wooden building in a cluster of scrubby trees. Tall windows lined the whole front wall, images of cacti and local wildlife carved into the wooden panels beneath each pane of glass.

Over the front door, a sign that appeared to have been welded from random bits of scrap metal read *Night Bloom Art Gallery*.

His eyebrows arched all on their own. He couldn't think of what to say.

Not that Addison seemed to notice. "I've been admiring all the art in your house," she said, talking a little faster than normal. "You have such a wide variety, and all of it is so beautiful. I looked at the website for this gallery this morning while you were sleeping, and I think you're really going to love some of the artists here. They're all local, too, so you won't see their work anywhere else in the world."

Mason was truly at a loss for words. He couldn't remember the last time someone did something this thoughtful for him. The last time someone paid enough attention to him to even realize how thoughtful this would be.

"Thank you," he managed at last, after he pulled into a spot and put the car in park. "This really means a lot to me."

Blushing with pleasure, she climbed out of the car, hurrying up to the bright turquoise-painted door. When he approached at a more sedate pace, she held the door open for him, gesturing for him to precede her inside with a sweep of one arm.

As soon as Mason entered the small gallery, he became mesmerized by the colors, the lines, the simplicity. He didn't have any art quite like this in his home, and that suddenly felt like a remarkable oversight.

Most of the paintings in his house had been acquired during his travels. It seemed only fitting that he find a painting to commemorate this first trip he took with another person.

A woman.

Addison.

After nodding politely at the man behind the counter, he walked slowly around the outside of the room, pausing several times to consider a particular piece that caught his interest. Addison trailed quietly in his wake, studying the paintings with a dreamy look in her eyes.

"You're a big fan of art," he observed when her breath caught at a painting of a desert sunset, a lonely cactus painted in shadow in the foreground.

"Look at these colors," she answered, her fingertip hovering an inch or so above the canvas as she traced along the lines. "I feel like this artist really saw the soul of the desert."

"Wow. I guess you're a *really* big fan of art."

Glancing his way, she laughed at his surprised look. "Granny was obsessed with art. I listened to her wax poetic about more paintings than you could ever imagine. I guess it rubbed off on me."

That she shared another of his greatest passions in life shouldn't have surprised him. Yet his mind reeled at the realization.

She's fucking perfect.

Putting that thought aside for another time, he continued his trek around the room.

"You like the ones of mountains best," Addison said as he stopped before yet another such painting.

"The mountains out here are so different from back home. The mountains around the Manor are over a hundred million years old, but these . . ." He trailed off, studying the stark, jagged lines. "These mountains are so young. So new."

Taking his hand, she leaned her head against his arm. "The purples and blues in this one would look amazing over your bed. I noticed you haven't hung anything there yet."

His chest ached again, but in a different way than he was used to. Almost like he was so happy it became painful, which made zero sense. "I've been waiting to find the right piece," he told her. "Looks like I finally did."

Grinning, Addison sauntered over to the counter, introducing herself to the man there, who turned out to be the gallery owner. They discussed the prices on the two pieces—Mason's mountains and her cactus at sunset. Because they planned to buy both, she managed to get a minor discount, and even free shipping back to Vermont.

Not bad. He probably would've been able to talk the man down even more, especially if he offered to pay cash. But she seemed so proud of herself that he didn't say a word.

Finally joining her at the counter, he pulled his wallet out of his pocket, reaching for his AmEx.

"Absolutely not," Addison said, pushing his hand away. "I'm buying these."

He gave her one of his sterner looks. "There's no way I'm letting you pay for art for my house."

No sign of her submissive nature in sight, she planted her hands on her hips and glared up at him. "This is a *gift*, Mason. To thank you for everything you've done for me. Everything you're still doing for me, in fact. Please let me do this for you."

He wanted to argue. To insist on paying for it himself. It's not like he needed anyone to buy him anything. Not at this stage in his life.

Mason couldn't help wondering if that instinct had something to do with the years of shitty birthdays and Christmases he had growing up. The pain and confusion associated with the receiving of presents year after year after year.

It occurred to him that he couldn't remember a time in his adult life when he'd accepted a gift graciously. He always either insisted he didn't deserve it, or assumed the other person gave it with ulterior motives.

Perhaps it was finally time to change that.

"Thank you," he said, forcing himself to step back. "That's incredibly kind of you."

Grinning at her triumph, Addison pulled her own wallet out of her little purse and handed her card to the gallery owner with an excited flourish. He watched her joke around with the man as she paid, his heart feeling fuller than ever before.

No matter where things went with Addison, he'd cherish this painting for the rest of his damn life.

CHAPTER 17

Addison

Their trip to the art gallery boosted Addison's mood for most of the day. Seeing Mason's joy as he took in all the paintings, the softness and gratitude filling his eyes when he let her buy his favorite for him . . . that was a high she thought she'd be able to ride forever.

As evening inevitably drew closer, panic crept back into her chest and chilled her to her bones.

This was it. Her last chance. She and Mason would leave New Mexico first thing tomorrow morning, starting their three-day drive back to Fairford Manor.

She supposed it would be easier to wait until she got home, have the ancestry site notify Steve that he had a new blood relative, and message him.

Remember that blonde in your bar who acted really fucking weird for three days before disappearing? That's me—the daughter you never knew you had. Surprise!

That felt so profoundly wrong to her. He deserved to learn of her existence face-to-face. Even though the idea scared the shit out of her.

"You're in complete control of this process," Mason said as they approached the door to the bar side by side. "If it doesn't feel right, don't force it. We can figure out a new plan together."

Some of the tension eased out of her shoulders. "Thank you." She took his hand, lacing her fingers through his. "I appreciate you being here with me."

He squeezed her hand, then pushed open the door for her.

Their footsteps echoed in the empty room as they slowly walked toward the bar. Addison looked around, taking in the chairs flipped upside down on top of tables, the silent jukebox in the corner.

When the place had been full of people, she hadn't noticed the large photograph hanging to one side of the bar. Walking over, she examined the grainy picture of what was obviously Frank Redford and a nine- or ten-year-old Steve. Her dad sat on the corner of the bar, his short legs dangling, hands folded properly in his lap. Frank, her great grandfather, leaned against the bar, one leg crossed over the other at the ankles, his shoulder touching his grandson's.

She couldn't help imagining another picture just like this one. Only it was a tiny Addison up on the bar, grinning joyfully at the camera. And Steve—or at least what she imagined he would've looked like in his late twenties—leaned over, bumping his shoulder against hers.

Tears stung her eyes.

Steve came out of the backroom hauling two obviously heavy boxes, one stacked on top of the other. He froze for a moment when he spotted them, then graced them with his disarming smile. "You two must have an even bigger drinking problem than I do," he joked with a wink, placing the boxes on the floor behind the bar. "Three nights in a row, and this time we're not even open yet. Come back in about an hour, okay?"

For a split second, Addison considered simply leaving. It was all too soon. Mason would help her figure out a new plan once they left New Mexico behind, just as he promised.

Mason placed a comforting hand on her shoulder and whispered, "I believe in you."

Taking a deep breath, she looked her father in their near-identical eyes and said, "Actually, do you have a minute? I was hoping to talk to you, if that's okay."

An emotion flashed through Steve's eyes, but it disappeared too quickly for her to figure out what it was. Motioning for her to take a seat at one of the tables, he moved around the bar to join them. He waited until they all got their chairs back to the ground and sat down before asking, "What can I do for you?"

"I guess there's no easy way to say this," she said, grateful when Mason wrapped his large hand around hers. "But I'm . . ." Goddamnit, why was this so hard? Taking a deep, bracing breath, she forced the words out before she lost her nerve. "I'm your daughter."

At first, Steve had no reaction at all, as if her words had truly stunned him. Then his lips spread into that Dennis Quaid smile she was growing to love. "What's your name, honey?"

"Addison Walker."

His smile turned a little bit sad. "Walker. I'll admit, I wondered as soon as I laid eyes on you. You look so much like Sharon."

Tears pricked at the backs of her eyes again. "You remember my mom?"

He chuckled. "She's a hard woman to forget. I'm sure I don't need to tell you that."

"I don't remember much about her, to be honest. She died when I was little."

His smile disappeared altogether. "I'm sorry to hear that." He swallowed, looking away and blinking rapidly. "Very sorry to hear it. I always hoped she was doing well."

"Would you mind, you know . . ." She struggled to find the right words, not wanting to upset him even more. "If you're willing, I'd really like to hear what you remember about her. About your time together."

Clearing his throat, he ran a hand through his slightly too-long hair. "Of course," he said, a little strength returning to his voice. "It's only natural you'd want to know." He stayed quiet for a while after that, staring off toward the bar as he gathered his thoughts. At last, he looked back her way and smiled. "Sharon was the kind of woman everyone would notice the second she walked into a room. She had this energy—I don't even really know how to describe it. Almost a star quality. Part of me always expected her to show up in the movies someday."

"When did you meet?" Addison asked, picturing this charming, magical version of her mom she never knew.

"Nineteen eighty-five." His gaze drifted over her shoulder, toward

165

the front of the building. "She walked through that door like she owned the place, and the second I saw her, I knew she was something special. She just got to town and needed a job. I convinced my granddaddy to hire her as a waitress."

Addison considered everything she knew about her mother. Her childhood in New York. Her drug addiction and death at thirty-three in Santa Fe. There were so many holes in her knowledge that she couldn't follow the path in her mind. It didn't make any sense. "What on earth was she doing here?"

"Wondered that for a while myself," he said. "Weeks went by before I figured it out. Turns out she was driving across the country, on her way to LA. She stopped at the old Bella Vista Restaurant down the way to grab some dinner, and her car refused to start back up. She didn't have any money to fix it."

Addison's breath caught in her chest. So many things had to go right—or, in this case, wrong—for her parents to meet. Her entire existence came down to a faulty car engine.

"Anyway, I was twenty-three," Steve said with a little shrug. "I'd never even been outside New Mexico. And here was this gorgeous, charming woman from New York who had eyes only for me. I'm sure you can imagine how fast and hard I fell for her."

That made Addison smile. She liked the idea that she came about as a product of love—even if that love may have been one-sided. "So what happened?" she asked, images running through her mind of how life could've gone if her mom stayed in Cedar Crest. God, why didn't she just fucking stay? Everything would've changed.

"I don't honestly know," Steve said, sighing. "She stayed a few months after she got her car fixed. I was starting to hope she'd stay for good. Then out of nowhere, she told me she found a better job somewhere else, and she was leaving. She didn't even seem to care—cold as ice. And that was that. I never imagined she might be pregnant."

She could hear the heartache in his voice. Even after all this time, he cared for her mother deeply. It made her wish she could give him a hug. "She didn't tell you where she was going?"

"Absolutely refused, and believe me, I begged. But she just got in her car and drove away." Steve wiped tears out of his eyes. "Remember, it was 1986 at this point. It's not like we had cell phones. The internet didn't even exist yet. She just up and disappeared, and I never saw or heard from her again."

"I'm so sorry," Addison whispered, choking back her own tears. She'd abandoned them both.

Clearing his throat again, Steve asked, "Where did Sharon go when she left?"

"Santa Fe."

He winced. "You've only been an hour away this whole time?"

Shaking her head sadly, she told him, "She died when I was six. I lived in a couple foster homes in Santa Fe after that, but I went to live with my granny in New York when I was eight."

He frowned. "You were in foster care? Why didn't anyone call me? I would've taken you in a heartbeat."

Addison burst into tears. "Fuck, I'm sorry," she said, trying to get herself under control. "I don't know what's wrong with me."

"Nothing's wrong with you." Mason, who had been her silent supporter up to this point, wrapped his arms around her. "Everything you're feeling right now is perfectly natural."

"I'm sorry," Steve said, turning to Mason for the first time in several minutes. "I know we've met the last couple nights, but I never even asked your name."

"Mason St. John." He held out a hand, and the two men shook. "Is it all right if I go get her a glass of water?"

Steve nodded, waving in the general direction of the bar, and turned his attention back to her. "How long have you known I'm your dad?"

"Nine days."

He ran his hand through his hair again, making it stand up in the back. "Sharon didn't even put my name on the birth certificate." He didn't sound surprised. Perhaps her sudden explosion of tears clued him in.

Shaking her head, Addison told him, "I only figured it out because I took a DNA test."

"I'm so glad you did." Steve's smile made the last of her tears melt away. "I signed up for all those ancestry sites years ago, wondering if I had any family out there I didn't know about. I'd given up on the whole thing until you walked through my door."

"Family you didn't know about?" Something about his tone caught her attention. "The way you said that, I don't think you're talking about a long-lost uncle."

His shrug was the definition of nonchalance, but a smugness shone out from his eyes. "Lots of tourists and hikers pass through this little town, and this is the only bar. You may not be able to see it now, but I was quite a looker back in the eighties and nineties."

Mason snorted from behind the bar. "Lots of potential for little Stephens and Stephanies you didn't know about?"

With another little shrug, Steve said, "Your perspective on things starts to change when you get old. You'll see what I mean in twenty years."

"But that means . . ." God, Addison could hardly breathe. Swallowing down the lump in her throat, she tried again. "That means you were looking for me, too."

"Yeah," Steve said, resting his hand on top of hers on the table. "Yeah, I was. I'm sorry if you had difficulties after Sharon passed away. It kills me that I've missed so much of your life, but I want you to know that I'm here now. And if you'll let me, I'll try to figure out how to be the dad you should've had all along."

Addison launched herself across the table, wrapping her arms around his neck. Her tears came back with a vengeance, but she didn't even care this time. Especially not when she realized he'd started crying too.

She had a dad.

After thirty-eight years, she finally had a dad.

She'd never felt more like she deserved to cry in her life.

Hours flew by like minutes as Addison and Steve talked. He called in one of his servers on her day off to tend bar, and they sat at a table in the corner farthest from the jukebox, filling in the details of their lives.

It wasn't until nearly eleven that Steve took a large gulp of his beer, cleared his throat, and said, "I can't help but notice you haven't mentioned a single thing from before you were eight. And you change the subject anytime I mention Sharon."

Addison's heart skipped a beat. Her gaze instinctively shot over to Mason, who perched on a nearby barstool for the last couple of hours without complaint, giving them some space. He lifted one eyebrow, clearly asking, *Do you need me?*

A deep breath, and a sip of her Jack and Ginger. The burn as it slipped down her throat centered her.

She could do this on her own.

Giving Mason the all-clear with a minute shake of the head, she turned back to her father.

"You don't have to tell me about it if you don't want to," he said before she could speak. "It obviously makes you uncomfortable. We've got the rest of our lives ahead of us, so nothing needs to happen tonight."

"No, it's okay." Another sip—more of the whiskey's exquisite burn. "It's just . . . not a very happy story. Most people don't like hearing about it."

Steve reached across the table to squeeze her hand. "Take your time, honey."

With another deep breath, she forced herself to ask the question that had been on her mind most of the night. "Was Mom on drugs when you knew her?"

He looked about as stunned as if she just smacked him upside the head with a two-by-four. "I'm sorry?"

"I'll take that as a no," she said, swallowing a large gulp of her drink. God, this sucked. Steve clearly loved her mom, perhaps had even created an idealized version of her in his mind after all these years. It broke her heart to have to shatter that image.

"No, I didn't—I mean, she never . . ." The rest of the sentence trailed away as he frowned down at his beer.

"Mom died of a heroin overdose," she said softly, hating the way he flinched. "They'd already taken me away by then. She left me home alone for almost a week when I was only six."

169

Steve's eyes had gone big and round. He stared down at his half-empty glass for nearly a minute, his hands clenched around it so tight she worried it might shatter. At long last, he picked up the beer and drained it. "Give me a sec," he murmured, stalking off to the bar to pour himself a refill.

While Steve huddled behind the bar, visibly shaking even from a distance, Mason sauntered over to the table. "Everything all right?" he asked softly.

"I just told him. About my mom."

Mason nodded, as if that's what he expected. "Can't be an easy thing to hear." Moving behind her chair, he began massaging her shoulders. "I'm so proud of you tonight. I hope you know how amazing you are."

Closing her eyes, she leaned into his hands, loving the feel of his strong fingers as they dug into her knotted muscles. "Better be careful," she teased. "If you're too nice to me, it might go to my head."

His chuckle washed over her like a warm breeze. "Just remember what I do to brats."

Addison looked over her shoulder at him and smiled. "Oh, I'm counting on it."

"Sorry about that," Steve said as he walked back up to the table, dropping onto his chair. His voice still had a strangled quality to it.

"I'll give you two some privacy." Mason leaned down, kissing the top of Addison's head, and returned to his barstool.

Steve watched him go, some of the tension leaving his eyes. "Your boyfriend seems like a good guy."

Her answering smile was small, almost shy. She wasn't quite used to the idea that Mason might be her boyfriend, and not just some guy she fucked on the weekends. "Yeah, he really is." Her first impression of him couldn't have been further from the truth.

"Sorry," Steve said again, looking down at where his hands rested on the table. "That wasn't the best reaction. I don't want you thinking I don't want to hear any more, cause I do. I'm not like those other people you mentioned. I just . . . I wasn't prepared for that. I am now."

Addison blinked away tears. "It's okay," she said, a catch in her voice. "I probably shouldn't have just come out and said it like that. You obviously cared a lot about her. I can't imagine what you're feeling right now, knowing how she died."

It took a second for Steve to react to what she said. As if he didn't quite comprehend it at first. When he lifted his head, something new burned in his eyes—something she didn't know how to name. "I'm not upset because of Sharon." He said it like the idea never occurred to him. "I'm upset because of you."

Addison's mouth dropped open. "Me?" What did she do?

"No child should have to live through that." His voice shook. "But you"—his eyes filled with tears—"are *my* kid. And you had to . . . fucking *six* years old . . ." He covered his eyes with his hand as he fought for control.

She had absolutely no idea what to say. Thoughts raced through her mind as she watched her dad struggle not to cry. Should she comfort him? Lie and say things weren't as bad as she made it sound?

By the time Steve let his hand drop back to the table, several bar patrons had begun throwing covert looks their way. One middle-aged woman in a paisley-print dress and cowboy boots outright stared. Addison had a feeling they weren't used to seeing their beloved bartender with any expression on his face but a charming smile.

"Oh, let them look," Steve said, noticing the way she glanced around the bar. "I don't care. To be honest, they should feel lucky. I almost threw my glass across the room, twice now."

"Only twice?" Addison quipped, trying and completely failing to lighten the mood.

"I don't know what happened to the Sharon I knew. She wasn't exactly the loving, nurturing type, but I never would've imagined she could . . ." He closed his eyes for a few seconds, taking a slow, deep breath. "Addiction is a disease. I'm not making excuses—for the love of God, don't think that. But things were so different back then. She wouldn't have been able to get any help even if she wanted it. The whole thing just breaks my damn heart."

"I'm really sorry I upset you." A few potential lies sprang to the tip of her tongue—little half-truths and downright fabrications that might make him feel better.

Steve shook his head, the look in his eyes suddenly urgent. "Don't.

Don't you dare apologize, honey. She's the only one who should apologize. She's the one who hurt you." *And me.* The words hung so heavily in the air between them, he might as well have said it out loud.

If only her mom could apologize. If she hadn't OD'd, if she'd gotten clean and they had a chance to reconcile when Addison got a little older . . .

No. She wouldn't go down that road. Like Mason's therapist told him, there wasn't any point in torturing herself over something that could never happen. She needed to focus on the future, not dwell on missed opportunities in her past.

"Now," Steve said, leaning back in his chair and making a show of getting comfortable. "You tell your story and stop worrying about me. You deserve to have someone who'll listen, and I promise you I'll be that person for you. Tell me all of it."

"All of it?" She made a be-careful-what-you-wish-for face. "I'm gonna need a lot more whiskey for that. And you might want to swap that out for a plastic cup, because it gets worse before it gets better."

"If I end up breaking a few pints, so be it," he said catching the eye of a server as he walked nearby, motioning toward her nearly empty glass. "Luckily for me, I own the bar."

CHAPTER 18

Mason

Returning to the Manor was bittersweet for Addison. It obviously broke her heart a little to leave her dad so soon after she found him.

The pride in Steve's eyes when she told him about the life she built as a baker, first in NYC and now at the Manor, had made her practically glow with happiness. When the man didn't even bat an eyelash upon learning what kind of establishment the Manor was, that endeared him to Mason even more. Not a lot of parents would be so openminded about their kid dating a professional Dom.

When the time came to head home, Mason worried she might stay behind. That he'd be making the trek back across the country on his own, and would never learn what might have happened between them with just a little more time.

Though staying in New Mexico, at least for a while, would've been an understandable decision, he selfishly rejoiced when she climbed into his car yesterday morning.

"Where are we going?" Addison asked as he pulled off the highway a little past Tulsa.

"I want to grab a bite to eat," he said, doing his best to sound like he wasn't up to something. Navigating the car through a green light, he scanned the signs in the short strip of businesses and restaurants for the one he wanted.

She gave the clock on the dash a pointed look. It read only a few minutes past four. "Bit early for dinner, isn't it?"

With a shrug, he turned into a small plaza with a pizza place, a karate studio, a twenty-four-hour diner, and a couple of other stores. "I've been driving for almost nine hours already. I need a break."

That seemed to satisfy her, and she climbed out of the car as soon as he parked in front of Aunt Bea's Diner—a place with a shabby sign and dirty windows. She glanced at the much nicer looking pizza joint a few storefronts away, but didn't argue when he pulled open the diner's glass door and stepped inside.

Jesus fucking Christ, he hoped this wasn't a mistake.

Once they got inside, Addison stepped up to the hostess stand, but he walked right past it, scanning the patched brown booths for a familiar face.

A short, stocky man with shaggy black hair and a crooked nose slid out of the corner booth, gaze locked on them.

"Table for two," Addison told the hostess as she approached, but Mason took her upper arm, pulling her into the aisle.

"The rest of our party's already here," he said softly to the hostess, though he didn't look at the woman. He kept his eyes on Addison, not wanting to miss even a millisecond of her reaction. Needing as much data as possible so he knew what to do next.

"The rest of our party?" she repeated, a deep line forming between her brows. "What do you—"

Looking into the dining room at last, her gaze locked on the man by the corner booth. She froze, her mouth still shaping her last word, her eyes as wide as he'd ever seen them.

"Hey, Addy," the man said with an awkward little wave.

"Ricky?" Her whisper came out so low, like she thought this was an illusion her voice would shatter.

Ricky grinned at her, his smile as crooked as his nose. "Yeah, it's me."

Addison flew down the aisle, hair streaming behind her, and

launched herself into Ricky's arms. "How?" She said it over and over, holding onto him so tight he actually winced.

Didn't stop him from wrapping her up in a massive bear hug. "Hey, I got you," he said, grinning at Mason over her shoulder. "It's all good. I got you."

When she finally let go, she looked up into the man's dark eyes, an expression of utter bewilderment on her face. "How in the actual fuck are you here right now?"

"Well," Ricky said, watching Mason as he walked slowly between the booths to join them. "I got an unexpected phone call yesterday. I assume you're Mason?"

Addison whipped around, staring at Mason with tears in her eyes. "Y-you? You did this? How? When?"

"I hired a private investigator. The day after you told me about him." He kept his expression utterly neutral, not yet sure how she'd take that news. When she didn't respond or react in any way, he found more words flowing out of him, impossible to stop. "You were so sad. I probably should've asked you, but I didn't want to get your hopes up in case the PI couldn't find him, and, well, it was obvious how much he meant to you. I thought for sure you'd want to see him again. When I got the report last night, and I found out he lived near Tulsa, it seemed like too good an opportunity to pass up."

Still nothing out of her. Not so much as the flick of an eyebrow.

"Please say something," he said as the silence dragged on.

"I—I can't—" Rapid, sharp breaths cut off the rest of her sentence.

"Breathe," Mason said, rubbing gentle circles on her back. "Sit down and breathe, little one." He helped her into the booth, wrapping a soothing arm around her shoulders as she struggled to regain control.

"Maybe we shouldn't have sprung it on her after all," Ricky said as he slid into the other side of the booth. He turned to Addison with apologetic eyes. "That's my bad. I really wanted to surprise you."

She started shaking her head before he got it all out. "No," she forced out between two slow, deep breaths. "Best surprise ever. I promise. Just give me a sec."

Ricky's grin lit up his whole face, and he waited patiently for her to get her breathing back under control. "Holy shit, Addy. I still can't believe you're really here. When Mason called me yesterday, part of me thought it was a sick joke."

Reaching across the table, Addison grabbed both of Ricky's hands, holding onto them for dear life. "I'm really here. And I'm not going anywhere until I know every single thing that's happened in your life since the last time I saw you, so you'd better get talking."

Ricky chuckled. "Oh God. I hope this place has bottomless coffee." He ran a hand through his shaggy hair. "Where should I start?"

"What are you doing in Oklahoma? Do you live here? What's your life like? Are you married? Do you have kids? Did you—"

"Whoa, whoa, slow down," Ricky interrupted, holding out his hands and laughing again. "One question at a time. Yes, I live here—about twenty minutes from here, actually. With my girlfriend. No kids, at least not yet. I'm working as a child welfare specialist in Tulsa."

"Child welfare—" Her eyes went very wide. "You're . . . you're working with foster kids?"

"Mostly I do home visits." Ricky sat up a little straighter, his eyes shining brighter. "Checking foster homes, or homes of people we have reason to suspect are harming or neglecting their children. It's my job to make sure the kids are getting the level of care they deserve. To keep them safe."

"Your literal job is to make sure no kid goes through what we did." Awe filled Addison's voice, and she wiped away tears. "God, Ricky. Do you know how incredible that is?"

Blushing, he picked up his coffee, swirling the dregs around the bottom of the cup without taking a sip. "I don't know about that," he said, clearly pleased but simultaneously uncomfortable with the praise.

Mason knew from experience how hard it was to accept a compliment when you never learned how as a child. His heart went out to the man.

"I *do* know about that," Addison insisted. "I couldn't be prouder of my big brother."

It was Ricky's turn to wipe tears from his eyes. "Okay, enough about me for now. I want to hear about you."

Sitting back against the plasticky fabric of the booth, Mason watched the pair as they gushed at each other. Their excited voices filled their little corner of the diner with so much joy the air around them seemed to literally vibrate with it.

He had a feeling they wouldn't make it back to the Airbnb in Missouri tonight. Not that he minded in the least.

They didn't end up in an all-night diner by mistake.

After nearly eight full days at Addison's side, being apart from her now fucking sucked. He couldn't glance at her whenever she entered his mind, drinking in her beauty, studying her expression, fantasizing about kissing those incredible lips. Nor could he touch her whenever the mood struck him, which felt like a fucking tragedy now. His skin itched to be in contact with hers. To grab hold of her and never again let go.

"Master Mason?"

The words yanked him from his thoughts, and he looked down at the redhead kneeling at his feet. "Forgive me, Tara," he said, brushing a gentle hand along her cheekbone. Thank God she was a repeat guest, currently on her seventh visit to the Manor. If he'd pulled this shit with someone new, it could've been a disaster. "I have a lot going on in my personal life, but that's no excuse for allowing myself to become distracted."

Tara ran her naughty little hands up his thighs, letting her fingertips graze his cock. She'd never been one to follow the rules. "Maybe I can do something to help you concentrate on the here and now, Master." She looked up at him with her big green eyes—eyes he'd lost himself in countless times in recent years.

They were the wrong shade of green, though. Addison's eyes were the most stunning green-blue he'd ever seen, with those incredible specks of gold throughout. Anything else seemed lackluster by comparison.

"You're such a good girl," Mason said, trying to force his full attention back to the kneeling sub before him. This was his job, goddamnit. His job, his reputation, and his best client. She deserved everything he could give her. "Take me in your mouth. Make sure I never think of anything but you again."

She purred her approval of his words, starting to unbuckle his belt with slow, seductive movements. Before she even managed to detach the leather from the prong, a scream ripped through the room.

"What the fuck?" Tara half-shouted, pushing up to her feet and running to the window. "Did that come from outside?"

Mason didn't wait around to answer. He ran from the study as fast as his legs would carry him, heading straight for the patio doors.

Addison. Her name repeated in his head in time with his heartbeat. He'd know her scream anywhere. If she was hurt . . . it didn't even bear thinking about.

Only slowing down enough to open the French doors without shattering the glass, Mason sprinted out onto the patio, gaze sweeping the garden for a glimpse of honey blond hair.

He found her kneeling in the snow beneath the kitchen windows, in between two square-shaped bushes. Her shoulders shook with her sobs.

"Addison?" he said hesitantly, skidding to a stop behind her. "What's—oh God."

She cradled an unmoving cardinal in her hand, his right wing bent all wrong, the bright red feathers sticking out at odd angles. "I h-heard something hit the window," she said, struggling to get the words out through her tears. "So I came out to check. And Alexander . . . he . . ." She dissolved into another fit of sobs.

Kneeling down beside her, he examined the tiny bird. "He's still breathing." The words left him in a rush. Thank fucking Christ he wasn't already dead. Flying into a window like that had the potential to snap a bird's neck. "We can try to help him."

Addison's head shot up, her puffy, red eyes finding his. "Do you think so?"

Standing, Mason stripped off his suit jacket, holding it out between his arms. "Put him in here," he instructed, carefully handing her the bundle once the little red bird rested against the black silk. Then he looked up, finding Luca and Kendra watching through the row of windows. "Bring us a box," he said, loud enough for them to hear through the glass. "Something with a lid."

Kendra sprinted into the pantry, disappearing from view for only a few seconds before she emerged with a large cardboard box, shaking what looked like onion skin from it as she ran to the door. "Here," she said as soon as she joined them in the garden, shoving the box against Mason's chest. "Will this work?"

"It's perfect, thank you," he said, holding it steady as Addison carefully lowered the injured bird into the box, nestled in his little silk bed.

Luca came out of the kitchen next, a long, thin knife in his hand. "Give me the lid," he said, and began poking holes in it as soon as Kendra handed it over.

While the chef worked, Mason pulled out his phone, keying in a quick Google search. "Look," he said, holding out his phone so Addison could see the screen. "There's a wild bird rehabilitation center less than an hour from here." Hitting the CALL button right over their address, he held the phone up to his ear.

Clutching the box to her chest, Addison watched him with worried, tear-filled eyes as the phone rang. "Did they not answer?" she asked a second before their voicemail message started.

"Shit," he muttered under his breath. "No, they didn't answer. Hold on." As soon as the beep sounded, he rattled off his name and number, then explained the situation. "Please give me a call back as soon as you can. In the meantime, we're on our way to you. We should arrive in less than an hour. I hope to hear from you soon."

"We're actually going?" Addison asked the second he ended the call. Her voice held equal parts worry and hope.

Checking to make sure his keys were in his pocket, he nodded. "Let's go. The sooner we get there, the better."

"Don't you have a guest, though?" she said, a catch in her voice.

"Fuck." He completely forgot about Tara. Opening his phone again, he hit the first name on his favorites list.

Jonathan answered on the third ring. "Jesus Christ, Mason. It's not even nine in the morning yet." Sleep clung to his voice. "Liz and I only went to bed a couple hours ago, so this better be good."

"I have an emergency."

The grogginess left his voice in an instant. "What is it? Is someone hurt?"

"Not exactly." He did his best to explain about Alexander as succinctly as he could. "I need to drive Addison and the bird down to the rehabilitation center to see if they can save him, but Tara's here again this week."

"For fuck's sake, man," Jonathan said, and he could tell his friend had run out of patience at last. "You can't just leave a guest like this. Especially not over a half-dead bird. Why do you even care?"

Mason had absolutely no idea how to answer. Not when Addison, Kendra, and Luca would hear every word.

After several seconds, Jonathan sighed. "It's not the bird. It's the girl."

He echoed his friend's sigh. There was no point in denying it. "Yes."

"Go." Now Jonathan sounded resigned more than anything else. "I'll take care of it."

Mason closed his eyes for a second as he breathed out a sigh of relief. Through every single thing that happened in the nearly twenty years of their friendship, he could always count on Jonathan no matter what. He only hoped he could fix this—that sometime soon, his best friend would be able to feel the same way about him again. "Thank you. She's in the study."

"Good luck," was all Jonathan said before ending the call.

"Okay," he said, placing a hand on Addison's back and leading her on the fastest route to his car. "Let's go."

CHAPTER 19

Addison

Addison sat in Mason's BMW for a long time after they returned to the Manor. He jumped out as soon as he turned the engine off, sprinting into the building in search of his neglected guest. But she didn't manage to drag herself out and head inside until the last of the heat seeped out of the car, leaving her shivering.

Good God, what a fucking day.

Alexander regained consciousness on the way to the rehabilitation center—sort of. What few movements he made remained sluggish for the rest of the trip. When the center called Mason back, the spectacularly calm woman on the phone explained he was probably stunned from the impact with the window, and based on what they described, likely had a broken wing at the very least. She promised to be ready and waiting the moment they arrived.

A team rushed from the small brick building as soon as Mason drove into the parking lot. Most of them hurried right back inside once Addison handed over Alexander's box. She watched them go, her eyes drifting over to the enormous circular aviary attached to one side of the building. She found herself wondering if they'd put Alexander in there once his wing healed or if they'd let him go.

The single person who stayed behind—a middle-aged woman with short brown hair—cleared her throat politely. "We'll do everything we can for him." As soon as the first word left her mouth, Addison recognized her as Phoebe, the woman they spoke to on the phone. Her promise sounded every bit as soothing as before. "We have a great team here. I feel confident that if it's possible, we'll get him flying again."

Mason asked so many questions, it made Addison's head spin. He wanted to know how many people worked at the center. What all their credentials were. Where they got their funding. If additional funding would help ensure Alexander's full recovery and, if so, how much they'd need. Would they be allowed to call the center for updates on Alexander's progress? If Alexander would be released back into the wild or, because of the previous injury to his leg, if they'd keep him here at the center. If he *was* released to the wild, would it be here, or up by the Manor to his original habitat?

The whole time, he held Addison's hand, pressing kisses to her knuckles while Pheobe gave them answers.

Addison stayed quiet as they drove back to the Manor. He clearly assumed it was because of Alexander, occasionally asking her how she was holding up or if she needed anything.

Though she was worried sick about the precious bird, he wasn't the reason she kept her mouth glued firmly shut. No, it was because of a revelation she had while Mason did everything in his power to ensure a random wild bird would live a long and happy life—for the sole reason that it mattered to her.

Somewhere along the line, she'd fallen in love with Mason.

Not a little bit in love. This wasn't some schoolgirl feeling that could either blossom into something bigger or fizzle out at the first test.

She was head over fucking heels in love with this man.

Having never been in love before, she must not have recognized it until it was too late. Somewhere in the midst of the cancelled Chile trip, the bunk beds, the way he helped her navigate everything with her dad . . . it just happened.

And then today. He dropped everything to help her yet again, treating both her and Alexander with so much tenderness that it made her heart ache.

Mason St. John was the most wonderful man she'd ever met in her life. She only wished she knew what on earth she was supposed to do about that. She'd had casual boyfriends before, and she'd had a long-term Dom before, at least until that whole thing blew up in her face. But she'd never been in a serious relationship in her life. How was she even supposed to tell him she wanted to start one?

Sighing, Addison pushed open one of the Manor's double front doors only enough to slip through, not wanting to let the cold inside. Time to head up to her room, take a long, hot bath, and maybe Google how to tell a guy you loved him without scaring him off. That seemed like a solid plan.

"I hope it doesn't get out that Mason abandoned his guest today," Zach said, drawing her attention over to the registration counter. He leaned on the wall behind his desk, arms crossed over his chest, a single eyebrow arched in clear accusation. "It would be a shame if the reputation we all worked our asses off for these last seven years got ruined over a bird."

Addison closed her eyes and counted to five. Then she looked Zach right in the eye and demanded, "What, exactly, have I done to offend you?"

The snide look disappeared from his face in an instant. His voice turned carefully neutral when he said, "I don't know what you mean."

"Bullshit," she shot back. "I've been nothing but nice to you from the day I met you. I see how you are with literally everybody else here, but the second I walk into a room, you're like a completely different person. If there's something going on I don't know about, please, for the love of God, just tell me already."

Zach opened and closed his mouth a couple times, then lowered his eyes, a blush reddening his cheeks. "I'm sorry." So much shame in those two words. It made her want to forgive him just to make him feel better. "It's not your fault. I promise. It's an issue with me."

Softening her own tone, she asked, "What does that even mean?" Instead of answering, he looked off toward the stairs, tears making his green eyes shine in the light of the crystal chandelier. "Just so you know, I'd love to be your friend if you'd let me."

Zach let out a shuddering breath, emotions flashing across his face in such quick succession she hardly kept up: shock, denial, pain, and finally longing. Such profound longing that she had to resist the urge to hug him, not sure how he'd react to such an affectionate act from her of all people.

"My shift just ended," he said, a catch in his voice. "Would you be willing to head into town with me? There's a coffee shop where we can sit and talk. I'll give you a ride back after."

She didn't even hesitate. "Absolutely."

Mere minutes later, they climbed into Zach's sky-blue Jetta. Music started playing as soon as he turned on the engine, and she followed his lead when he remained quiet throughout the drive.

Downtown Fairford was a quintessential quaint New England town, with little brick shops and restaurants lining the only real street, their lights glittering in the darkness.

Zach found a spot near the coffee shop, and they managed to go inside, wait in line, order, and even sit at a table with their drinks without trading more than two words. It was almost impressive, really. Though it didn't bode particularly well for how this so-called "talk" would go.

"So," Addison said, cradling her mug of English breakfast tea between her hands. "What do you want to talk about?"

"Give me a minute." He closed his eyes, his face screwing up in what looked like actual pain. "Sorry, this is really hard for me. I've never told anyone this."

Her mouth dropped open, but she snapped it shut before he reopened his eyes. "Wow," she said, trying to sound honored rather than shocked, and sort of succeeding. "It means a lot to me that you trust me."

His lips quirked up into his usual half smile, and for the first time since she entered the lobby that evening, some of his customary humor danced in his eyes. "It's okay. You can say, 'Why are you trusting me with your deepest, darkest secret when you've been a total bitch to me for two months?' I won't be offended."

Addison returned his smirk. "You weren't a *total* bitch. At the New Year's Eve party, you gave a toast in my honor."

"Did I?" He chuckled. "Sounds like something I'd do."

"I'm sorry about whatever changed things between us."

He started shaking his head before she got more than half the sentence out. "No, please don't. I meant what I said before. You've done nothing wrong. This is one hundred percent a me problem."

When he didn't elaborate, she took a slow sip of her tea, then prompted, "If you tell me what it is, maybe I can help."

Groaning, Zach leaned his head from side to side, stretching his neck muscles. "Okay, fuck it. Time to just rip the Band-Aid off and get it over with." He closed his eyes and blew out a long breath. Then he spoke so fast, the words all ran together. "I've been in love with Mason since the day I met him."

Addison hadn't quite figured out what to expect, but none of her varied ponderings had even been close.

"Oh, shit." What else was there to say?

"Yeah," Zach said gloomily. "Exactly."

"Damn, that's . . . wow. Is he bi, or pan, or anything that would include—" She gestured vaguely in Zach's direction.

With a morose shake of the head, Zach said, "The man is straight as an arrow. I've known almost the whole time I had a snowball's chance in hell, but the heart wants what the heart wants, right?"

"Right," she agreed, reaching across the table and taking his hand. "I'm so sorry, Zach. I can't imagine how hard the last couple months have been for you."

Zach gave a bark of humorless laughter, though he only had kindness in his eyes. "I can't believe you're consoling me. After the way I've treated you? You should hate me."

"There are very few people in this world I hate," she answered. "Probably fewer than I should, to be honest, but nothing you've done even gets you close to that list."

Zach rolled his eyes. "Raging bitch, remember?"

Snorting, Addison said, "Oh no, he made a couple snide comments after I started dating the man he's in love with. Better cast him out forever."

Looking down at their joined hands, he smiled, without a single trace of snark or sarcasm. "Well. When you put it like that." Slipping his hand carefully out from under hers, he wrapped his hands around his

cappuccino, drumming his fingertips against the mug. "It's sort of liberating, finally telling someone."

"I'm surprised you didn't even tell Olivia," Addison replied. "Isn't
she your best friend?"

"Best friend I've ever had," he agreed. "But if I told her, she'd have to
tell Aiden. Aiden would tell Mason, and I just wasn't ready for that yet."

Her eyes widened slightly at his use of past tense. "Does that mean
you're ready now?"

Zach gave a lethargic shrug, like he didn't care one way or the other.
The truth was written all over his face, though. The notion fucking
terrified him.

"I'm not going to tell Mason unless you want me to," she promised.
She didn't like the idea of keeping secrets from him, but this . . . it
wasn't her secret to tell.

When Zach slumped back in his chair, relief filling his eyes, she
knew she made the right decision.

"Thank you," he whispered. "I don't know if I'll ever be able to
thank you enough."

The pair sat in silence for a while after that, pondering the revelations of the day until their drinks ran dry. "Should we head out?"
Addison asked, spotting a couple of teenagers eyeing their empty mugs
as they searched the busy coffee shop for a table.

"I just have a question before we go," Zach said, staring down at his
hands for several seconds before he went on. "Do you love him?"

Her head jerked back in surprise. She considered his closed-off
expression before saying, "I don't know how you want me to answer
that."

Zach lifted his head, forcing himself to meet her gaze. It looked like
it took monumental effort. "I just want you to tell me the truth."

Hoping this wasn't a huge mistake, she said, "Yes, I do. More than I
ever thought possible."

He let his breath out with a soft sigh. "I'm glad. Because I'm positive
he's in love with you."

Heart thumping madly in her chest, she asked, "Are you sure?"

"Oh, come on. He literally drove you to New Mexico."

Addison blushed. "Yeah, okay. Fair."

"Since having him for myself isn't an option, I just want him to be happy." He gave her a watery smile. "He's happier now than I've ever seen him. So I'm glad you feel the same way."

Relinquishing their table to the teenagers, they headed back out into the cold.

Addison barely even felt it. She was in a sort of a daze, practically floating along the sidewalk to Zach's car.

Mason loved her.

And she was sick and tired of wasting time.

CHAPTER 20
Mason

What a fucking week. After abandoning Tara for the emergency trip to the wildlife center, he paid extra special attention to his most loyal guest for the rest of her stay. Luckily, she felt so fucking good by the time Saturday morning rolled around, Wednesday's fiasco was long forgotten.

But that meant he hadn't been able to do more than send Addison an occasional text for the last few days. Given how succinct her replies had been, he had a feeling she wasn't too pleased about that. Time to head to the kitchen and start making it up to her.

He rounded the stairs into the back hallway just as Jonathan came out of the study. The head Dom stopped in his tracks, regarding Mason for a few seconds before a determined look firmed in his eyes. "You have a minute?" Jonathan asked.

Mason nodded. Addison's shift didn't end for another twenty minutes anyway. "I actually wanted to talk to you, too." He followed his friend into the study, shut and locked the door behind him, and settled into one of the leather armchairs.

Pouring them each two fingers of scotch from one of the decanters on the sideboard, Jonathan handed him a tumbler before claiming the chair opposite.

"Can I please say something before you tell me all the ways I've been fucking up?" Mason said, setting the drink on an end table without taking a sip.

Surprise flitted across Jonathan's features, but he didn't even try to deny it, instead gesturing for Mason to continue.

"I'm sorry. It's probably deeply inadequate to say that, though I hope it's at least a start." He sighed, running a hand through his hair. "I haven't handled things particularly well for a while now, but I had no idea why until recently, so I couldn't figure out how to fix it. None of you should've had to put up with my bullshit. I just hope you can all forgive me in time."

Jonathan's hard, determined look melted away, concern bringing out faint wrinkles around his mouth and eyes. "Are you willing to talk about it now that you know?"

Staring down at his hands, Mason didn't answer at first. Could he talk about this? Telling Addison had felt like lifting the weight of the world from his shoulders, but this was Jonathan for Christ's sake. The only concrete detail he'd ever shared with the man was that he no longer spoke to his family because they were assholes.

But Jonathan had been the one to convince him to find a therapist back in their California days. He probably already knew a lot more than Mason gave him credit for, in fact. The man was far too observant for his own good.

With a sigh, Mason said, "I never told you how alone I felt when I was a kid. But I'm sure there were signs."

Emotions Mason didn't know how to name flashed through Jonathan's eyes. "You want to know what I thought the first time I met you?" he asked, a slight catch in his voice.

"Oh God, do I?" Mason tried to chuckle, but it came out more like a strangled groan.

Jonathan's answering smile was kind. "I thought you looked like you believed it was you against the entire world, and no matter how shit the odds were, you were going to make damn sure you came out on top."

Tears sprung to Mason's eyes. "You're making that up."

"Ask Leo," Jonathan said with a little shrug. "I'm pretty sure I said that to him almost word for word right before we introduced ourselves to you outside the dining hall."

Mason swallowed and looked down at his hands again. "It always *was* me against the world. Growing up, my mom spent half her time telling me I'm a piece of shit who doesn't deserve to be loved, and the other half completely ignoring me. That's all I knew."

"The thing is," Jonathan said, his voice as soft as Mason had ever heard it. "It hasn't been you against the world for almost twenty years now. You've had us."

"It feels like I'm losing all of you, though." He forced the admission out before he could stop himself, and immediately wished he could take it back. Jesus, his friends would all think he was completely fucking pathetic when Jonathan told them about this conversation.

Jonathan stayed quiet for almost a minute—so long Mason almost fled from the room. Then he let out a long sigh. "I know what you mean. When I came up with the idea for the Manor, I had this perfect picture in my head of what our lives would be. But that never happened, even for a single day. It's never been the four of us like I imagined. I've had to figure out how to live with that."

Images and feelings coursed through Mason as he remembered the days and months after Leo ran off with Sophie. The unanswered texts, the sound of Leo's voicemail message. The frustration on Jonathan and Aiden's faces as the three remaining partners tried to make decisions about renovations and policies without their fourth vote, because Leo was too busy creating his new life in Manhattan without them.

But also the joy on Leo's face when they managed to get him on a video call. The ease with which their friend spoke, as if he'd finally found the answer to all his life's questions.

Mason never found it in himself to blame Leo or Sophie for what happened. Same when Aiden met Olivia, or when Rafe found Nell. His friends were happier.

They were *better*.

He had a feeling Addison made him better, too.

Finally, Mason forced himself to meet Jonathan's gaze again. "Everything changed so fucking fast, and I felt like I was losing control of my life, and I just . . . I don't know. I lost it for a while. But I'm figuring out how to live with it all, too."

Leaning back in his chair, Jonathan took a long sip of his scotch, eyeing him over the rim of the glass. "Have these new revelations perhaps been brought on by a sassy blonde who makes a mean cinnamon roll?" His eyes crinkled at the corners.

Mason rolled his eyes. "You know damn well they were."

"And another mighty bachelor has fallen," Jonathan said, raising his glass in a mock-toast. He knocked back the rest of his drink in one. "God save the rest of us."

Christ, what a fucking relief. Part of him had worried he'd damaged their friendship beyond repair. But if Jonathan could still joke with him, everything would be okay. "I really am sorry."

"You don't need to keep apologizing," Jonathan said, his smile turning kind. "I forgave you before you even said it the first time."

"You did?" Disbelief filled his voice. "Why would you do that?"

"Why wouldn't I? You're one of my best friends." When Mason continued to look unconvinced, he said, "Look, I knew something was going on with you—something I didn't know about or understand. I'm not an idiot." Jonathan lifted a single shoulder in a lazy shrug. "You know what a patient man I am. I was more than willing to wait while you figured your shit out."

Mason considered that for a bit. "How pissed are the others?"

"Rafe will come around, and Aiden's worried about you, not pissed. None of us have seen you wound this tight since the year we started our company."

Mason almost smiled at that. "The year you strongarmed me into finding a therapist, you mean."

"Admittedly, my plan for this conversation was to strongarm you into finding another one," Jonathan answered with a half-smile. "It worked so well the last time."

He couldn't argue against that. Therapy had turned his whole life around. "And Camden?"

Jonathan chuckled. "You know him. Nothing bothers him for longer than it takes to find the next hole to stick his dick in."

With a short huff of laughter, Mason said, "Truer words have never been spoken."

"So." Reaching across the space separating them, Jonathan took the discarded drink, taking a small sip before continuing. "Can I take it this means you'll behave at all future Saturday meetings?"

Mason's answering smile could only be described as rueful. "I'll do my best."

"It's good to have you back, man," Jonathan said, draining the second tumbler before standing.

Climbing to his own feet, Mason hesitated for a moment, but then thought, *Fuck it*. He pulled his oldest friend into a hug. "You've always been there for me. Thank you."

Jonathan froze at first, but then laughed softly and returned the embrace. "This girl is good for you," he said as they broke apart. "And for the Manor, I might add. Liz went on about Addison's cinnamon rolls for three days."

Christ, the fucking cinnamon rolls again. It would always be the cinnamon rolls. "Who can blame her?" he said with half a smile.

With a final chuckle and a, "See you tomorrow," Jonthan patted him on the shoulder and left the room.

Mason took a minute to just let himself breathe. Everything would be all right in time. He was sure of it.

He'd need to talk to the other guys soon. Each and every one of them deserved an apology for how he'd acted the last year or more, but that would have to wait.

For now, only one thing mattered.

Addison.

"You're awfully quiet this morning," Mason said as he unlocked his front door. She'd barely spoken on the drive over.

Addison moved toward the little table where her collar waited without saying a word, but he put a hand on her shoulder to stop her.

Only half turning toward him, she asked, "Don't you want me to get ready, Master?"

Okay, he wasn't imagining it. Something was definitely off. "I'm sorry I couldn't talk much the last few days," he said, watching what he could see of her face for her reaction. "I needed to be extra attentive to Tara after I ran out on her like that."

She turned the rest of the way, peering up into his face with a confused frown. "Do you think I'm mad at you?" It sounded like genuine surprise in her voice.

"Aren't you?"

Her smile eased the building pressure in his chest. "Not even a little bit."

"You put on your application that you don't ever want to be shared or have scenes with other people," he said, feeling the need to explain how he jumped to this wrong conclusion. "Then you were so quiet after I ran off to be with Tara, so I wasn't sure . . ." He let the sentence trail off.

She huffed out a little laugh. "I know you have a job to do, and it doesn't bother me at all. Honest. Not wanting to be double teamed or passed around is a whole different thing." She wrinkled her nose, and it was fucking adorable. "I can't be the only kinky girl to feel that way."

"Not even remotely," he assured her. "But there *is* something wrong, though. Isn't there?"

She studied his face for several seconds before a decision gleamed in her gold-flecked eyes. "Do you think maybe we can keep being Mason and Addison a little bit longer? I kind of want to talk to you about something."

Alarm bells went off in his head. That wasn't quite a gravely delivered *we need to talk*, but it was damn fucking close.

Don't do this. The desperate plea filled his mind, his heart, all of his senses. *We'll figure out how to make this work somehow. Don't give up before we even try.*

Outwardly, all he did was nod, leading her over to the living room with a hand on the small of her back. He waited until they settled on the sofa, both partially turned to face one another, to ask, "What's on your mind?"

"Why did you drive me to New Mexico?" she asked, her expression unreadable.

Mason's mind cycled through the different possibilities of where she could be going with this. None of them seemed particularly good. "You needed help, so I helped you," he said, choosing his words carefully.

"That's all?"

Frowning, he tried to figure out what the hell that was supposed to mean. Wasn't that a perfectly good reason to do something nice for someone else?

Unless . . . perhaps she really did mean it when she accused him of helping with ulterior motives.

"If you're asking if I only drove you down there so you'd keep sleeping with me, I—"

"No," she interrupted, laying a soothing hand on his thigh. "That's not what I'm asking. I'm sorry I ever said that. I wasn't thinking rationally at the time."

Mason looked down at her hand, wishing he had the courage to place his own hand over it. Since when had he become such a fucking coward?

In the end, he decided the truth was the only way out of this. "Addison, I'm going to be honest with you. You're scaring the hell out of me right now. What's the matter?"

Grimacing, she said, "I'm sorry, I'm doing this all wrong." She heaved a sigh that he felt in his bones. "I'm trying to ask if you did that just because you're nice, or if you"—she gulped—"have feelings for me." She couldn't look him in the eye anymore.

Mason sat in stunned silence for a handful of rapid-fire heartbeats. And then he smiled in a way he couldn't ever remember smiling before. With his mouth, his cheeks, his eyes, his forehead—his whole face. He hadn't even been sure if the muscles in his face worked the way they did for other people until that moment.

Grabbing her around the waist, Mason hauled her onto his lap, positioning her so they faced each other. A startled laugh bubbled out of her, and her hazel eyes met his. "Addison Walker, are you asking me if I'm in love with you?" he said, still grinning like a fool.

Her smile turned shy. "Maybe."

"Christ," he said, laughing. "I thought you were breaking up with me."

"God no! Fuck, no wonder you were being so weird."

The horror on her face made him laugh some more. His heart had never felt this light in his entire life.

"Little one, from the moment you walked into my life with your absurdly delicious food, you've turned every single aspect of my world upside down." He cupped her face between his hands. "You've made me happier these last few months than all the other years of my life put together."

Tears glistened in her beautiful eyes. "No one in my life has ever been there for me like you. Not even close." When she blinked, the tears made twin trails down her cheeks. "It literally fucking hurts when I'm not with you. Every time something happens—even tiny, stupid little things—I want to tell you." She leaned into his touch. "And I can't wait to hear every little thing about you. That's love, right? That has to be love."

"If there's another word for it, I have no idea what it is." Leaning in, he pressed his lips softly against hers. "I love you."

"I love you, too, Mason," she whispered against his lips. "I love you so much."

Their mouths collided as they both surged forward. Addison laughed at the fumble, but Mason merely took tighter hold of her face, keeping her where he wanted her as he slanted his mouth over hers.

He'd never tire of kissing this woman. She arched her body when he commanded it with dominating hands, making herself soft and pliable and entirely his to control.

He wanted to feel her skin against his. He wanted to feel it everywhere.

Lifting her to her feet, Mason made quick work of her clothes, tossing them onto the floor without his usual care. His clothing joined the pile as fast as he could shed them, and then they were back on the sofa, Addison straddling him as he surged up into her waiting pussy.

"You're *mine*." Mason growled it against her neck, digging his fingers into her ass as he lifted her. He slammed her back down onto his cock with enough force to make her teeth rattle. "If anyone else even thinks of touching you, I'll snap their fucking neck."

"Yours," she promised, her eyes drifting closed as he lifted her again, arching his hips as he pulled her back down. "Only yours."

Mason couldn't think of anything he wanted more.

They fucked until they were both breathless, their bodies slippery with sweat. "I love you," Mason said, voice strained as he lifted his hips again. He loved the way his muscles tightened and protested as he pushed them to exhaustion. "I love you. I love you."

Sweet fucking Christ, he was so close. Licking his thumb, he lowered it to her clit, doing his best to keep up a constant rhythm as she writhed and bounced on top of him.

Eyes shut tight and head thrown back in ecstasy, she rocked her hips in the most delectable way, screaming when her orgasm finally shattered through her.

Her pussy clenched around him as she came, squeezing his cock with enough force to drag him over the edge with her.

Addison collapsed against him, panting. As he held her with exhausted, sweat-slick arms, still buried deep inside her, he couldn't imagine ever being happier.

Hours later, as they lay in bed together beneath the painting of purple and blue mountains, Mason whispered, "Little one?"

"Yes?"

"You're not leaving, are you?"

She went extremely still for several seconds, not even seeming to breathe. "What do you mean?" She sounded genuinely confused.

"When your trial period is up in a few weeks," he explained, trying to keep the fear out of his voice. "You're going to stay, aren't you? You're not moving back to New York?"

Propping herself up on her elbow, she looked down at him with the sweetest smile he'd ever seen. "I'm not going anywhere."

Relief warmed him from the inside out, and he closed his eyes for a few seconds as his middle-of-the-night anxieties drifted away. When he opened his eyes again, Addison was looking down at him with so much love written all over her face, it took his breath away. "Will you live here? With me?"

Her eyes went big and round. "Are you serious?"

Mason frowned. "I can't tell if you're upset or not."

"Of course I'm not upset," she hurried to say, placing a calming hand in the center of his chest. "I'm just . . . wow, do you really mean it?"

In answer, he rolled onto his side and opened his nightstand drawer. Pushing a neat stack of books and the case for his glasses aside, he picked up a thin, rectangular box, then sat up against the headboard.

"Maybe this will convince you how serious I am," he said softly, opening the box and holding it out for her. "I ordered this while we were in New Mexico."

Inside, a gold collar sat nestled against the black velvet lining—five thin chains attached to a large golden O ring. The chains were the perfect length for the ring to rest securely against the base of her throat.

Addison stopped breathing again.

"It was our second night there. I couldn't sleep, and it took me until almost dawn to figure out why."

Running a single fingertip along the length of one gleaming chain, she whispered, "What was the reason?"

"Because I'd fallen in love with you. I'd never been in love before, and I had no idea what I should feel or what should come next." Removing the collar from the box, he undid the clasp and held it up, suspended between both hands. "It wasn't until I ordered this that I finally fell asleep."

Addison looped a finger through the ring on her leather collar, still buckled around her neck. "Is that"—she nodded toward the gold collar —"like Olivia's?"

"Do you mean, would I want you to wear it all the time, not just when we're here?"

When she tried to answer, no words came out, so she nodded instead.

"I would like that," he admitted, his voice softer than intended.

"Very much. That's something we need to decide together, though. If that's not something you want yet, or even ever, I'll understand."

She held out her hand, and he draped the new collar over her palm, letting the ends dangle off the sides. "It's lighter than I expected," she said, still whispering. "It's so beautiful, Mason."

"As incredible as you look in leather, the gold will be stunning on you. It'll bring out the gold in your hair, and the flecks in your eyes." Wrapping a hand gently around her throat, he pressed just hard enough to make her breath catch. "It suits you better. You deserve something as classy and beautiful as you are."

Addison drew in short, sharp breaths as his hand tightened, but didn't even try to pull away.

"Tell me what you're thinking," he said, not quite a command, but with his hand partially cutting off her air, not exactly a request either.

"I'm remembering how shocked I was when Olivia told me her collar is permanent." Her voice came out as a delectable rasp. "That only Aiden knows where the key is. I couldn't imagine wanting that. Being brave enough to let people judge me."

Every bit of lust and excitement left him in an instant. "Oh," he said, letting his hand fall to his lap. "I—I didn't realize. I can—"

He started to reach for the golden collar, not wanting to look at it anymore, desperate to get it out of his sight. But her hand fisted around it.

Mason stared at her hand for several seconds, uncomprehending. Then he dragged his gaze up to meet hers.

"I used to be afraid of what people thought of me. Afraid that if I let them in all the way—if they saw the real me, with the flaws and the fucked-up childhood and the fears and the kink and all the rough, jagged pieces—they wouldn't want anything to do with me. So I filed myself down as smooth as I could, and pretended that's all there was to me. And you know what? It fucking sucked."

Her lips lifted into a jagged, crooked smile, and he felt the heavy threat of tears at the backs of his eyes. "I know it did," he said, placing his hand over her fist. "You don't have to do that anymore."

"I'm not going to." It was a declaration. "I refuse. Did I tell you I called Kate on Thursday?"

"Your friend in New York?"

She nodded. "I told her *everything*. All the secrets I've been keeping because I couldn't stand the thought of losing her."

"Let me guess," Mason said with half a smile. "She thinks you're every bit as wonderful as I do."

Her laugh made the room seem brighter somehow. "Something like that. I'm going to tell Lola next. I'm done pretending."

Mason leaned forward, pressing his lips softly against hers. "I'm proud of you, little one. That was an incredibly brave thing to do."

"I want to wear your collar, Mason. I want everyone to know I'm yours." Her hand shook as she unfurled her fingers and held out the gold chains. With a slight tremor in her voice, she added, "I don't ever want to feel like I'm alone again, even for a second."

Pride swelled in his chest, the feeling so enormous he wasn't sure his body could contain it. Reaching up, he removed the leather collar, dropping it onto the bed between them. Then he picked up the new collar, letting the delicate gold chains flow over her hand like water as he lifted them.

His own hands shook slightly as he wrapped the collar around her neck and clasped it in place.

The precious metal glinted in the light from the nightlight when she swallowed.

So beautiful.

So fucking perfect.

Mason brushed his lips across the golden ring at the center of her throat.

His.

EPILOGUE

Addison

"Guys, if you don't come out right now, we're doing this without you," Addison said, giving the Doms around the dining room table a scolding look.

Rafe arched his eyebrows at Mason. "You going to let her talk to you like that?" he said in his low, gruff voice. When she first met him, those words would've half-terrified her. Rafe seemed right on the verge of turning her over his knee at the best of times. After nearly five months at the Manor, though, she knew she didn't need to worry. He was amused, not angry.

Besides, they all knew what the gold chains encircling her neck meant. Mason would fucking kill anyone who touched what was his—a fact he never let anyone at the Manor forget.

Mason only shrugged in response, a smile lurking in his lapis lazuli eyes.

"If you would be kind enough to wait five more minutes," Jonathan drawled from his place at the head of the table. "We're almost finished with our meeting."

"Don't say I didn't warn you," she said, flipping her hair over her shoulder as she turned away. The door swung closed behind her as she hurried back across the kitchen, heading straight out onto the patio.

The spring flowers were in full bloom, blanketing the garden in so much color it almost hurt to look at it. She couldn't think of a more perfect place for this to happen.

Addison headed straight for the small crowd gathered at the edge of the patio nearest to the trees. Phoebe from the wildlife rehabilitation center stood in the middle of the group with a plastic animal crate at her feet.

Zach, Olivia, and Nell all gave her expectant looks as soon as she moved within earshot. Even Gabriel and Kendra, who had come in on their day off for the occasion, watched her with interest.

"Well?" Olivia asked.

"Jonathan told me to wait five more minutes." Her tone made it abundantly clear how she felt about that.

"Screw Jonathan," Zach said, rolling his eyes. "Did you tell him Alexander's freedom is way more important than his stupid Saturday meeting?"

She shrugged. "I made it clear we're not waiting." Even if she was willing to keep Alexander cooped up any longer than necessary—spoiler alert: she wasn't—she and Mason had a flight to catch. They'd already delayed their trip by twenty-four hours after Phoebe called, and she had no intention of pushing it back again. Time was a luxury she didn't have today. "If they want to miss it, that's their problem."

No sooner were the words out of her mouth than the kitchen door crashed open behind her. All five of the Manor's Doms filed out into the garden, Mason in the lead.

Addison grinned so wide, her face hurt. She knew he wouldn't let her down.

A hell of a lot of things had changed in the past two and a half months. Addison's plans to move back to New York long forgotten, she'd accepted a permanent position at the Manor. She loved her kitchen, her coworkers, and the guests.

She especially loved reading what people wrote about her food on the Manor's subreddit. Her cranberry-ginger cinnamon rolls were almost as famous as Camden's dimple at this point.

Mason took a page out of Aiden's book, cutting back his hours and doing everything he could to go home with Addison each night. Things didn't always work out the way they wanted, of course. Even when they did spend the night together, they often spent hours side-by-side on their laptops, researching and answering emails. The charity foundation they were in the process of starting—its sole mission to support foster kids around the country—took more work than she ever could've guessed.

As long as they kept facing each bump in the road together, the whole thing seemed possible. Especially since Olivia and Nell were always there to help when things got confusing or hard. If anyone understood what she was going through right now, it was those two.

With the slew of changes overtaking Addison and Mason's lives, only one thing remained constant: their love grew every single day. As long as that stayed true, the rest would work itself out in time.

As soon as the Doms joined the group, Mason moved up behind Addison, wrapping his arms around her. "Sorry we're late, little one," he murmured in her ear.

She craned her neck, giving him a mischievous smile. "I think you owe me an extra hour of driving lessons for this."

A smile played at the corners of his lips. "Done."

They'd turned Addison's quest to finally learn how to drive into a little game, letting her earn time behind the wheel by being a good girl. At this rate, she'd have her license in no time.

Once everyone settled down, Phoebe swept her gaze around the group, giving them all a welcoming smile. "I'm so glad you were all able to join us today as we release Alexander back into the wild. These are our favorite days at the center, and it makes it even more special to share these moments with the amazing people who brought the animal to us in the first place."

Addison felt her heart fill with pride, and she crossed her arms over Mason's.

"As some of you already know, Alexander's wing was broken in two places when Addison and Mason brought him to us." Phoebe's smile had vanished, replaced by a somber look. "Our veterinarian partner performed surgery on the wing the day after he came to us. Once the bones had a chance to heal and he responded well to physical therapy, we moved him out into our flight complex. We monitored him for several weeks as he regained strength in his wing."

They'd even let Addison and Mason visit a couple times during that stage, watching Alexender flit around the huge aviary attached to the main building. It had been amazing to see his progress through the weeks.

"We were unsure if we'd be able to release him back into the wild because of the previous injury to his leg." Pheobe spread her hands wide, smiling again. "But given Addison's testimony of his abilities before the broken wing, and our own observations in the flight complex, we feel confident he has every chance to live a long and happy life here."

Mason tightened his arms around Addison, kissing the top of her head. He'd been right there at her side as she argued Alexander's case, ready to jump in if she needed it. His support gave her the strength she needed to not give up until she ensured Alexander would be freed if his wing made a full recovery.

"Now," Phoebe said, gesturing down to the crate. "Just a couple more things before we get to the main event. One, when Alexander exits the crate, you may notice a small aluminum band around his leg. The band is a tag engraved with Alexander's unique number. This way, if anything else ever happens to him, the people who help him will know he spent time at our facility before, and we'll be able to give them all the information we have on him."

Addison glanced around, taking in a few concerned faces. "Don't worry. I already grilled her about this."

"That's a fact," Phoebe muttered with a snort.

Smirking, Addison said, "The tag won't affect him at all. Scientists do this all the time, and the birds live perfectly normal lives, like the bands aren't even there."

The crease between Zach's brows disappeared, and he gave Phoebe an expectant look. "What was the second thing?"

"Yes, thank you for keeping us on track," Phoebe said with an amused half-smile. "The second thing is that we all need to stand behind the crate when I open it. If Alexander sees us huddled around him, he might get scared and refuse to come out. But if he sees those trees over there"—she gestured toward the forest bordering the garden—"he'll fly right out and go home. Now, does anyone have any questions before we get started?"

When no one responded, Phoebe moved directly behind the crate, motioning for everyone to stand behind her and to the sides. As they shuffled into place, Zach held up his phone for Addison to see. "I'll record everything for you," he promised with a smile. "You just enjoy the moment, okay?"

She gave him a grateful smile. "Thank you so much." Then she moved into place on Phoebe's right, Mason at her side.

"Everyone ready?" Phoebe asked. When they all nodded their assent, she bent down and unlatched the door, swinging it out of the way.

Addison held her breath, afraid to even blink in case she missed it. Her heartbeat thundered in her ears as she waited.

When Alexander burst from the crate, his bright red feathers shining in the spring sunlight, she couldn't have held back her tears if she tried.

"Shit, did you remember to send out the video of Alexander?" Mason asked the question as the bellman carried their bags into their hotel room in Santiago. "I promised you I wouldn't let you forget, but then I forgot."

"Don't worry," Addison said moving over to the nearest window. Even at nearly two in the morning, the city below buzzed with life and light. It was fucking beautiful. They planned to spend three days in Chile's capital before moving onto the next leg of their trip—exploring the glaciers of Patagonia. "I sent it to everyone on the way to the airport."

Several people in her life had taken a keen interest in Alexander's story, regularly asking for updates on the little bird. She and Mason had barely started the four-hour drive down to Boston when she shot off the texts.

The video went to Ricky first, and then to Lola. As her granny's best friend, the woman was a consistent presence in Addison's life once she moved to Manhattan. They'd only grown closer in the nine years they were business partners.

None of that compared to now. Lola cried through long portions of their conversation back in March, when Addison finally opened up about all the hidden parts of her life. Tears of sadness and pain as she learned about Addison's life before moving to New York. But also of joy, to know that she didn't intend to conceal huge pieces of herself any longer.

"No one should have to hide who they are." Lola's words had stuck with Addison for months now. She only wished she'd been brave enough to be honest sooner.

The other person she sent the video was Steve. She and her dad kept in close contact since she left New Mexico, texting each other several times a day, and having video chats at least once a week. They were very much still in the getting-to-know-you phase, which was a little awkward at times. She didn't know how to be a proper daughter any more than he knew how to be a dad.

Every day—each conversation—got a little better than the last. The simple fact was, she genuinely liked him as a person. She had no doubt that, with enough time, that feeling could grow to love.

Steve had been particularly interested in how she'd handle her first ever flight, having never been on a plane himself. He told her repeatedly that taking a fourteen-hour flight for her virgin voyage was absolute madness.

"What time is it in New Mexico right now?" she asked, pulling out her phone as the bellman left.

Mason checked the clock on his own phone, then did some quick math. "Almost ten."

"Good. Then he'll be awake to see this." Opening their text chat, she sent several messages in a row. Only a few seconds passed before the three dots appeared. When his response followed shortly thereafter, she smiled.

> Greetings from South America

> I almost had a panic attack right before takeoff, but Mason got me through it

> Flying is fucking glorious. First class is even better than in the movies
>
> P.S. I intend to see the entire world before I die

Glad to hear it, honey.

Now get some sleep. You must be exhausted.

She fired off a quick text to Kate, too, even though it was later in New York. Kate always put her phone on do not disturb when she went to sleep anyway. That time, she put her phone aside without waiting for a reply. She had more important things on the agenda.

"Mason," she said coyly, walking up behind him as he pulled a cell charger out of his laptop bag.

"Hmm?"

"How many hours has it been since we left the Manor?"

He let out an amused huff. "God, it feels like a thousand." Calculations flashed through his eyes as he turned around. She knew he was adding up the drive down to Boston, the super involved check-in process at Logan, the long-ass customs line in Chile, and everything else they went through today. "Though I suppose it was closer to twenty-three. Why do you ask?"

"Well," she said, sliding her body up against his, wrapping her arms around his neck. "It occurs to me that I've wanted you to fuck me for the last twenty-three hours. And I hoped that, now we're finally here, you can do something about it."

"Hmm," Mason said again, looking down at her with a wicked glint in his eyes. "You're telling me you had twenty-three hours to find a way to seduce me in public, and you failed?" He made a disappointed tutting sound as he reached between them, unbuckling his belt. "I expected better of you."

Liquid heat pooled between her thighs. *Fucking finally.* "I'm sorry, Master."

"Not yet," he said, a dark promise in his words. "But you will be." He pulled his belt free of his beltloops with a soft *swish*. "I'm a firm believer that the punishment should fit the crime. So I think you've earned twenty-three lashes—one for each hour of your failure."

God, it was hard to keep a smile off her face. "Whatever you command, Master."

"Strip," Mason ordered, an adorably superior look on his face. He was having fun with this too, and that made her deliriously happy. "Then bend forward with your hands on that windowsill."

Eager to get started, she followed his directions as quickly and succinctly as she could. Though she still folded her clothes, stacking them neatly on a chair the way he liked it. He could get peevish when things got messy. Even on the rare occasions he created the mess himself.

Body completely bare, she moved over to the window, bending at the waist to brace her hands on the low windowsill. "What if someone sees?" she said, eyes wide as she looked out over the city.

"We're on the fourteenth floor," he pointed out, moving into place behind her and slightly to the left.

She resisted the urge to roll her eyes. "We're surrounded by skyscrapers. Anyone could be looking at me right now."

"It's two in the morning. Which means no children should be awake. As I recall, that was your only objection to being on display." Smug satisfaction dripped from every word. "I suppose anyone else who happens to look at this specific window will see a very naughty girl getting her ass painted red by her Master's belt."

She pressed her thighs together, trying to relieve the aching throb of her pussy. Before she made any progress, Mason forced a hand between her legs, prying them apart.

"Keep your legs spread wide. I want to see how much wetter you get with each stroke."

Addison whimpered. "Yes, Master."

"Good girl."

God, even that made her pussy wet as a fucking river.

"Now let's begin. There will be no need to count."

He brought the belt down across her ass with enough force to drive the air from her lungs.

"Do you think there's someone out there right now, watching you?"

Mason asked, bringing the belt down twice more. "Someone who likes seeing bad little girls be punished."

She raked her gaze across the nearest building, searching for any sign of movement in the dark windows. "Oh, I hope so, Master."

With a bark of laughter, he laid twin lines of fire across her upper thighs. The sweet bite of pain brought tears to her eyes.

"Brace yourself," he ordered. "I'm not stopping again until we're through."

Addison tightened her grip on the windowsill and waited, every inch of her body tingling with anticipation, her ears straining for the sound of leather slicing through the air.

He stood behind her, utterly still and silent, letting her wind herself up tighter and tighter as she waited. Just when she became sure she couldn't stand it for another second, the belt cut through the air, landing across her sit spots with a pain so perfect she started to cry.

True to his word, the belt fell again and again without reprieve. Eighteen strokes in a row, each one driving her need higher and higher.

By the time he tossed the belt aside and pressed into her, she was about ready to die. "Don't hold back," she begged, arching her back, trying to find the perfect angle for him.

"Wouldn't dream of it." He forced it out through clenched teeth as he pounded into her from behind, reigniting the fiery welts on her ass with each stroke.

Addison twisted her hips ever so slightly, gasping when his next stroke hit her G-spot. Her pussy tightened around him, making him dig his fingers even harder into her hips.

"Fuck," he said, his rhythm faltering for only a moment. Then he was right back at it, sending surges of pleasure racing through her. "Come for me, Addison. Let them see you come with my cock buried inside you."

His words were the last little push she needed before she toppled over the edge. A scream tore free from her throat as pleasure slammed into her like a fucking tidal wave, so hard and fast that nothing else existed.

Next thing she knew, she lay cocooned within crisp white sheets, gloriously cool against her bare skin. Disappointment filled her when she found the bed empty beside her.

Though every light was off, she could see the whole room with ease. A mere sliver of window remained visible between the mostly closed curtains, right in the middle.

Mason stood bathed in colorful, neon light as he gazed out into the city.

Pushing the sheets aside, she climbed out of bed, padding across the plush carpet on bare feet. He must not have heard her coming, because he jumped when she placed a hand on his back.

"What are you doing out of bed?" he asked softly, wrapping an arm around her and nestling her against his side.

"Looking for you," she answered honestly. "I got worried when I woke up alone."

He gave her shoulders an apologetic squeeze. "Sorry. I think I slept too much on the plane. Don't let me fuck up your sleep schedule, too."

Addison heard the lie in his voice. An experienced traveler like him knew how to beat jetlag. Something else was keeping him awake.

Lifting her head, she gazed up at his reflection in the window. He was so profoundly beautiful as he surveyed the city below, like a fallen angel or a dark, calculating god.

And he was hers. She still had trouble believing it sometimes.

"Hold me while I fall back asleep?" she asked.

Finally tearing his gaze away from the lights of Santiago, he looked down at her with a loving smile. "Of course."

Grabbing the edge of the curtain, Addison closed it the rest of the way, plunging the room into darkness.

Mason stiffened beside her. "Are you sure?"

She held onto him a little tighter than before, but the usual panic didn't rise through her. "You'll never fall asleep with all this light." He didn't grow up in the city like her, and spent the last near-decade in the literal wilderness.

"But—"

"I promise to tell you if I start to panic. Right now, I feel okay." She paused, taking stock of her body, her emotions, making sure that wasn't a lie. She smiled as a sense of calm drifted over her. She could do this. "Come to bed with me?"

Settling together in the center of the king-size bed, Mason pulled her body against his, enveloping her in his warmth.

"You don't have to worry," he whispered against her hair. "I'm right here. I'm not going anywhere."

With his arms around her, and the gold collar a constant, calming weight against her throat, it was impossible to feel alone.

Addison smiled as her eyes drifted closed. "I know."

The End

Acknowledgments

This book literally wouldn't have been possible without the incredible help and support of my editor, Karen Washo at Utterly Unashamed. You pushed me to keep digging deeper and deeper, until I finally found the heart and soul of this story. Thank you for your honesty, your kindness, your brilliance and creativity, and your belief that I could turn this book into something beautiful.

The gorgeous eBook on your screen or the stunning paperback in your hands were only possible because of three people. Shari Ryan at MadHat Studios took an ugly, basic Word document and turned it into an actual book. You continue to amaze me with your skills. Robin Johnson at Florida Girl Design has created two more perfect covers for me. I couldn't be prouder to have your covers represent my work. And Virginia Carey, you continue to be the best proofreader an indie author could ever hope for. Your attention to the tiniest of details allows my readers to get lost in the story.

A very special thank you goes out to Linda Russell and the rest of the team at Foreword PR & Marketing. Because of you and your team, every cover reveal and release day has been special beyond my wildest dreams. I have the most beautiful teaser graphics in the world. And you help me figure out the best moves for my career, offering endless support as I turn those plans into reality. I couldn't have done any of this without you.

Every single person who has taken the time to message me, email me, interact with my social media posts, enter my giveaways, post ratings and/or reviews—all of you are my heroes. You have no idea what that all means to an author, and especially an indie author in her very first year of publication. You give me the strength and energy to keep chasing that next story idea, to type deep into the night after my family has gone to bed, to edit and rewrite until I have a story I'm proud to share with you. Thank you from the bottom of my heart.

Sam, I can't thank you enough for how enthusiastically you volunteer to be my first reader every single time. You're a beautiful person and a wonderful friend.

A quick thank you to Z for giving Addison a name and this book a title, though she'll be horrified if she ever finds out I did this.

And of course, endless appreciation and love to Jason, my prince charming, my best friend, and my favorite person. Your never-ending love and support mean everything to me. I love you as big as the whole universe.

Also by Bay Sinclair

Fairford Affairs

Fixing Olivia

Unravelling Nell

Fairford Affairs Novellas

Rewarding Sophie

Liberating Zach (Coming Soon!)

About the Author

Bay Sinclair is the author of steamy romance with broken girls, sexy Doms, and lots of heart. She writes contemporary romance—though she was one credit away from a history minor in college, and historical romances hold a special place in her heart. When she isn't writing, she's an avid foodie in search of the next great culinary adventure, and she drinks entirely too much green tea.

Connect Online
BaySinclair.com

f facebook.com/100092035117400

instagram.com/authorbsinclair

a amazon.com/author/baysinclair